Best Wishes
Love R. Aslov

HANNAH

HANNAH

June R. Asker

The Book Guild Ltd
Sussex, England

The Book Guild Ltd
25 High Street,
Lewes, Sussex

First published 1992
© June R. Asker 1992
Set in Baskerville

Typesetting by APS,
Salisbury, Wiltshire
Printed in Great Britain by
Billing & Sons Ltd.,
Worcester.

A catalogue record for this book is
available from the British Library

ISBN 0 86332 727 3

1

The wind whistled round the house and the rain lashed heavily against the dirty little windows, windows that were barely covered by the faded, orange flowered curtains, hanging dismally on a sagging piece of string.

Hannah stirred gently, aware of the two little bodies pressed either side of her in the bed.

Her sister Maureen, who was six years' old and her darling little sister Betsy, who was just four.

She looked lovingly at Betsy and thought how pretty she looked with her long, fair hair washed the evening before and bedecked with blue ribbon that she had insisted on wearing through the night; for it was Christmas Eve and she wanted Father Christmas to know a special effort had been made in honour of his visit.

Although Hannah was only eleven years old, she often felt much older, more like a mother to Betsy who she had taken under her wing since she had been released from her mother's breast.

Her mother was more than happy to abandon Betsy to her for in addition to her sisters, there was another baby asleep in the bedroom next door with her mother and father.

The latest addition was a little boy and her parents were thrilled with him for they had wanted a boy on each occasion the girls were born.

Although not especially cruel to the girls, it was painfully obvious who was the apple of their eyes for little Colin was pampered and petted and picked up the moment he made a noise. He rarely cried, mainly because when he was not sleeping he was being fed, changed or just cuddled. But in spite of all this attention he was not a very robust child, in fact he was quite small and pale.

At birth he had been a lusty nine pound baby but it seemed

5

as though his life was in reverse for instead of getting bigger and stronger as time went on he appeared to get smaller and weaker.

His father had noticed that he was not progressing as he should but he knew to draw attention to the fact would only upset his wife.

A few weeks earlier he had said to her 'Why don't you take Colin to the clinic to have him weighed and have a natter with the other women?'

'I've enough to do with all you lot to look after without wasting my time at the clinic' she'd replied sharply. 'Anyway, Elsie Watson will be there with her Tom. I had enough of her sarcasm when I met her at the butcher's last week.'

'"Hello Aggie," she said. "How's your little Colin getting on? Has he picked up at all?"'

'Anybody would think he was sick or something. My Colin might be little but there's nothing wrong with him, at least he doesn't look like a big red-faced navvy like her boy Tom.'

'I don't understand you at times Aggie,' John had said, 'you and Elsie have been friends since you were at school together and now you go out of your way to avoid her and you don't ask her round for a cup of tea or anything. You two used to go everywhere together at one time; she's been a good friend to you, especially when you've been having children. Who's always the first to come round and do your washing and cleaning 'till you get on your feet?'

'I've done the same for her!'

'I know, that's why I can't understand what's gone wrong between you two.'

'Well I just haven't got time for her now, so let it drop.'

With that John did, for the time being anyway, for he was aware that Aggie was afraid of something being wrong with Colin, although she would not admit it to herself or anyone.

Maureen started to jiffle and Hannah said, 'Keep still Maureen, you're letting all the cold air come in the bed.'

'I can't help it,' said Maureen, 'I want a wee.'

'Well get up and go and have a wee then,' said Hannah, although she could understand Maureen's reluctance, because it meant climbing out of bed onto the cold linoleum floor, then going down the stairs, through the kitchen, down the garden to the draughty little shed that housed the wooden lavatory.

'But, it's raining,' said Maureen.

'I can't help that,' said Hannah, 'either keep still or get up.'

'It should be snowing, not raining,' said Maureen, 'it's Christmas Day.'

'Well, it doesn't always snow on Christmas Day,' said Hannah.

'Yes it does,' said Maureen, 'In every comic or book you see it is always snowing on Christmas Day. Are you sure it's Christmas Day, Hannah?'

'Yes, I'm sure,' said Hannah. Then she saw Maureen's lips begin to quiver so she said kindly, 'It's very early, perhaps it will snow later. You can tell it's very early because Father Christmas hasn't been yet.'

'I don't like going to the lavatory when it's dark, it's creepy down the garden,' said Maureen. 'Come with me, Hannah.'

'Don't be silly, there's no sense in both of us getting wet; tell you what, I'll watch out of the bedroom window so I can see you going down the garden and I'll stay there until I hear you shut the kitchen door when you come back.'

'Oh, all right,' said Maureen uncertainly. There was a pause and then her skinny little body leapt from the bed.

'My mac is in the hall,' said Hannah. 'Put it on but don't let it drag on the floor in the lavatory.'

The sudden movement disturbed Betsy. 'Has He been yet?' she asked sleepily.

'No, love, it's still night time, go back to sleep. I'll wake you when He's been.'

She looked to the bottom of the bed where three pillow cases hung, looking whiter than they had ever looked when they were on pillows; their mother had made a special effort to get them that clean. The pillows looked strange without their covers; they were stripy and dingy.

'I wonder what I'll get,' she thought, 'there's so many things I need. I'd want a pillow case as big as a house to get them all in. Still there's no fear of that. If we're lucky we'll get an apple, an orange, some nuts and please,' she prayed, 'a lovely bar of chocolate all to myself.'

Hannah did not expect anything else from her parents (she knew there was no Father Christmas), but she could be sure of a nice present from Antie Lil.

Auntie Lil lived in London and did not have any children of

her own but she always came on Christmas Day with presents for her sister, Aggie's, children.

Oh, she did love Auntie Lil, not just because of the presents but because she was fat and jolly and always smelt lovely. She wished she did not have to bring her husband with her; for although Uncle Bill was also fat and jolly Hannah did not love him the way she did Auntie Lil. He always wanted Hannah to sit on his lap and when no-one was looking he would fiddle with her bottom; Uncle Bill never hurt her or anything but it was strange and she did not like it. Then he would wink at her as if they shared a secret and this puzzled her even more.

Her thoughts were interrupted by Maureen scrambling up the stairs. Just before she reached the top she slipped and screamed out in pain as she fell back down again.

'Hannah, Hannah!'

'All right love I'm coming.'

'What the hell are you kids playing at, at this time in the morning?' came their father's voice from his bedroom.

'Maureen's fallen down the stairs,' said Hannah.

'Well, get her back to bed and keep bloody quiet or you'll wake Colin up.'

Bugger Colin, what about poor little Maureen? thought Hannah, as she helped her up the stairs. Maureen was trying to cry quietly but yelled out loud when they were in the bedroom and she saw her bleeding knee. 'Don't cry, love,' said Hannah gently, 'Nobody should cry at Christmas. I'll soon make it better for you.'

'But it hurts badly, Hannah, and look at all that blood?' wailed Maureen.

'I've a nice piece of clean rag under the pillow, I'll put that on your knee and you'll look just like a wounded soldier. I just hope you and Betsy don't need to wipe your noses as I haven't any more rag,' said Hannah.

She wrapped the cloth round Maureen's skinny little knee and as they were thoroughly frozen by now, jumped into bed and hugged each other to get warm.

'Night, night, Maureen; go back to sleep now.'

The younger child quickly fell asleep, tired from all her crying; but Hannah was no longer tired so she just lay very still keeping the others warm with her little thin body. She looked across the bedroom to the little empty fireplace. Oh, she thought wouldn't it be lovely if there really was a Father Christmas and when they woke up there'd be a lovely fire burning and they could sit round it, lovely and warm, drinking big mugs of cocoa.

The only time there'd been a fire in the bedroom was when she had had a bad bout of tonsillitis and had to stay in bed for a week.

When I get married, she thought, it will be to a very rich man so my children can always have a fire in their room and always be lovely and warm.

Muffled voices were coming from her parents' bedroom. 'Come on Aggie.'

'No, go back to sleep John.'

'Oh, come on Aggie, it is Christmas Day.'

'It's always Christmas Day as far as you're concerned, you hossy old bugger.'

'Please Aggie.'

'Shush, you'll wake the baby up.'

'No, I won't, I'll be very quiet.'

'You won't be happy until I've had another four children will you?'

'I'll be careful I promise.'

'I've heard that before!'

'Just let me kiss you then.'

A rustling of the sheets and then, 'What are you doing down there! You said you were just going to kiss me!'

'I know I did, but I want to kiss you all over!'

It went quiet and Hannah thought it was all over, but then she heard soft moans coming from her mother. 'Oh, John, you know how to fire me, I can never refuse you for long.'

Then she heard the bed springs softly squeaking, then louder and louder with both her parents moaning and grunting and whispering; then finally, one loud grunt from her father and then silence.

They are just like pigs thought Hannah in disgust, don't they know I can hear them? But of course they don't; and I would never dare mention it to them. Thank goodness Maureen and Betsy are asleep; but one day when they're a bit older they will hear and start asking questions. Still, by then Mum and Dad will be older too and perhaps they won't do it so much.

A similar scene was being enacted in the flat belonging to the

Huggins in London.

Lil was savouring a lie-in and thinking with pleasure about her trip down to Norfolk where her sister Aggie and family lived.

She wished she could feel more comfortable at her sister's house. Although she knew Aggie did her best for her family and had done extra spring cleaning in anticipation of her visits, the house and the children always had that not quite clean smell about them, but she loved them all very much in spite of their lack of hygiene.

Lil's biggest regret in life was her inability to have children.

When she and Bill had married ten years ago, she being just twenty-five years old and Bill being ten years her senior, her dearest wish was to have children but it just never happened.

There was absolutely no reason for her barren state. They had both had tests at their local GP's and then later by specialists who all agreed that there was no medical reason why she could not get pregnant. But after a decade of hoping she had now resigned herself to being childless.

It's a funny old world, she thought to herself. There's Aggie and John with more children than they can afford, and here's us. Although not rich, we could give a couple of chidren a very comfortable upbringing. Still, enough of this brooding. She gave herself a mental shake. I have a lot to be thankful for.

My little shop for instance, suitably called Floral Corner as it was situated on a corner in one of the small streets in London off the main thoroughfare and while it was not commercially well situated it suited Lil down to the ground. She was able to do the majority of work herself with one full-time assistant and an accountant one day a week. She would never to able to make a fortune with the little shop but she earned enough to keep herself very well dressed and with (her one weakness) a good supply of expensive perfumes.

Although she was a rather large lady she liked to look and smell pretty; thus the shop and herself were complementary to each other.

And then there was her Bill. Although he was no earth shaker he had a good, steady job with a well-known estate agency in the city and the year before had been promoted to manager, so he now received a very good salary. Bill's one fault, if it could be called such, was that he was abnormally sexually active and expected Lil to comply every morning as regular as clockwork. But in spite of this she loved him dearly and counted herself very lucky. She stretched like a contented cat and put her arms around him. Quick as a flash he responded and proceeded to make love to her.

'My God girl,' he said. 'I certainly got my money's worth when I married you. It was the best day's work I ever did. Come here and I'll give you your Christmas present.'

Why, thought Lil, does he always act as if he is doing me a favour? Little does he know I'd deem it more a favour if he gave me a day off now and then, for although he's a lovely man and I love him dearly, it's so much a routine I rarely get any pleasure from it.

But as usual she pretended an orgasm and the obvious joy she gave him made up for her lack of a climax.

With a mighty grunt Bill rolled onto his back, puffing and panting, as if he'd just completed a marathon.

He really should go on a diet, thought Lil. He's much too fat and this is the only type of exercise he takes. I don't want him to die of a heart attack, even though he'd jokingly said that every man would like to die on the job, preferably with his mistress.

Little did she know that when Bill had remarked about getting his money's worth when he'd married her it had a double implication, for, before he had met Lil, when he lived with his old mother (now dead), Bill used to cruise around Piccadilly, picking up prostitutes, quite often paying for their company for the whole night.

He'd met Lil when she had gone to the estate agents with a view to buying Floral Corner, where she had previously been employed. He handled the purchase of the shop for her and on completion had invited her to dine with him.

She had been really impressed when he booked a table at the Savoy. They had a wonderful meal, complemented with a bottle of Bollinger champagne.

He had been wonderful company and things progressed very quickly from that night onwards and within six months they had both sold their individual flats and bought a larger, more luxurious one. They had twin personalities, both being large, jolly people and they were very contented and compatible.

It was only 8 am but still Lil was no longer sleepy, so she

decided to get up, take a nice long bath, breakfast and then prepare for the two hour drive to the little village where her sister Aggie lived.

She ran a bath, pouring in bubble bath and bath oil, frothing it with her hands. Her leg was in mid-air, preparing to step in, when she felt a gush of warm liquid. Looking down, she was dismayed to see blood running down her legs.

Oh my God, she thought. What's wrong with me?

She had noticed in recent months little spots of blood after making love, but nothing like this.

Don't panic she told herself. Things like this happen sometimes for no reason at all.

She took her bath, taking special care with the rest of her toilet. By now there was no sign of any blood so she decided to say nothing to Bill and to put it to the back of her mind until after Christmas and then if she were still worried, to visit her doctor in the New Year. Meanwhile, there was no point in worrying Bill unnecessarily.

The drive down to Norfolk took longer than expected, because the rain had turned to sleet, making the roads hazardous and by the time they reached the Fens in Norfolk where Aggie lived it was snowing quite steadily.

Hannah awoke and peeped down to the bottom of the bed. The pillowcases were now hanging at an untidy angle, which meant that there was something in them pulling them out of shape.

Thank goodness, she thought. She had been afraid that her parents might fall into a deep sleep after their romping earlier and forget to fill the children's cases.

Where the dingy curtains didn't quite meet in the middle, she could see the rain had stopped and a few flakes of snow were falling.

She reached her arm out to the bottom of the bed where her cardigan lay and put it on over her vest and knickers.

When she had outgrown her pyjamas last year they'd been handed down to Maureen with the promise of a new pair for Hannah before the winter, but somehow or other there never seemed to be money to buy them.

She slipped out of bed, opened the curtains, tiptoed back to bed and gently touched her two little sisters.

'Maureen, Betsy, he's been.'

The children awoke instantly and looked first to the pillow-case and then to the window.

'Oh Hannah, it's snowing, it's snowing,' shouted Maureen in glee. 'Didn't I tell you it always snows on Christmas Day, didn't I, didn't I?'

Hannah looked at their radiant little faces and thought Thank You God, for making it snow.

They reached to the bottom of the bed for their pillowcases, trying to keep the blanket round them and at the same time delve for their presents. They each took out the contents which comprised an apple, an orange and a little bag of mixed nuts. Although there were no bars of chocolate, Aggie had made some treacle toffee for Maureen and Hannah and for Betsy there was a box of dolly mixtures.

The main present for Betsy was a little rag doll, which she fell in love with instantly. The two older girls had crayons and a colouring book and a lovely new pencil with a rubber on the end.

Now that they had satisfied their curiosity, they decided to get dressed and go down for breakfast. They had heard their parents go down earlier and Hannah guessed that by now there would be a fire lit in the grate in the little kitchen.

Maureen dressed herself, but Betsy needed help, so Hannah pulled her jumper over her head, thinking to herself that if the jumper had just one more wash it would be too matted to pull over her head. It had been passed down from Hannah to Maureen and now to Betsy, so it was on its last legs and goodness knows where the next one would come from. Next her little corduroy skirt that had worn almost smooth, then her grubby little socks and lastly a pair of buckle shoes with a buckle on one and a safety pin in the other.

Hannah quickly slipped on her skirt and jumper which were only slightly better than Betsy's, then down the draughty staircase to the kitchen.

John was outside feeding the animals – chickens, pigs and rabbits – and Aggie was sitting on a three-legged stool in front of the fire. Colin was sitting on the mat like a statue.

'Come on baby, come to mummy, there's a good boy.'

13

Colin looked at his mother, grinned and dribbled, but made no attempt to move towards her.

'Look what mummy's got for you,' she said, holding out a buttered crust to him, but still he made no attempt to move.

'You really are a lazy little boy' she said. 'Still, in a few weeks you'll be a year old; perhaps you'll start to crawl then.'

'Betsy was walking when she was as old as Colin' said Hannah. 'He really is lazy.'

'You mind your business, miss,' said Aggie. 'When I want your opinion I'll ask for it.' She gave Hannah a sharp slap around the ear.

Hannah's eyes filled with tears not because she wasn't used to being smacked, but today her ears were bright red with the cold and the smack seemed to ring right through her head.

Betsy looked round-eyed at her mother, then at Hannah, and promptly burst into tears.

'That's right, now you start,' said her mother impatiently. 'Hannah, get those kids up the table and have your breakfast.'

'Can't we come and sit by the fire, Mum?' said Maureen.

'No, you can't, you're not squatting about like animals.'

'You and Colin are sitting near the fire, why can't we?' asked Maureen.

'You kids are getting far too cheeky,' said Aggie giving Maureen a hefty slap on her little thin arms. 'Now you can have a cry as well like the others. Hannah, pull the table away from the wall and get up on the stool and have your beakfast.'

The table was a scrubbed wooden one and the stool, which was long enough for all three girls to sit on, was also wooden with nails sticking up, which had been made by their father.

They climbed onto the stool and because they were very hungry forgot their tears and began to eat from a large plate in the middle of the table filled with chunks of bread and margarine.

Aggie then handed each of them a big chipped enamel mug full of hot tea which they took gratefully, wrapping both hands around it to get warm.

When they'd eaten all the bread and drunk their tea they felt much better and the fire was now sending some warmth across the room.

Hannah climbed down from the stool, took the plate and mugs to the sink and washed them under the cold tap, and left them to drain on the wooden draining board. She daren't dry them with the tea cloth because they only had one decent one and that had to be kept clean for when Aunt Lil and Uncle Bill were here. Aggie knew that when they'd all had Christmas dinner her sister Lil would insist on drying the plates and saucepans and she wouldn't let her know that they usually dried the plates on some old rag that had once been a sheet.

The children spent the rest of the morning sitting at the table with their colouring books and eating their nuts.

Colin was now asleep in his pram, after being fed with a large bowl of bread and milk.

In the front room the cockerel, which John had killed and plucked the day before was now slowly cooking on the big black cooking-range along with a big pan of potatoes, sprouts and carrots. Aggie had made a huge batter pudding and a plum pudding complete with three silver threepenny pieces for the children to discover.

They would be allowed to go into the front room when Aunt Lil and Uncle Bill arrived and spend the rest of the day in there as it was Christmas. The front room was only used for special occasions or if they had visitors, which was very rarely.

The clock on the kitchen mantlepiece showed that it was one o'clock. I hope they get here soon, thought Hannah, as she was beginning to feel uncomfortable sitting on the hard stool for so long. But she knew they wouldn't be allowed to leave the table until the visitors arrived.

At last she heard the swish of car wheels. They had arrived.

They came in the kitchen door, bringing a flurry of snow with them; two large, jolly people with arms full of presents.

'Is anybody home?' Uncle Bill shouted.

The children scrambled down from the table and threw themselves at him, nearly knocking him over in their excitement.

Aunt Lil kissed Aggie and John, then hugged and kissed the children in turn. 'Look at our little Betsy,' she said, 'she gets prettier every time I see her. The ladies in London spend pounds and pounds at the hairdresser's every week to try and get their hair that beautiful colour.'

'I don't know who she takes after,' said Aggie. 'Nobody in our family ever had lovely hair like her and John's sisters have mousy hair like me.'

'It must have been the fairies,' said Maureen, 'cos they can do magic; they must have waved their wand over it.'

'Or the milkman,' said John, giving Auntie Lil a wink.

The joke was lost on Maureen and she couldn't understand why the grown-ups laughed so heartily.

'Give me your coats,' said Aggie, 'and we'll go through to the front room and have a drop of Christmas spirit.'

Bill and Lil were taken to the best seats, on the brown leatherette couch, and John poured a whisky for himself and Bill and a sherry for Lil and Aggie.

The children waited for the grown-ups to sip their drinks, almost dancing with excitement, wondering what the gaily wrapped parcels held. Then Lil put down her sherry and said, 'Look at their little faces, I can't make them wait any longer, who wants to be first?'

'Colin, cos he's the baby,' said Hannah.

So Aggie sat Colin on the floor and Lil placed a parcel next to him.

'You can unwrap it for him, Maureen,' said Aggie.

So while the others watched, wide-eyed, a lovely woolly poodle dog was revealed, mounted on wooden wheels with a wooden handle to push it along with.

The baby looked at it in fascination and tentively touched it, pulled his hand away sharply then touched it again. He did this a few more times then gradually got more confident and tried to poke its eyes out.

Now that Colin was happy, it was Betsy's turn; her parcel was even bigger so they all helped to take the paper off and a lovely little dolls-house appeared. Next it was Maureen's turn and her present was a baby doll with a pink china face.

'Oh, isn't she lovely!' she exclaimed, giving the doll a big hug and kiss. I'll love her for always and always.'

'Oh thank you Aunt Lil', said Hannah, on being handed *Little Women.* 'How did you know I wanted this book?'

'Well,' said Aunt Lil, 'I remember you telling me you were reading it at school last year and how much you loved it, so now you've got your own book to read whenever you like.'

'Oh, it's lovely,' said Hannah. 'I'll cover it with brown paper like we do at school, to keep it clean.'

'We musn't forget Mum and Dad must we?' said Uncle Bill, so the last two parcels were unwrapped. Two pairs of thick woollen socks for Dad to wear inside his boots and two flowery aprons for Mum.

'I don't know how to thank you Lil,' said Aggie, 'I feel quite ashamed because we couldn't afford to buy anything for you.'

'Don't give it another thought,' said Lil. 'Being invited to spend Christmas Day with you and the kids is our gift.'

It was now time for dinner so Aggie and Lil went into the kitchen to fill the plates and John and Bill took the opportunity to snatch a quick smoke before they came back.

'Hannah,' called Aggie, 'come and fetch the stool and get the kids up to the table for dinner.'

So Hannah placed the stool between the wall and the table so that the children wouldn't fall backwards.

The men carried the chairs from the kitchen to the front room for the grown-ups and they all sat down to eat.

John carved the cockerel, giving himself and Bill a plump leg each. The women were given a good portion of breast and the rest was divided between the children. The grown-up's glasses were filled and the children were each given a cup full of lemonade.

Oh lovely, thought Hannah, why can't every day be like Christmas? When I leave school and get a job I'm going to buy the kids a bottle of lemonade every week.

Next came the plum pudding and although it was too rich for Hannah she happily ate her small portion and as her teeth hit something hard she squealed in delight and took a silver threepenny piece from her mouth. She then helped Maureen and Betsy find theirs and when they'd sucked them clean she put them in her pocket for safe keeping. By the time the meal was over the grown-ups were rather joyful and flushed from the effects of the drinks.

Aggie and Lil started to clear the table, both a little unsteady on their feet, but they managed to carry the plates to the kitchen without mishap.

Uncle Bill just managed to totter from the table to fall clumsily on to the couch and John fell in beside him.

Hannah lifted the children down and took the stool back into the kitchen where Aggie and Lil were attempting to do the washing up with much giggling and banging about. Colin had been put back in his pram and was sleeping, despite all the noise.

'Make us a cup of tea, love,' said Aunt Lil to Hannah. 'I need something to sober me up, I feel quite tiddly.'

'So do I,' said Aggie. 'I think I'll have to go upstairs for a lay down. Are you coming Lil? Hannah can bring our tea up to us.'

So they finished the washing up and clumsily stumbled up the stairs to Aggie's bedroom where they fell onto the bed and promptly went to sleep.

By the time Hannah had made the tea and took it upstairs they were both sound asleep so she put the cups on the dresser and crept down.

Betsy and Maureen were very tired and full up from their exceptionally large dinner so Hannah carried them upstairs to their bedroom for a sleep. They both went quite happily when Hannah said they could take their presents with them.

It was bitterly cold in the bedroom so Hannah didn't undress them. She put them into the bed fully dressed, covered them up, gave them a kiss and then went downstairs to the front room.

Now, thought Hannah, I can have a nice quiet read in the kitchen while everyone's asleep. She crept in to get *Little Women* and tucked the book under her arm, but before she reached the door to leave John stirred.

'Is that you Hannah, didn't you make me and Uncle Bill a cup of tea?'

'I thought you were asleep,' said Hannah.

'Well I'm awake now and my mouth tastes like the bottom of a bird's cage. How about you Bill?'

'I could murder a cup of tea,' came the reply. 'Make us one Hannah and I'll give you a tanner to buy some sweets.'

Impatient as she was to read her book, she knew she'd never make another sixpence quite so easily, so she went to the kitchen where the blackened kettle was always kept on the boil, perched on the little fire grate, and made two more cups of tea, which she carried into the front room.

'Hannah,' said Uncle Bill, 'come and give us a kiss and I'll give you your tanner.'

So Hannah put the cups down and went towards him. He swung her up in the air and began kissing and squeezing her until she said, 'Put me down please Uncle Bill.'

'Hark at her John,' said Bill, 'she thinks she's getting too big to be kissed and cuddled.'

'Well, don't give her the tanner then,' said John.

'Oh, I don't know,' said Bill, 'I think I'll give it to her if she just gives me one nice big kiss for Christmas.'

So Hannah put her arms around his neck to reach up and kiss his cheek but he turned his face and made her kiss him long and hard on his mouth.

'There, that didn't hurt did it?'

'No,' said Hannah, but she was very glad when he put her down for he'd made her feel very strange and a little afraid, for some reason she couldn't understand.

She started to move away but Bill said, 'Come and sit here with us.'

'No thank you Uncle Bill, I'm quite all right.'

'Don't be so bloody rude,' said John. 'What's the matter with you girl? Do as you are told.'

So she sat on the couch with Uncle Bill's arm around her and tried to read her book but she was too uncomfortable to concentrate. Uncle Bill kept kissing and squeezing her, causing her to blush, which made him and John laugh at her.

John finished his tea, gave a loud belch and got up from the couch. 'I think I'll go and feed the animals,' he said. 'It will be dark before long, and don't forget, when you go Bill, there's a dozen new laid eggs for you to take home with you.'

'Thanks,' said Bill, 'do you want me to come and help you with the animals?'

'No, you stay here in the warm, it'll only take me about half an hour; then if the women are awake we'll have a drink and a game of cards.'

On John's leaving the room Bill turned to Hannah. 'What shall we do until he gets back? Do you fancy a little game?'

'No thank you Uncle Bill, I'm quite happy with my book,' said Hannah.

'You'll have plenty of time to read that when we're gone,' said Bill, 'Let's have a game of hunt the thimble. We'll use my handkerchief as the thimble; you can go first. I'll cover my eyes while you hide it.'

So Hannah reluctantly joined in the game and hid the handkerchief under her book, which she put on the table.

'Are you ready?' said Bill.

'Yes, you can look now,' replied Hannah.

Bill came towards her and began to run his fingers over her body.

'Is it here?' he said feeling her chest.

'No,' said Hannah.

'Is it here?' he said, putting his hand up her skirt.

'No,' said Hannah loudly, 'it's not on me'.

'I don't believe you,' said Bill, 'I think you hid it in your knickers.'

'I *didn't* I *didn't*' said Hannah in alarm.

'Well, I think I'll just make sure anyway,' he said putting his hand down her knickers.

'No Uncle Bill, please don't, it's not there honestly,' said Hannah, beginning to feel very frightened.

But Bill carried on feeling inside her knickers and then he started stroking her.

'What's this then? Something here feels all soft and warm. You really are a lovely little girl; give you uncle another kiss,' he said.

'Please don't Uncle Bill, you're frightening me,' said Hannah.

'Don't be silly girl, I wouldn't hurt you for the world. You know you're my favourite; I only want to make you feel good.'

Just then a cry came from the kitchen.

'It's Colin, I must go to him,' said Hannah.

'He'll be all right, he's in his pram, leave him,' said Bill.

'No,' said Hannah, 'he'll wake the others up.'

'That's true,' said Bill, 'we don't want to wake your mother up, do we? Go and see to him and then come back.'

Hannah quickly ran to the kitchen, crying and shaking with fright. Then Betsy's voice came from the bedroom. 'Hannah, can we come down, we're cold?'

'Yes, love come down, I'm in the kitchen with Colin.'

She wiped her eyes and straightened her clothes. She didn't want the children to see she'd been crying, it would only frighten them.

'We're hungry,' said Maureen.

'You're always hungry,' said Hannah, 'it's not long since you had your dinner. You'll have to wait until mother gets up; I know she's made some jam tarts for tea.'

'Coo, can we have one now?' said Marueen.

'No you can't,' said Hannah, 'they're for tea and anyway

20

we'll have to eat our bread and butter first or she won't give us one. I'll make you a nice hot cup of tea to warm you up.'

When they'd finished their tea Hannah wondered how to amuse them until the grown-ups woke up, but just then her mother and Aunt Lil came into the kitchen, shivering.

'My God,' said Lil, 'it's freezing; how do you stand the cold in this house? It's a wonder the kids don't get ill, they must be tough little buggers.'

'Oh, you've got soft since you moved to London,' said Aggie, 'although I must confess it is exceptionally cold this Christmas, and I think there's a lot worse to come. Make us a cup of tea,' she said to Hannah.

'I don't know what you'd do without your Hannah,' said Lil. 'She's like a little mother to those kids.'

'Yes, she is good with the young ones,' said Aggie grudgingly. 'Still she should be doing something for her keep now; she is eleven and she can't just sit around eating her head off until she leaves school and gets a job when she's fourteen.'

John came into the kitchen, stamping the snow off his boots on to the mat. 'It's not easing up much,' he said.

'You don't have to bring all that snow in with you John, why couldn't you have taken your boots off outside?' said Aggie.

'You must be barmy woman if you think I'm going to piss about outside taking my boots off just to keep your kitchen tidy. It's cold enough to freeze the balls of a brass monkey out there.'

'There's no need for that kind of language John' said Aggie.

'Oh don't put your airs and graces on, your sister's heard it all before and Bill is a man of the world, aren't you Bill?'

Oh dear, thought Hannah, please don't let them start rowing. There weren't many days that passed without them fighting and arguing but she'd hoped Christmas Day would be the exception.

'Well shut the door then,' said Aggie, 'do you want to guide the German planes down here?'

This remark caused a hush in the conversation, for, on 7 October, just a month after the outbreak of war, the first bombs had been dropped in the area, just a few miles away on the outskirts of the town of King's Lynn.

An air raid warden had been on patrol at 12.30 am in woods just outside the town and had heard the sound of approaching aircraft. On looking up he'd seen the light under the aircraft which meant that the bomb doors were open. A few moments later he'd heard the crunch of falling bombs. What surprised him almost as much as the falling bombs was the fact that the planes had driven over the sleeping town to drop their bombs in woods; the only damage caused was to some electric cables. The local people concluded that the German air-crew were under training. Nevertheless, it brought home to the people that they were indeed at war; until this occurrence it had just been war-talk.

With these sobering thoughts John quickly stepped inside and closed the door.

The rest of the afternoon passed amicably, with the grown-ups playing cards and Hannah and the children playing Snakes and Ladders.

They decided on an early tea, for Bill had a long drive back to London ahead of him. Aggie had a tin of salmon she'd been saving for months and now came the pleasure of opening it.

The grown-ups enjoyed the large plate of salmon sandwiches and the children had bread and butter followed by jam tarts and big mugs of tea.

All too soon it was time for the Huggins to begin their journey and after many hugs and kisses for the children they set off.

It had been snowing all day, so by now the snow was quite thick on the ground. The worst part of the journey was immediately ahead of them, driving through the twisting country lanes, but once on the main roads it would be easier.

'Take the kids up to bed now Hannah,' said Aggie.

So Betsy and Maureen said, 'Night, Night' to their parents and Aggie gave them a cold peck on the cheek.

'Good night, Mum.' said Hannah, winding her arms around her mother's neck, and giving her a big hug and kiss.

'Get off with you,' said Aggie, pushing Hannah roughly away. 'You're a bit too big for all that slopping about.'

'She wasn't so keen earlier,' said John, 'when Bill wanted to kiss her.'

'That was different,' said Hannah.

'I don't know how,' said John.

No you wouldn't thought Hannah, for I don't really under-stand it myself. I only know it wasn't right, somehow.

22

2

'Hannah,' shouted Aggie from her bedroom, 'have you got them kids up yet? You're back to school today, remember? If you don't get a move on you'll miss the bus.'

'Yes, we're up,' Hannah called back, jumped quickly from the bed, dragging Maureen and Betsy with her.

'Come on, quick, we're late,' said Hannah to Maureen. 'I go up into a new class this term. I don't want to get on the wrong side of the teacher the first day.'

Maureen began to dress slowly, complaining about the cold. 'I'm freezing,' she said.

'Well, you will freeze if you creep about like that' Hannah replied. 'Come on, jump about a bit quicker then you'll get warm,' She had already put on her clothes, (feeling very snug in her new knickers and stockings that Aunt Lil had bought her for Christmas) and was dressing Betsy, who was feeling unhappy at the thought of her sister going to school without her.

'Don't go to school today, Hannah,' she said, 'I'll be on my own. Just have one more day's holiday, and go to school tomorrow.'

'I wish I could,' said Hannah, for she knew that Betsy would be very lonely until they returned this afternoon, 'But if I don't go to school the inspector will come after me and take me to jail,' she said dramatically. 'You wouldn't want that would you?'

'No,' sniffed Betsy miserably, 'but if he did come, I'd hide you up, I wouldn't let him take you.'

'Come on now, cheer up, we'll be back home before you know it. If I am allowed to bring a book home from the school library I'll read you a story tonight.'

'Are you kids ready yet?' called Aggie.

'Yes Mum, we're now going down,' replied Hannah, dragging her reluctant sisters with her. It was warm in the kitchen

23

for John had been up for hours and had lit a fire and was now down the fields, mucking out the pigs.

They huddled round the fire while Hannah made them a mug of tea and cut some bread and butter for their breakfast. She cut a few slices extra which she wrapped up in two packets, one each for Maureen and herself for their lunch.

'Can I have some lunch?' asked Betsy.

'You don't go to school,' said Maureen.

'Please Hannah.'

'Oh all right,' said Hannah, 'if you promise not to cry any more, I'll make you some lunch, but don't eat it as soon as we're gone, save it for later.'

Breakfast over, they put on their coats and waterboots and set off.

Hannah had given Betsy a pencil and some paper and told her to draw her some nice pictures and to stay away from the fire until Mother got up.

They had a two mile walk ahead of them to where the school bus would pick them up and they'd only been walking for about five minutes and already their fingers and toes were aching with cold.

It was hard work trudging along the country lanes, for the snow was a foot deep and all around them nothing but fields broken only by a tree here and there.

It was beginning to snow again; not big flakes but small powdery snow that blew in gusts and settled around their upturned collars and the tops of their waterboots. They battled on, heads bent against the wind, both too cold and miserable to speak. At long last they turned a corner and the red barn came into view.

'Come on, we're nearly there' said Hannah. 'Five more minutes and we can shelter in the barn until the bus comes.' For this was where the school bus stopped to pick up the girls. But it was fifteen minutes later when they reached the barn, for the snow was thicker now and every step they took made their legs ache more.

When they did eventually reach it they were unable to shelter inside because the snow had piled up outside the doors making it impossible to open them.

Maureen couldn't control her misery any longer and began to cry loudly, drops running down to her chin, almost freezing on the way.

Hannah fumbled in her pocket for the piece of rag she kept there for wiping the children's noses, her fingers so numb with cold she could hardly hold it.

'Please don't cry Maureen,' she said, tears running down her own face. 'Come on, let me wipe your nose, you'll only make yourself feel worse.'

But Maureen was beyond being comforted and just cried all the more loudly, her nose now beginning to bleed.

Hannah wiped her nose as best as she could with the inadequate scrap and then they wrapped their arms around each other and danced around to try and get warm.

This was the scene that met the bus driver as he rounded the corner a few minutes later, – two little snow covered figures jumping around like pixies in a glen.

Poor little buggers, he thought, as he pulled to a halt to allow them to climb into the bus, it's cruel to turn animals out in this weather, let alone kids. Although he'd picked up other country children along the way, they hadn't had a two mile walk like the two little scraps he now collected.

Maureen quickly sought out her friend and went to sit beside her and Hannah joined her friend, Pam Bates, who had saved a seat for her.

Although Pam's family were quite well off (they owned a little fruit and vegetable shop), she wasn't at all stuck up, like some of her classmates.

'Oh Hannah, it's good to see you, did you have a nice Christmas, what did you get? Come and tell me, I've missed you since last term,' she said.

She tucked her arm through Hannah's. 'Come and sit close to me and get warm. Oh, and by the way I saved you a present from our Christmas tree.' She handed Hannah a parcel.

Hannah rubbed her hands together to get some feeling back in them and untied the parcel, with Pam looking excitedly over her shoulder.

The parcel revealed two little white handkerchiefs with pink checked borders.

'Oh, aren't they pretty,' she said, 'they're much too nice to wipe your nose on. Thank you Pam, they're just what I wanted, but I haven't got anything for you,' she added miserably. 'We didn't have presents on our tree, just paper chains.'

'That's all right I didn't expect you to get me anything,' said Pam, 'there's really nothing I need.'

'Would you mind if I gave one of the hankies to Maureen?' asked Hannah, 'only she had a nose-bleed while we were waiting for the bus and I had to throw the rag away.'

'No, of course I don't mind,' her friend replied, 'you really are good to your sisters. I wish I had a sister like you. I know I have my brother Ken but it's not the same. He's a boy and just because he is older than me he doesn't talk to me much. He thinks girls are soppy and he'd rather fight with his rough mates.'

'How old is Ken now?' asked Hannah, trying to appear only mildly interested, for secretly she thought he was the most handsome boy she had ever met.

'Nearly fourteen,' answered Pam, 'and don't we know it? He's so big headed, he thinks he is a grownup now his voice is breaking, I have quite a laugh at him sometimes, for one minute he is talking in a deep voice and then his voice breaks and he talks all squeaky. I can't help laughing at him but if he hears me I get a clip round the ear, but it's worth it, it's so funny.'

Hannah couldn't help giggling with her friend but then thought of herself. No wonder Pam is such a happy girl she has got everything anybody could want, a nice house, a kind mum and dad, and best of all, a handsome brother.

But in spite of this, Hannah didn't begrudge her anything because she loved her dearly.

They arrived at the school to find the playground filled with noisy children playing snowballs. They all skipped happily off the bus intent on joining in, but just then the school whistle sounded so there was no time.

Hannah walked over to where Maureen was talking to her friends and gave her her lunch and one of the hankies. She still looked very cold and miserable but she cheered up on being given the lovely new hanky.

'Don't lose it,' said Hannah, 'and use it if you have to and I'll wash it for you tonight so you can have it clean again for tomorrow.'

Another blast from the whistle and the children formed files and paraded into the school.

Hannah and Pam looked for the door marked 'Miss Gibbard 1B' and walked into their new classroom apprehensively.

I wonder why they never have young teachers, thought Hannah, looking over to where their new teacher stood in front of the blackboard. She had to be nearly forty, with her hair pulled back in a bun and wearing a neat grey cardigan over a pale grey blouse, dark grey woollen skirt, thick stockings and stout black shoes.

I wonder if teachers look like teachers when they are babies, she thought and giggled to herself as she imagined Miss Gibbard as a baby, lying in a pram with her hair in a bun and a dummy in her mouth.

'What are you laughing at?' asked Pam.

'I'll tell you at playtime,' whispered Hannah.

'No more talking, find your seats please,' said the teacher, 'you can sit where you like this morning and I'll move you around if I find it necessary.'

Pam and Hannah seated themselves at the front of the classroom and the rest of the girls chose their seats, next to their friends where possible.

'Now,' said Miss Gibbard, 'starting with you two girls' (pointing to Hannah and Pam) 'I would like you to stand up one at a time and tell me your names. It will probably be a few days before I remember them all so you'll have to bear with me and remind me of your names as we go along.'

Pam stood up first. 'Pamela Bates,' she said. Then Hannah, 'Hannah Hardy,' and so it went on until all the girls had introduced themselves.

That over, Miss Gibbard said to Pam, 'Pamela, is it?'

'Yes Miss,' came the reply.

'Right, you and your friend?'

'Hannah,' said Hannah.

'Yes, you and Hannah come to my desk and give out a pencil to all the girls. Now, these pencils will be given out each morning by Pamela and Hannah and collected by them every afternoon, and as we go through the day the rest of you will be given similar duties which you will carry out for one week and then change to different duties for the next week.'

Hannah felt very important at being chosen to give out the pencils. Miss Gibbard doesn't seem to be too bad she thought, at least she can't be as bad as last year's teacher, 'Miss Cat'.

She was a thin, miserable old spinster and none of the girls liked her. They used to say (behind her back) 'Cat by name - Cat by nature.'

The pencils all distributed, Hannah walked back happily to her seat.

'Hannah,' said Miss Gibbard, 'come out to the front, please.'

Hannah left her seat and went to Miss Gibbard's desk.

'What are you wearing on your feet?' asked the teacher.

'Waterboots,' said Hannah.

'I can see they're waterboots. What I mean is, why are you wearing them in class?'

Hannah shifted uncomfortably.

'Well answer me,' said Miss Gibbard.

'Don't know Miss,' said Hannah with her head down.

'Speak up, I can't hear you.'

'Don't know Miss,' said Hannah speaking more clearly.

'You don't know. Well I'll tell you something you will know in future. You do not come into my classroom wearing waterboots. Now go to the cloak-room and take them off.'

Hannah stood rooted to the spot in embarrasment.

'What are you waiting for?' asked Miss Gibbard. 'Go now quickly, you're holding up the class.'

So Hannah went from the classroom into the corridor, tears rolling down her face. She went to her peg in the cloakroom where her coat hung and put her waterboots underneath.

What do I do now? she thought, I can't go back with my boots on and I can't go back with nothing on my feet. I wish I were dead, she thought miserably.

Just then she heard approaching footsteps and coming down the corridor was Miss Cat.

Oh no, she thought, I can't face her. So she quickly ran from the cloakroom before Miss Cat could reach it, and back to the classroom.

When she walked in Miss Gibbard had her back to the class and Hannah went quickly to her seat. Pam reached for her hand and give it a squeeze as if to say 'Chin up, I'm here with you.'

This gesture of kindness brought tears to her eyes again, which she wiped away with her new hankie. She then took a big breath and pulled herself together, and concentrated on the lesson for the rest of the morning.

Miss Gibbard looked at the clock on the wall and waited until both hands were exactly on the twelve and then rang a little bell that stood on her desk.

'Dinner time girls, make sure you're back in the classroom promptly at 1.30, enjoy your dinners and try not to get too wet playing snowballs,' she said, with a smile.

The girls gasped, and looked at each other in astonishment. Miss Cat would have said something like 'If I see anyone playing snowballs they'll get the cane'. And she would have carried out the threat with sadistic pleasure.

With a loud scraping of chairs they all stood up and began hastily leaving the classroom.

As Pam and Hannah were about to leave Miss Gibbard said, 'Hannah, you stay behind.'

The rest of the class filed out and Pam loitered near the door while Hannah went up to the teacher's desk.

'Do you think you're funny?' Miss Gibbard asked Hannah.

'Please Miss, I don't know what you mean,' replied Hannah.

'I think you do know what I mean and I also think you're trying to be clever in front of the other girls.'

'I'm sorry Miss Gibbard,' Hannah replied meekly, 'but I still don't know what you mean.'

'Why did you come into my class wearing waterboots?'

'Please Miss,' came Pam's voice from the doorway, 'Hannah is a country girl and she has to walk two miles to catch the school bus. That's why she has to wear rubber boots.'

'Oh I see,' said Miss Gibbard. 'I'm sorry you have to walk so far in this weather but that's no reason to come into class wearing boots, and why, when I sent you to take them off did you not put your shoes on? Did you think you'd have some fun with me?'

'No Miss, not at all, you see, I haven't got any shoes.'

'Do you mean you forgot to bring them to school?'

'No,' interrupted Pam. 'She hasn't got any shoes; she wore them out last term and her mother hasn't brought her another pair yet. She only has the rubber boots to wear.'

'Oh I'm sorry, I didn't realise that,' said Miss Gibbard kindly. 'Why didn't you say so before?'

'Some of the other girls poke fun at her,' said Pam, 'just

29

because she's a country girl and her family are very poor.'

'Well, they won't do it if I can help it,' said Miss Gibbard, 'but in spite of this Hannah is a lucky girl to have a friend like you, Pamela. There's not much I can do about the situation today but we'll sort something out temporarily. What size shoe do you take?'

'Size 1,' replied Hannah.

'Right, come with me. You can come too, if you wish Pamela,' she said and took them down to the gymnasium.

'Wait here,' she said, and walked to the far end and had a few words with the gym teacher, Miss Ramsbottom.

A few minutes later she came back carrying a pair of navy-blue plimsoles.

'Here you are Hannah' she said. 'You can have these on loan until you get some shoes, but you must leave them at school every afternoon.'

'Thank you very much Miss Gibbard,' said Hannah, tears of gratitude filling her eyes.

'Well, run along now and have your dinner and don't be late back in class,' said Miss Gibbard, 'and forgive me for appearing harsh but I didn't understand the situation.'

The two girls ran off happily, hand in hand.

The rest of the day passed quickly and happily with children and teacher getting to know each other and very little real work getting done.

Normally, school fnished at four o'clock but as the weather was so bad it was decided to let the children go home early at 3.30, so they all ran to the cloakroom, delighted at being let out early.

Hannah put on her waterboots and took the plimsoles back to Miss Ramsbottom in the gym and was told to collect them again in the morning before class started.

Outside, it was snowing heavily and already the daylight was disappearing and it was getting quite dark.

The bus was waiting to take the girls back home and after Hannah had checked that Maureen was there they all climbed aboard and the driver set off slowly.

When they reached the Red Barn the driver stopped to let Hannah and Maureen off. He looked with concern at the girls. 'Will you two be all right on your own, or is someone coming to meet you?'

'No, we'll be all right, we always go home on our own,' said Hannah.

'Well, I'm not very happy about you being on your own today,' he said. 'The weather is terrible and it is almost dark, but' he shrugged, 'there's nothing I can do about it, so get home as quickly as you can and I will see you in the morning.'

The children waved and said goodbye and the bus moved off.

Hannah glanced over to the barn and was puzzled to see that the snow had been cleared away from the doors.

Who on earth could have done that and why? she thought. She couldn't imagine the reason for anybody doing it because for as long as she could remember the barn had never been in use; it just appeared to be a landmark.

'Come on Maureen,' she said, 'let's go home as fast as we can.' She didn't want Maureen to know she felt suddenly afraid. And then the barn doors opened, causing them both to scream in alarm.

'Boo,' came a voice from within.

'Who's there?' asked Hannah.

'Boo,' came the voice again.

'Whoever you are, come out and stop trying to scare us,' said Hannah, with more bravado than she felt.

'Guess who?' said the voice.

'I don't know and I don't care,' said Hannah. 'it's too cold to play games with you, whoever you are, we are going home.'

'Wait a minute Hannah, it's only me,' came the voice and out stepped a figure.

'Billy Wilson, you crazy fool, what on earth are you doing out here on a day like this?'

Billy was a large man, about twenty years old with the brain of a child and everyone knew Billy was a bit 'tetched' in the head. He had a larger than normal sized head with one eye lower than the other, big, bad teeth and ears that stuck out like jug handles. He was quite a frightening sight, if you didn't know him, but harmless as a baby.

Hannah had once gone to his defence when a gang of children were throwing stones at him and he'd been her devoted slave ever since.

'I brought you an apple, Hannah,' he said, 'but I was too late to catch you before you got on the bus so I ate it myself.'

'Have you been here all day?' asked Hannah in horror.

'I told you, I was too late to catch you when you went to school so I just waited for the bus to come back.'

'Oh Billy, you silly fool, you must be half dead with the cold. Don't you ever do that again,' admonished Hannah.

'I thought you wuz my friend, now you're shouting at me,' he said, his big lips quivering and dribbling.

'I am your friend. I'm sorry, I didn't mean to shout at you. Come on, you can be our bodyguard and take us home safely.'

A big grin appeared on his face and he ambled over to the girls.

'What did you do all day in the barn?' asked Hannah.

'I read my comic and then I went to sleep in the straw until I heard the bus come.'

'Weren't you cold?' asked Hannah.

'No, I was lovely and warm in the straw.'

'Are you cold now?' asked Hannah.

'No, feel,' and he put out his big hand towards her. She felt it, and to her surprise it felt quite warm.

'You feel warm enough,' she said.

'You see,' he said happily, 'I'm lovely and warm so don't be mad at me any more.'

'I'm not mad at you, Billy, I was just worried about you. Come on, we'd better get home or your mother will be out looking for you.'

'Do you want a piggy-back Hannah?' he asked

'No, thank you Billy,' she replied.

'Do you want a piggy-back?' he asked Maureen.

Maureen looked at Hannah, questioningly.

'I'm strong,' said Billy, 'I bet I could carry you all the way home.'

'It's all right, Maureen, you can have a piggy-back, then you feet won't get cold and wet.'

So Billy bent down and Maureen climbed on his back.

'Off we go,' said Hannah, pleased at having some company for the long walk home, even if it was only poor Billy. She knew she would come to no harm. Billy would protect her with this life if necessary.

They seemed to get home quite quickly for Billy was strong and moved along briskly, hardly aware of Maureen on his back and Hannah had a job keeping up with him, so she was very warm with the effort by the time her house come into view. Maureen jumped down from Billy's back.

'Thank you Billy,' she said, 'that was a lovely ride and you kept me lovely and warm.'

Billy's face broke into a grin, exposing his big ugly teeth.

'Yes, thank you Billy,' echoed Hannah, 'that was very kind of you. Now you go straight home and stay there while the weather is so bad and we'll see you again when the snow has gone.'

It was about two miles further to his house but Hannah knew he would do as he was told so she wasn't worried about him.

'You're not mad at me any more, are you Hannah?' asked Billy.

'No, of course not, I told you, we're friends, now. Off you go and we'll see you another day.'

So off he went, grinning like the Cheshire Cat.

3

March came in like a lion.

There had been very little let up with the weather. The snow refused to go and the older folk were saying it was one of the worst winters they could remember.

Icicles hung on every possible ledge, some as big as six feet long, and although the sight of them fascinated the children they couldn't work up much excitement for it had been a long, hard winter and they'd suffered with coughs and colds for weeks. All through the nights the sounds of their coughing rang through the house and they'd grown very thin and pale.

Even Aggie, usually very robust, had grown haggard from lack of sleep. Consequently, she was very short-tempered and she and John were constantly bickering.

Hannah could hear their voices now, raised in anger, coming from the bedroom next door.

'How do you think I can cope with another one?' Aggie's voice enquired of John.

'I'm half out of my mind with worry. You bloody men are all the same. All you think about is your own selfish pleasures and never mind the consequences.'

'That's not true,' came the reply, 'I'm as worried as you but I think you're jumping the gun a bit. Perhaps your cold has got something to do with it.'

'I think that's wishful thinking on your part, John; if I'd just missed one it could be possible, but not two.'

'Come on Aggie, have a heart, if you are pregnant you know I didn't do it on purpose. I know as well as you, we can't afford any more kids.'

'We can't afford the ones we've got.' wailed Aggie, as she burst into tears.

Colin, normally very placid, had been sitting up in his cot, looking from one to the other of his parents, and on seeing his mother in distress he promptly joined her and began to cry and cough uncontrollably; so much so that he held his breath and went very red in the face. John leapt from the bed and snatched him from the cot and began patting his back and shaking him to make him breathe, but still he held his breath.

Aggie panicked and grabbed him from John.

'It's all right baby, don't cry,' she said, but still he wouldn't breath.

'Oh my God, do something,' she screamed, so John took him from her and continued shaking him and just when they thought he would never breath again he filled his lungs and cried out.

Aggie was still crying, but now it was with relief, 'I'm so sorry baby, we didn't mean to frighten you,' she said, wiping his face and soothing him.

Colin's cries gradually quietened down to little sobs as she rocked him in her arms.

John pulled on his trousers and said to Aggie, 'You stay in bed for a while and try to get some sleep. Hannah will look after the others and I'll bring you a nice hot cup of tea.'

'Do you think we should have the doctor out to look at Colin?' asked Aggie. 'I know all the kids are poorly but Colin seems to have a temperature. I've been giving them all a dose of glycerine, honey and ipicac every day but it doesn't seem to be doing any good. I think he needs something stronger.'

'Let's see how he is today,' said John, 'and if he's not better by tomorrow I'll bike over to the village and ask Fred Bates if I can use his phone to call the doctor.'

He finished dressing, then popped into the children's bedroom.

'Hannah, your mother's not very well so she's staying in bed with Colin. You and the others stay in bed as well and keep warm, there's no point in getting up yet, it's too cold and I haven't lit a fire yet.'

'Can we have a drink please Dad, our throats are sore and we all have a headache.'

He looked at them and thought, They really do look poorly with unnaturally flushed faces.

'I'm just going to put the kettle on,' he said, 'so I'll bring you all a mug of tea.'

Hannah sank back gratefully in the bed. She really didn't

feel well enough to go downstairs for a drink but she would have made the effort for the sake of Maureen and Betsy.

Ten minutes later he came back into the bedroom with the tea.

Hannah helped Maureen and Betsy to sit up and wrapped her cardigan around their shoulders so they wouldn't freeze while they were drinking it.

The inside of the bedroom window had been covered in ice for weeks and it was so cold in the bedroom that their breath came from them like steam.

'Stay in bed until I get back,' said John. 'I'll see to the animals and get back as early as I can. Behave yourselves, for Colin is very poorly and he needs some rest.'

The children couldn't have gathered up enough strength to misbehave even if they'd felt like it. They drank their tea as hot as they could and then huddled together under the covers to get warm and went to sleep.

When John returned from the fields, hours later, they were all still in bed.

He popped his head in to look at Colin, just as Aggie woke up.

'You've had a good sleep,' he said.

'What's the time?' asked Aggie sleepily.

'It's two o'clock,' he replied.

'I must have been more tired than I realised,' said Aggie.

'How's Colin?' asked John.

'He's been sleeping nearly all the time you've been out with hardly a cough but I don't like the look of him, he seems to be burning up with fever. We'll have to get the doctor out to him tomorrow.'

When John had lit the fire he called out, 'Hannah, you can get up now, if you like.'

But they all felt too tired and weak to get out of bed so John took some more tea and a plate of bread and butter to the bedroom and Hannah and her sisters had a picnic. She then read some of her book to them until they fell asleep again.

Aggie slept very little that night for Colin appeared much worse and she woke John as soon as it was daybreak to go down and fetch a drink for the baby. He came back with a bottle of orange juice, lifted Colin from his cot and put him in bed with Aggie.

She cradled him in her arms and attempted to give him his bottle but although he seemed to be very thirsty, every time he swallowed a little of the juice he cried.

With a lot of coaxing, she managed to persuade him to drink about half the contents of the bottle but gave up after that because he now began to cry loudly and she noticed that his throat looked very peculiar, covered with a greyish-white membrane.

'What on earth's wrong with him, John?' she asked. 'His throat looks very infected.'

'We won't give him any breakfast until the doctor has seen him,' said John. 'I'll go for him now but I think it's useless to try and bike in the snow so I'll walk, so don't worry if I seem to be taking a long while. I'll get back as quickly as I can and pray that the doctor isn't out.'

He arrived at the little village shop before it was open and banged on the door until Hannah's friend, Pam, opened it.

'I'm sorry to disturb you so early love,' he said. 'but would you ask your dad if I can use the phone? I need to call the doctor.'

'Of course you can, Mr Hardy. I know Dad won't mind but I'll let him know you're here. There's nothing wrong with Hannah, I hope' she couldn't help adding.

'Well, she and the other girls are poorly but it's Colin we're really worried about. He seems to be much worse than them.'

She gave him the doctor's number, then went to fetch her father.

'Hello John, what's up?' said Fred Bates coming in to the back room of the shop as John was replacing the phone.

John explained, adding that fortunately the doctor was in and would be there within an half an hour.

'If it's all right with you Fred, I'll wait here, and the doctor will pick me up on the way through, to save me the walk back.'

'Yes of course you can,' said Fred, 'come through to the kitchen and have a cup of tea while you're waiting. Peg is just brewing up.'

Peg, his wife, was a fat jolly woman with cheeks like rosy, red apples and it was easy to see from whom Pam inherited her happy-go-lucky nature.

'Come and sit down and get warm, you must be frozen,' she said. 'I'm sorry to hear the kids aren't well. Let me know if there's anything I can do to help.'

It was nearly an hour and two cups of tea later before the doctor arrived.

He came hurrying in, shaking the snow from his hat and apologising for taking so long, but, he explained, his old car was a bit temperamental in the cold weather. He'd have to try and get a new one before next winter, although how he'd manage this he had no idea at the moment, for country doctors didn't earn much money. But, something would have to be done, he thought worriedly, for human lives would depend on his speed.

'Would you like a cup of tea?' asked Peg.

'That's very kind of you, but I can't stop now, I'll just warm my hands and get off to see young Colin.'

With that he hurried out, John at his heels, adding, as he reached the door, 'If I have time, I'll call on the way back for a cup of tea, for I might not get another chance today, with so many children sick.'

'You sound as though you're very busy,' said John, as they started off.

'I'm rushed off my feet,' replied the doctor. 'I've had little or no sleep for weeks and I don't have time to eat properly. I think I've lost weight recently and my wife's very concerned about me but what can I do? I know it's not fair to her, myself, or my patients to work until I drop but I can't get any help, for all the neighbouring villages have epidemics of one strain or another so there's no help to be had. I just hope I'll be able to keep going until things improve.'

When they reached the house, Aggie met them at the door.

'Oh thank God you're here,' she said. 'I'm sure Colin has worsened even since you left.'

'Come, come,' said the doctor, 'I'm sure things aren't as bad as you think. Calm down, now, or I'll have another patient on my hands.'

'I'm sorry,' said Aggie, 'but I just know he's very ill.'

'I'll be the judge of that,' answered the doctor. 'Where is he? Let's have a look at him.'

They took him through the hall and up the staircase to the bedroom where Colin sat tearfully in his cot, waiting for his mother to return. On seeing a stranger entering he began to wail loudly, holding out his arms to Aggie.

'It's all right baby, it's only the doctor, he won't hurt you.'
But he refused to be consoled and clung to Aggie for all he was
worth.

'Come on old chap, let's see what all the fuss is about,' the
doctor said, attempting to take him from his mother, but he
clung on, refusing to be separated from her.

The doctor allowed him a minute or two to calm down but
when he still couldn't coax him away from his mother he
suggested that she sat on the bed with Colin on her lap, while
he examined him.

With much difficulty, he managed to look him over and with
a few taps here and there and a good look at his throat he
concluded his examination.

'What is it doctor, what's wrong with him?' Aggie asked
fearfully.

'I'm sorry to inform you that Colin has diphtheria' the
doctor said quietly.

'Oh my God, I knew it, I knew it,' screamed Aggie. 'He'll
die, won't he? He'll die.'

'Not necessarily,' replied the doctor. 'It is very serious but
I've seen a lot worse cases than this pull through. With luck
he'll be all right. I'll give him some medicine to try to contain
the infection. We must try to stop it reaching his heart.'

'What happens if it does?' asked John.

'Well,' explained the doctor, 'if that does happen there's a
danger of it affecting his heart muscles and leaving a weakness
there. But even if the worse comes to the worst it's not the end
of the world. I've known people badly affected who've lived a
long life with proper care. But do try not to be too alarmed, it
won't help if you allow your worries and anxieties to affect
Colin. If you like, John, I can give you a lift back to the village
to pick up the medicine. The sooner he starts the course the
better. Now what about the girls? I'd better take a look at them
while I'm here.'

'They're all right,' said Aggie. They've just got colds. Its
Colin we've got to worry about.'

'Nevertheless,' said the doctor, taken aback by her lack of
concern for her daughters, 'I would like to make sure they're
free from infection.'

'If you want to waste your time that's your business,' said
Aggie. 'I'll get them up and bring them down to the kitchen.'

'There's no need for that. Mrs Hardy, just take me to their bedroom. I don't want to disturb them more than I have to.'

'If you insist,' said Aggie.

'I do,' replied the doctor beginning to feel annoyed with her. It's incredible, he thought, how can a mother be out of her head with worry over one child and not care tuppence about the others? I've never met anyone like her before.

'Don't take any notice of her, doctor,' said John, 'it's not that she doesn't care about the girls, it's just that she's half crazy with worry over Colin.'

'That may be so,' said the doctor, 'but she shouldn't have to be reminded that she has four children, not just one.'

He tapped on the girls' bedroom door and went in. They weren't alarmed because they'd heard most of what was said next door.

What a pathetic sight, he thought, no wonder she didn't want me to come in to their bedroom.

He'd got used to sights of poverty but it still disturbed him every time he came across it.

The bedroom was quite dark, because the one little window was so frosted up it kept most of the light out. The only furniture was a big bed and a broken chair on which the children put their clothes. The floor was covered in cheap canvas, so old and worn that the pattern had almost disappeared.

The children were almost lost in their bed. They'd huddled down so far that only the top half of their faces showed above the thin covers that served as blankets.

'Hello Hannah,' he said. 'I hear you're all a bit poorly.'

'We're all right, thank you doctor,' Hannah replied politely. 'We've just got colds, that's all, it's Colin who's really ill.'

'Well, that may be so but as I'm here I might as well have a quick look at you and Betsy and Maureen, if that's all right with you?'

So he examined the girls, satisfied himself that they were free of infection and explained to Hannah about Colin's illness, adding that until he was better they were not to go near him.

'Your father is coming back with me to fetch some medicine for Colin and I'll also send some linctus for you and your sisters; you're big enough to take charge of it. Take one teaspoonful three times a day. Can you remember that?' He didn't want to leave it in Aggie's charge for he feared she wouldn't bother to give it to them.

'Yes, I can remember that, I'll look after the others, don't you worry.'

The doctor smiled, thinking to himself, Here's one little girl who's had to grow up before her time. 'I'm sure you will Hannah,' he said. 'I'll be calling in again in a couple of days' time to see how you're all getting on.' He went downstairs to where Aggie and John were waiting.

'Will Colin be all right, doctor?' asked Aggie. 'Please say he'll be all right.'

'He has every chance of pulling through,' replied the doctor. 'I'll do my best, you do your best and after that, the rest is in God's hands.'

She didn't even ask if her daughters were all right, thought the doctor, as he and John went to his car.

Aggie watched the car slither away and rushed upstairs and immediately ignored the doctor's advice by picking Colin up and fussing and crying over him and in turn, making him cry.

'It's all right baby, Mummy's here, don't cry, you'll be all right, I won't let anything happen to you, we'll have you better soon.'

And so she carried on, getting herself in a state, stifling Colin, making him hot, uncomfortable and very bewildered. Hannah, on hearing the commotion, tapped on her mother's door and walked in.

'Don't cry Mum, you're only making yourself and Colin worse. Remember what the doctor said about keeping calm.'

'It's all very well for him to say keep calm, it's not his baby that's ill and as for you, you don't care, all you care about is them two next door.'

'That's not true Mum, I do love Colin, we all do, it's just that you won't let us get near him, you like to have him all to yourself.'

'Don't your dare answer me back, you cheeky little bugger, get out of here and stay out,' said Aggie and swinging her arm round, she caught Hannah a fierce blow round her face, 'and take that with you, to teach you a lesson.'

The blow caught Hannah unawares and lifted her off her feet and as she fell she hit her elbow on the iron bed-frame. She staggered to her feet. Her head felt as if it had been pumped full

41

of cotton-wool and there were red dots swimming around before her eyes. Blood flowed from her arm which lay open like a scarlet painted mouth.

When Aggie saw the blood she screamed at Hannah, 'Get out of here, you'll get blood all over my bed.'

She's going mad, thought Hannah, as she stumbled drunkenly back to her bedroom.

Maureen and Betsy were sitting wide-eyed, shaking with fear and cold on the edge of the bed.

'Oh Hannah, what ever has she done to you?' asked Maureen.

'It's all right, when I've washed the bloo—.'

'Hannah, Hannah, Hannah.' Voices coming from far away. 'Hannah please wake up, please Hannah' and then two tear-stained faces came through the mist, went, and came back again.

'Hannah, please, wake up.' She could hear the voices but she was floating and warm and she didn't want to be disturbed. She smiled and tried to slip back into the lovely, light feeling of nothingness, but this time, hands gently shaking her.

'Please Hannah, you're frightening us.' The two little faces came back and this time they stayed, and steadied.

Consciousness came back and with it a knife-sharp pain in her arm and twin hammers in her head and as they helped her to sit up floods of tears gushed down her face.

'Where am I? What's happened? Did I fall?' and then she remembered.

'I'm going to tell a policeman about Mum,' said Betsy. 'Then he'll take her to jail and she won't be able to hurt you any more. Poor Hannah.'

'It's all right, I'm feeling better now, I must have fainted, I don't think Mum meant to hurt me so much, she just meant to give me a slap and I fell. She's so worried about Colin, we must try and keep out of her way and be very quiet until he's better.'

But Betsy wasn't convinced and she cried and hugged her beloved Hannah.

'Come on, cheer up. I feel better now, really I do. When I've cleaned up my arm it won't look half as bad.'

'You can have my hankie to tie round it if you like,' said Maureen.

'That's very kind of you Maureen but once my arm is

42

cleaned up I can put my hankie round it, I just hope the blood won't spoil it.'

She went down to the kitchen, poured some water into a bowl and added some salt (for she'd remembered being told it was a good antiseptic if nothing else was available), then gingerly dipped her elbow in it. She gasped with the pain and her eyes filled with tears. I must have put too much salt in, she thought.

She gently patted it dry, put a piece of rag on the gaping wound, then wrapped the hankie round it. She had to sit on the stool for a few minutes then for she felt quite faint again. When her head stopped spinning she took a few deep breaths to compose herself and went back to the bedroom.

'Here I am, all patched up,' she said brightly to her two worried little sisters.

'Is it all better now, Hannah?' asked Betsy.

'It doesn't hurt so much now,' she lied bravely, but I'll have to sleep on the outside of the bed, just in case one of you accidently knock it and makes it bleed again.'

On his word, two days later, Doctor Lawson returned, to be met by Hannah at the kitchen door.

'Hello Hannah, how are you today? Are your coughs any better?'

'We're better in the daytime but the coughs get worse again at nights but your medicine has made our throats better, they're hardly sore at all now, thank you,' she replied.

'Where's your mother, is she out?'

'Oh, no doctor, she's been in the bedroom with Colin nearly all the time since you last came. She only comes out to go to the lav' or to make a cup of tea.'

'Where's your father?'

'He's down the field seeing to the animals.'

'So, who's been looking after you and your sisters?'

'I've been looking after them, I'm quite big enough, I am nearly twelve.'

'Hm,' said the doctor, 'and who's been seeing to your meals?'

'We've had bread and butter mostly but we haven't been very hungry and this morning I made us all some toast on the fire and that was lovely. Maureen and Betsy ate a big plateful and we all had two mugs of tea, but don't tell Mum, we're only supposed to have one.'

'You're a good girl, Hannah and one day you'll make a good little mother.'

He then noticed the grubby handkerchief round her elbow.

'What's wrong with your arm, have you had an accident?'

'Sort of,' and she explained what had happened, adding quickly, 'it wasn't Mum's fault, she didn't mean to hit me so hard, it was my fault for answering back. Please don't say anything to her about it.'

He noticed that she looked very frightened, so he said quickly, 'No of course I won't but I think I'd better have a look at it.'

The blood had congealed and the handerchief had stuck to it, so he took off his coat and poured some water from the kettle into a bowl. He opened his little black case and took out some lint and bandage and a little bottle of TCP.

'We'll have to get that hankie off and put a clean dressing on,' he said 'or you're going to have a sore arm for a very long time. This will sting a bit, Hannah, so you'll have to be very brave.'

He very gently bathed her arm until he could get the hankie unstuck, then he put some fresh water in the bowl and a few drops of TCP and bathed it with cotton wool.

'Oh you poor child' he said, 'that's a very nasty gash, it should have had a couple of stitches. I'm afraid you'll have a scar, but,' he said 'it seems remarkably clean, and there doesn't seem to be any infection.'

'That's because I bathed it in salt,' Hannah said proudly.

He patted it dry and wrapped a bandage round it. 'There,' he said, 'that should do the trick, I'm sorry if I hurt you, you've been very brave. It should be all right now but I'll leave you a clean bandage in case it needs re-dressing before I come again. Now, let's go and have a look at young Colin.'

Hannah tapped quietly on her mother's door and said, 'The doctor's here, Mum,' showing him in.

Aggie looked at Hannah's arm. She didn't say anything, but she thought, No wonder he was a long while before he came up, pampering to that child instead of coming straight up here to my baby. Hannah noticed the sour look and quickly ducked out.

'Good morning, Mrs Hardy, how are we today?' inquired

the doctor, trying to ignore the foul-smelling air in the room. 'I'm glad to see you've lit a little fire, but don't forget to open the window a bit to change the air.'

Aggie sat on the edge of the bed, nursing Colin.

'How has he been these last two days? Does the medicine seem to be doing any good?'

'I don't think he's any better or worse,' she replied, 'but at least he's quieter so we've been able to get some sleep.'

'Have you been out for some fresh air? You haven't been sitting here all the time I hope.'

'Yes, I have, I can't leave him. There'll be plenty of time for fresh air when he's better.'

'That may be so but you should take yourself out a couple of times a day for some fresh air; otherwise, you'll be ill and then who will take care of him?'

'But, if I leave him, who'll look after him? You won't let the kids come in here, so what can I do?'

'When he's sleeping it won't hurt to leave him for a while. He's quite safe in his cot, he can't fall out and when John comes home, why don't you let him come up for a while? Then you can go downstairs for an hour and listen to the wireless or read the papers, to take your mind off your troubles.'

'No thank you, there's no pleasure in the wireless or the papers nowadays. All we hear, or read about is the war. I've got enough to worry about in my own house, without worrying about the rest of the country.'

'Even so we *are* at war and you should keep in touch with the outside world. Just by ignoring it won't make it go away. There haven't been any more bombs dropped in our area since October. Enemy planes have been spotted, but they've just been flying in as far as the Wash and then turning back. Most strange, people are beginning to call it "The Phoney War".'

'Perhaps that's all it is so I'm not worrying myself to death over something that might not happen.'

Doctor Lawson let the subject drop then. It was impossible to hold an intelligent conversation with someone as illogical as Aggie.

He took Colin from her arms, with no protest from the baby this time, examined him carefully and put him in his cot.

'Now Aggie, you do as I say and have a little break from the sick-room.'

45

'Do you think he's any better?' asked Aggie, ignoring his remark.

'He's no worse, at least,' he said. But he's no better either, he though to himself. 'He seems to be holding his own but I'll come in again in a few days time. If at any time you're at all worried or he seems to get worse, don't hesitate to call me, and don't forget what I said about taking care of yourself.' For although he had little time for the selfish woman he appreciated that she needed to take care of herself so she would be able to care for the sick baby.

'Good-bye,' he called to Hannah, 'take care of yourselves, I'll see you in a few days' time.'

46

4

During the next two weeks, Hannah, and her sisters' colds gradually receded.

Colin was pretty much the same. Aggie still stayed entombed in the room with him and the doctor was growing increasingly concerned with the baby's lack of response to his medicine.

Hannah had her twelfth birthday and with it, her first period. She felt no need to inform her mother about it for the year before, Aggie had handed her a package saying, 'Keep these in your bedroom, you'll need them one day.'

She'd given Hannah no explanation as to the contents (which turned out to be hand stitched sanitary squares). She had learnt all about periods and babies at school so she wasn't at all perturbed.

She had received three birthday cards, one from Miss Gibbard and the girls in her class, wishing her a happy birthday and a speedy return to school, one from Pam, with a hankie inside (Pam had heard about the ruination of the other one due to Hannah's cut elbow) and one from Aunt Lil, containing a postal order for 25s., for which she thanked God (and Aunt Lil). Now she could buy some shoes to go back to school in. Her father had given her a half-a-crown, so if she were very careful she could buy some new socks as well.

She felt very excited at the prospect of returning to school wearing new shoes and of seeing Pam, although they'd kept in touch with notes which Doctor Lawson had kindly passed back and forth.

She missed having someone her own age to talk and laugh with for there'd been very little to laugh about lately.

Aggie had become very withdrawn and a little peculiar, her whole world revolving around Colin, hardly noticing Hannah and her sisters.

John had taken to going into King's Lynn for a drink, if he

could beg a lift, usually from fellow pig and chicken dealers he came in contact with at the market. He was very fortunate in some respects, for, having no transport of his own, he was usually given a lift to market when he had chickens or pigs to sell.

Today he'd taken some chickens to market. If the prices were poor he would bring them home and take them back another week when the prices were better; if they were good he would probably go into town for a drink before returning home.

A toot-tooting on a horn announced the arrival of the baker's van; Mr Rake called twice a week.

'Mum the baker's here,' called Hannah,

'I can't come down, you'll have to see him, get two loaves and tell him I'll pay him on Friday.'

The van came to a halt, the door opened and out stepped Elsie Watson.

'Hello lovie,' she said to Hannah, 'I was asking Mr Rake how you were all getting on and he said he'd give me a lift out here to see you and pick me up on the way back, when he's finished his rounds.'

Hannah collected the bread and she and Elsie went into the kitchen. Hannah told Aunt Elsie (as she liked to be called) all about their colds and Colin's sickness and her mother's state of mind, whilst making a cup of tea.

Maureen and Betsy had heard voices and had come gingerly to the kitchen door to see who was there.

'Hello, my little lovies, come and give your old Aunt Elsie a kiss.'

Their eyes lit up with pleasure when they saw who it was.

She enveloped them in her big fat arms and kissed and cuddled them until they had to come up for air.

'Oh, you little lovies, I could eat you all up,' she said, 'if I ever have any little girls, God willing,' she added 'I'm sure I'll kill them with kindness. I love my little Tom, bless his heart, but I hope he'll have some sisters one day. If not,' she said, 'I'll ask your mother if she'll sell you to me' with a wink at Hannah. Maureen and Betsy looked at Hannah.

'She's only joking,' laughed Hannah.

'Well, if Mum ever does sell us, I hope Aunty Elsie will buy us. I wouldn't want to go with anyone else,' said Maureen half

48

seriously.

'Where's Tom?' asked Betsy.

'He's got a bit of a cold so I've left him with his Auntie Annie', said Elsie. 'Now, I've brought something for good little girls. Have you been good Betsy?'

'Have I Hannah?' asked Betsy.

'Yes, you've been as good as gold, and you,' she said to Maureen, who was looking at her questioningly.

So Elsie handed the two girls a lovely big red lollipop.

'I got something else for you Hannah, though how you can enjoy that rubbish is beyond me. Still, I know you and your friends like it' and she handed her a bag of liquorice wood.

'Oh lovely,' said Hannah, 'I can make a stick of that last me all day, so there should be enough here to last me all the week. I haven't had any for ages, thank you ever so much Aunt Elsie.'

They all sat talking and drinking tea for quite a while. It was so comfortable in Elsie's company and she obviously enjoyed talking to the girls.

Aggie's a lucky bugger, she thought, I'd give my right arm for a little girl and she's got three and doesn't give a rap for any of them. I don't begrudge her her good fortune but I wish she'd realise how fortunate she is and not look upon them as nothing but nuisances.'

Maureen and Betsy were sitting on the stool, all their attention concentrated on their lollipops. Betsy had the sticky substance running down her chin and was trying to capture it with her tongue.

Hannah saw the mess she was getting in and took out the ever-faithful piece of rag and mopped her up, at the same time straightening her hair ribbon and tucking her hair behind her ears.

Elsie's heart ached as she watched Hannah unconsciously playing the role of mother. She's such a little thing; she thought, somebody should be mothering and fussing over her. The strange thing was that although Hannah didn't receive any love or attention from her parents, she had all the love in the world to pour on her little sisters and quite suddenly she felt very sorry for Aggie for being unable to appreciate all these treasures under her roof.

'Are you going to ask your mum to come down? I don't

suppose she knows I'm here.'

'I'll go and tell her,' said Hannah, who was in the process of filling the kettle and replacing it over the fire.

She tapped gently on her mother's door and put her head in. 'Aunt Elsie's come to see you Mum, are you coming down?'

'Can't she come up here?' replied Aggie, 'I don't like leaving Colin, you know.'

'Just come down for a little while, it'll do you good, Colin's asleep and we'll be very quiet so we'll hear him if he wakes up,' said Hannah. 'Come on Mum, just for five minutes.'

Aggie got up reluctantly, 'Oh, all right but just for a few minutes.'

Hannah felt elated at being able to coax her mother from the bedroom. Although she knew it was due to Aunt Elsie's presence, for whatever reason, it was a step towards normality.

When Aggie walked into the kitchen Elsie tried to disguise her shock. Aggie's hair was limp and greasy, her clothes were grubby and crumpled as if she'd slept in them and she was very pale with dark shadows round her eyes; her stockings were wrinkled around her ankles. All in all she looked ten years older than when they had last met.

Elsie stood up. 'Come and sit here, by the fire, love, you look perished. I'll make you a nice cup of tea, have you had anything to eat?'

Aggie walked over to her seat which Elsie had just vacated.

'Hello, Elsie, it's good to see you. Did they tell you about Colin?'

'Yes love, the baker told me so I thought I'd come and keep you company for a little while.'

Aggie looked over to Hannah. 'Take Betsy and Maureen upstairs to play, so me and Aunt Elsie can talk in private.'

'Don't send them out on my account Aggie, it must be bloody cold upstairs.'

'Oh, they're all right, they're as hard as nails, and they'll be able to hear Colin if he wakes up.'

So with great reluctance, they left the warmth and comfort of the kitchen and Aunt Elsie.

'Are you looking after yourself Aggie? You don't look very well. Have you lost weight since I last saw you?'

'To tell you the truth, Elsie I'm worried to death.'

'Oh come on Aggie, I'm sure things aren't as bad as you

think.'

'They're worse than you know, and if I've lost weight that's a bloody miracle, for by all accounts I should be putting it on.'

'How do you make that out Aggie? From what I hear from Hannah, you're hardly eating a thing, so you're bound to lose weight.'

'There are other ways to get fat, besides eating,' she replied.

'Oh, you don't mean,' began Elsie.

Aggie put her face in her hands, and began to cry. 'Yes, I think so; in fact, I know so, I haven't seen anything since before Christmas.'

'You could be wrong.'

'Yes, and pigs could fly but they don't. Oh I'm sorry Elsie, I didn't mean to bark at you but I've felt so bloody awful since Christmas and I've had nobody to talk to. It's a good job I haven't got a gas cooker for I'd have stuck my head in it before today.'

Elsie went over to her and put her arms around her friend's quivering shoulders.

'Come on Aggie, I know things are bad but we've had bad times before and we always manage to come through them together.'

Elsie's sympathy was just too much and Aggie cried long and hard for about five minutes. Elsie didn't say anything but just kept her arms around her and let her cry it all out. It'll do her good to have a good old blar, she thought, she's been bottling things up for too long. Let her get it all out of her system, then perhaps she'll be able to think rationally.

'Right, now you've got that lot out we'll have a nice hot cup of tea. We have always been able to sort our problems out over a cuppa,' said Elsie.

Aggie blew her nose and looked up to Elsie. 'You're a good sort, Elsie, I don't know what we'd do without you.' And she didn't just mean her family. Elsie was often called upon by the villagers for helping to bring a baby into the world or laying out someone who'd died, for she managed to make them look lovely and happy in death and in so doing brought great comfort to the grieving families.

She made a fresh pot of tea, by which time Aggie's sniffling had almost stopped.

They sat sipping their tea in companiable silence for a few

minutes, enjoying the comfort it gave them and toasting their legs before the fire.

Aggie gave a huge sigh. 'Thanks Elsie, I feel a lot better now, you're as good as a tonic.'

'Talking of tonics,' replied Elsie, 'do you want me to make an appointment for you at the surgery so Doctor Lawson can give you a check up?'

'He'll only tell me what I already know and anyway I can't leave Colin.'

'Don't worry about that, I'll make the appointment for a time when I can come and look after Colin until you get back. You really ought to go and see him. You do look a bit peaky. Perhaps he'll give you a tonic or something.'

'I must confess, I do feel worse than I usually do when I'm pregnant but I think it's because I'm so tired from sitting with Colin.'

'Yes, I expect that's what it is but it won't do any harm to have a checkup. Then, if your worst suspicions are confirmed I'll put you down in my diary for I'll know when I've got to come and do for you' she said with a smile. 'At least' she added, 'you don't kick up a fuss like some. You'd think it was the end of the world the way some of them create, whereas you make it look as easy as shelling peas.'

Aggie couldn't help smiling at this. 'Well I tell you what Elsie, I'll be more than glad when the pea season's over; I think my pod has popped enough times.'

They were now more comfortable and relaxed and spent a happy hour talking of other things and inevitably the war and the German planes over King's Lynn were mentioned, but on this subject Aggie started to tense up again. So Elsie quickly changed the subject, thinking to herself, I'll have to be very careful not to talk about unpleasant things, for in Aggie's state of mind she couldn't cope with unhappy thoughts.

The sound of a horn tooting announced the arrival of the baker's van.

Hannah, Maureen and Betsy tumbled into the kitchen to say goodbye to Elsie, who gave them all a kiss and a cuddle, including Aggie, to whom she said, 'I'll let you know when I've made the appointment for you. Meanwhile take care of yourself and try not to worry too much, you'll only make yourself ill.'

As soon as the van had rounded the corner Aggie headed back towards the bedroom.

'Can we have something to eat, please?' asked Maureen.

'Hannah, cut them some bread and jam and look after them until your dad comes home,' and with this she was gone.

John hadn't returned by eight o'clock. Hannah assumed he'd had a good day at the market and had gone for a drink so, she washed her sisters and took them to bed.

She was unable to sleep straight away, thinking about her mum and how strange she was becoming and about her poor little brother, who just didn't seem to be getting better, and then there was Dad who was drinking more than ever and was probably drunk by now and half the money he'd got at the market would be in the till behind the bar at The Woolpack or The Eagle.

She could understand him having a drink now and then to cheer himself up for, his life was not much fun with her mum at the moment. But on the other hand, they were very hard up and the money he wasted at the pubs could have been spent on the kids. They were beginning to look very thin from not having proper cooked meals but at least Hannah saw to it that they had plenty of bread and butter and tea, so they wouldn't starve.

She slipped into an uneasy sleep.

She was walking down the High Street in King's Lynn wearing only her knickers. She had one leg longer than the other and was walking with one foot on the path and the other in the gutter so nobody would notice.

'Why didn't I put my clothes on?' she thought. 'Still, I'm nearly at the shoe shop and when I've got my new shoes I'll be able to walk properly.'

She walked into the shoe shop, which was full of people, but nobody noticed she had no clothes on. She chose a pair of lovely, shiny, black shoes and gave the lady behind the counter her money. But instead of giving her the shoes, the lady gave her a pint of beer.

'I don't want beer, I want a pair of shoes,' she said.

'We don't sell shoes, so take this beer or I'll call the police,' replied the lady.

People were starting to look her way, and she bobbed down so they wouldn't see her.

'Please, I want some shoes,' she said.

'You haven't any money.'

'Yes I have, I gave it to you.'

'Oh, no you didn't, don't be cheeky,' The woman said, hitting her in the face.

She started to cry and then she saw Pam's brother Ken and his friends coming into the shop, wearing very, very long football scarves. Oh, he musn't see me, she thought in horror. They were in the shop, and the door banged loudly behind them.

The door banging woke her up with a start. Her heart was thumping and she was in a sweat. Thank goodness, I was only dreaming, she thought in relief.

Another bang from downstairs in the kitchen and John's voice.

'Who the bloody hell left the stool out for me to trip over? Where is everybody? Aggie, Hannah, where's my tea?'

Aggie's voice came from the bedroom. 'Hannah, go down and make your father a sandwich and a cup of tea before he wakes the whole house up.'

'I daren't Mum, he sound as though he's drunk. You go down.'

Colin started to whimper. 'There, what did I tell you? He's woken the baby up now. Go down and see to him, he won't hurt you.'

'Don't go Hannah,' said Betsy, sleepily, 'I'm frightened, stay here with us.'

'It's all right,' said Hannah. 'Dont' worry, I'll just quickly make him a sandwich and I'll be back before you can say Jimmy Riddle.'

Her father was slumped in a chair by the fire.

'Hello dad, did you have a good day at market?'

'Pretty fair, pretty fair. Where's your mother? As if I don't know. Is it too much trouble for her to come and get me some tea?'

'You know she doesn't like to leave Colin,' said Hannah.

'How the hell does she expect me to go out and earn money for her if she can't be bothered to cook me some food? I'll have to sort that bloody woman out once and for all.'

'Please don't upset her tonight dad, she's not very well. Auntie Elsie's been here today and she's going to make an appointment for Mum at the doctor's.'

'It's a bloody head doctor your mother wants, I swear she's going round the twist.'

'Don't say that Dad,' said Hannah beginning to cry, 'she's just so worried about Colin it's made her ill.'

'I'm sorry Hannah, I didn't mean to upset you. You're a good girl, come and give your old Dad a kiss,' and he picked her up, swaying drunkenly, and nearly toppled over.

He held her tight, smothering her with kisses and breathing his beery breath over her.

'Please Dad, put me down, you'll fall over,' said Hannah, trying to wriggle free.

He dropped her abruptly. 'Have I got the bloody plague or something?' he asked. 'I can't get near my own wife and my kids treat me like muck. I should have stayed at the Woolpack. At least they're always pleased to see me.'

He slumped back in the chair and started to doze. Hannah cut him some cheese sandwiches and made a pot of tea.

'Here you are Dad,' she said, gently rousing him. 'I'm off to bed, good-night.' She hurried up to her bedroom and climbed into bed, heaving a sigh of relief.

About a half hour later, she heard her father stumbling up the stairs and crashing into his bedroom.

'Hello Aggie, my love, have you been waiting for me like an impatient virgin?' No reply. 'Come on, don't pretend to be asleep, look what I've got for you.'

'Shush John,' said Aggie quietly from under the blankets.

'Don't you shush me, woman, I said I've got something for you, don't you want to see it?'

She peeped out cautiously. He stood beside the bed, wearing only his shirt and socks, holding his huge penis in his hands.

'There, isn't he a beauty? And aren't you a lucky girl?' he said, waving it about.

'Move over Aggie, I'm about to explode.'

'How can you behave like that when your baby is ill in the same room?' asked Aggie contemptuously.

'Look here woman, I've had just about enough of your excuses. You haven't let me get near you for weeks. I know Colin is ill and I know you're pregnant but I'm a man with feelings and with or without your consent I'm exercising my rights, so you might as well get used to the idea.'

He got into bed and started fumbling and mauling her, 'Open your legs,' he said.

'No John, please don't.'

'Open your legs,' he said in a louder voice.

'Don't shout, the kids will hear you.'

'Are you going to let me in or not?'

'No, I'm not,' she said, pressing her legs tightly together.

'All right, if you want to play games,' he said, getting out of bed.

She pulled the blankets up to her chin.

'Open your mouth.'

'What?'

'You heard me.' He was kneeling beside the bed with his penis close to her face. 'It's time we had a bit of variety in our lives.'

'Oh no John, I couldn't,' she said.

'Oh yes, you could and you will.'

He took hold of her face with both hands and guided his penis towards it. But, with her wriggling about and his penis jumping about in excitement, it was impossible. He stood up.

'Sit up,' he said angrily and when she made no move, he pulled her up to a sitting position. 'Now, it's up to you. We can do it the hard way or the easy way.'

She struggled and screamed and he gave her an almighty slap and while she was half stunned he put his penis in her mouth and began to move it in and out until he came, with a grunt, exploding in her face. She coughed and gagged and began to be violently sick.

Hannah had heard her mother shouting and unable to contain herself she pushed her mother's door open to see her father standing over the bed with his dripping penis and her mother being sick on the floor.

'Get out!' her father yelled at her.

'What have you done to her?' she said.

'I said get out, or do you want me to take my belt to you?'

'Go back to bed, I'm all right,' said Aggie, coughing and spluttering.

So Hannah backed out, as her father moved towards her, too drunk to realise the sight he portrayed to his daughter – a sight she would remember for the rest of her life.

5

It was arranged for Aggie to visit Doctor Lawson the following Friday.

Elsie had come to the house on an early bus in order to stay with the children until she returned and had persuaded Aggie to let Hannah go into town with her.

The surgery was situated down a cobblestone courtyard off the market square and going off the square in the opposite direction was the High Street where there were two shoe shops.

Aggie would probably have to wait an hour or two in the surgery. Even if she got there on the dot of nine o'clock there would already be a queue of townspeople ahead of her so, during this period, Hannah could get her postal order changed at the post office and buy her new shoes.

They had planned to walk the two miles to the bus-stop. Fortunately the weather was a bit better, although there was still snow underfoot, for which Hannah was grateful, for she would have been very embarrassed walking down the High Street in waterboots if the weather had been fine.

Aggie was in quite good spirits as they set off. Although she was reluctant to leave Colin she knew that Elsie would take care of him as well as herself.

Hannah was outgrowing her mac, which she'd had for a couple of years and had worn so much that it no longer afforded any warmth and Aunt Elsie had insisted upon her borrowing her long knitted scarf. It was wrapped around her neck, crossed over her chest and tied behing her back. She was wearing a clean pair of school stockings so at least she wouldn't be ashamed to take off her boots in order to try on new shoes. She was so excited at the thought of new shoes that she wanted to run all the way to the bus-stop but because she was with her mother had to contain her exuberence.

Because of the scene Hannah had witnessed in her mother's

bedroom there was an uneasy tension between them but after a few minutes the fresh air seemed to exhilarate Aggie and she loosened up and was talking to Hannah quite agreeably.

She can be quite nice sometimes thought Hannah. Perhaps, when Colin is better she won't be so peculiar and then perhaps, Dad won't drink so much and then we'll all be happier.

A toot-tooting on a horn interrupted her thoughts and she stepped in close to the verge to enable the oncoming vehicle to pass, but as it drew level with them it stopped and a voice said,

'Morning, ladies, can I give you a lift?' It was Fred Bates, Pam's father.

'Thank you very much,' said Aggie as she and Hannah climbed into his van.

'Where are you two ladies off to?' he asked.

Aggie explained the reason for their trip to town (but not her expected pregnancy).

'What time are you planning to return, Aggie?'

'That's a very good question, Fred, but you know what Doctor Lawson's surgeries are like. I'll be lucky if I'm out within two hours.'

'Well,' said Fred, 'the reason I asked is because my business will take me a couple of hours. I guess I'll be returning about twelve o'clock, so, if you've done your business by then, be at the corner near the bank and I'll give you a lift home.'

'That's very good of you, Fred, I really appreciate it, if you're sure we're not putting you out.'

'Not at all, my pleasure ladies,' he said, doffing his cap theatrically.

Hannah enjoyed the ride to town. It was lovely and warm in the van and a treat to talk to somebody as nice as Mr Bates.

In no time at all, it seemed, they arrived at the market square.

They thanked Fred, in the hope that they would be able to meet him at 12 o'clock for the return journey.

Hannah walked with her mother down the courtyard to the surgery. It was packed full, with only standing room, but a gentleman vacated his seat for Aggie.

Hannah left her mother to go and buy her shoes. She knew exactly what to get and then she was to return to the surgery. She changed her postal order and went to the nearest shoe shop. She saw what she wanted in the window, priced at 23s.

but she didn't want to rush in and buy them until she'd looked in the other shop at the far end of the High Street. An identical pair of shoes were in the second shop window but this time, priced at twenty-two shillings and sixpence, so feeling very glad that she hadn't rushed in and bought the first pair she saw, she went inside.

'What do you want, little girl?' asked a toffee-nosed lady.

'Please, I'd like to try on the black, lace-up shoes that are in the window' she said.

'They're twenty-two and sixpence. Do you have enough money?'

'Oh yes, I have my birthday money,' said Hannah, smiling to herself, as she thought, thank goodness I'm not back in my dream, I'd be getting a clip round the ear about now.

She tried on a size one and walked up and down the shop enjoying the squeeky sound of the new leather.

'They seem a trifle big,' said the shop lady. 'Do you want to try a smaller size?'

'Oh no thank you, my mum always buys them a bit big, so they last longer.'

'Is there anything else I can get you?'

'Yes please, how much are white socks?'

'One and six a pair.'

'I'll have two pairs, please.'

'That will be twenty five shillings and sixpence, please,' said the lady, after she'd wrapped them. 'Do you need any polish?'

'How much is it, please?'

'Sixpence a tin.'

'Yes, I'll have one please,' said Hannah.

She paid for her parcel, which had been wrapped in brown paper. If I'm careful, thought Hannah, I'll be able to use the paper for covering books.

She wrapped the remaining one shilling and sixpence in her hankie, tied it securely and put it in her pocket. Her shopping had taken her about an hour so she decided to return to the surgery to wait for her mother, as it was too cold to go window shopping and anyway, she had her precious shoes so there was really nothing else she wanted to see.

Aggie had been in to see the doctor but there was still an hour before they were to meet Fred Bates for the ride home so they sat for a while in the waiting room, reading the books.

'Are you hungry, Mum?' asked Hannah.

'Yes, I am, are you? Still, we'll have to stay hungry till we get home. I haven't any money to buy anything in town.'

'Could you eat a bag of chips, Mum?'

'Where do you think I'm going to get money for chips? I told you, I haven't any money. I know, I've saved the bus fare, thanks to Fred, but I need a bag of sugar and luckily I've brought my ration book with me, so we'll go and get one now in case he's early.'

'Mum, guess what? I've brought my shoes and socks and I've got one and six left over so I can buy three penn'orth of chips for you and me and take two bags home for Maureen and Betsy and I'll still have sixpence left to save.'

'I don't like taking your money, Hannah, but I must confess I could eat a bag of chips.'

So off they went across the market square down the High Street and off the High Street at the very top, into Norfolk Street.

They could have found the chip shop blindfolded for the aroma of fish and chips wafted down the street, teasing their taste buds, and just two doors away was The Eagle where John spent much of his time and money.

Coming towards them, tucking into a large package of fish and chips was Billy Wilson and his mother.

'Yo ho, Hannah,' he yelled at the top of his voice, jumping with joy on spotting his friend.

When they drew level with him he said 'Do you want a chip? Go on have one, they're lovely.' He thrust his fish and chips under her nose.

'No thank you Billy, we're just going to buy some.'

'Can I come and play with you one day, Hannah?' he asked.

Aggie scowled at Hannah in disapproval.

'Yes, of course you can,' replied Hannah, 'but not until the snow has all gone, it's too far to walk from the village when the roads are bad.'

His mother, Old Ma Wilson, as she was called, stood beside Billy, patiently, waiting for him to finish his conversation, tucking in quite unselfconciously to her fish and chips. She was a peculiar looking woman, very small, under five feet, always wearing waterboots, summer and winter, and a head scarf tied tightly under her chin. Nobody could remember seeing her with the head scarf off and they wondered if she had any hair. She had hair sprouting from a large mole on her chin and tiny little piggy eyes.

It was difficult to believe she had given birth to Billy, who was so large. Everyone guessed that his father must have been a very big man but nobody knew who he was. He could have been anyone of a hundred and any nationality, for before his birth, his mother and a handful of other low women used to frequent the docks area, earning money by going with the men off the boats that came to King's Lynn regularly.

The men, from all countries, were very generous to the Dock Lillies as the local people called them, especially the big Dutch men who, as well as giving them money, used to supply them very generously with cartons of cigarettes and bottles of gin. The women used to drink some of the gin but mostly they sold it to the locals, who were very partial to it. They said it was much stronger than the British equivalent, so because of their usefulness they turned a blind eye to the Dock Lillies.

Very often the women, including Billy's mother, would be smuggled aboard the boats and spend the whole night there. But in doing this they took a huge risk for if they were caught the men would be instantly sacked.

Old Ma Wilson had taken pregnancy in her stride and after the birth found work cleaning houses and washing and ironing. Although illiterate, she was nobody's fool, and always managed to provide for and take care of her big son and never needed to ask for anyone's help.

She kept herself to herself and never caused any bother and was secretly admired by some for being such a good mother and devoting her life to her son. It didn't seem to worry her that he was 'tetched' in the head; he was simply her son and she worked hard and spent all her money on feeding and clothing Billy and together they were happy and content.

Her one big fear was that, if anything happened to her there'd be nobody to take care of Billy, for she had no other family and she knew, as sure as eggs were eggs, he'd end up in a mental home. He was no trouble at all; he was never violent and all it took to keep him happy was plenty of food and a good supply of comics. He couldn't read them of course, but he could 'read' the pictures and would spend hours at a time poring over them.

'We're now going to catch the bus, are you coming on the bus?' asked Billy.

'No, we've got a lift home with Mr Bates, but I'll see you another day.'

'Oh, all right,' he said, looking downcast.

'Come on Hannah, if we don't get a move on we'll miss Fred and then we will have to catch the bus' said Aggie, concerned in case she had to spend her precious money on bus fare.

They went into the little fish and chip shop and put in their orders, asking the girl behind the counter, to wrap two packets especially well, as they were taking them home.

The shop was very tiny but they'd squeezed a wooden table and two benches up the corner to enable six people to sit down and eat.

As it was still quite early the lunch-time rush hadn't started so they sat at the table to eat their chips.

Hannah felt very important sitting there, especially when Ken and his mates came in to buy chips.

She smiled up at him and said, 'Hello Ken.'

He glanced over and saw his sister's scrawny little friend with her equally scrawny mother.

'Oh, hi,' he said, thinking to himself. How bloody embarrassing, I hope my mates don't pull my leg for talking to her. But they were intent on flirting with the girl behind the counter and his exchange with Hannah went unnoticed. He mentally mopped his brow in relief.

Hannah tried to make her chips last out until Ken was served so she could look into his face again but he and his friends ate their chips at the counter, talking and laughing with the girl, so, reluctantly, on her mother's insistence, they left.

They went to the shop to buy the sugar and Hannah, still hungry, thought to herself, lovely bread and sugar for tea tonight. They all loved bread and sugar, dipped in tea, when Aggie wasn't looking.

They arrived at the bank, where they were to meet Fred ten minutes before twelve but he was already there, so they got into the van, thankful that they wouldn't have to stand around in the cold. They rounded the corner at the bus stop next to St Nicholas church and there stood Old Ma Wilson and Billy.

'Poor sods,' said Fred. 'They'll be frozen before the bus comes, it's not due for about forty minutes; I'd give them a lift but I haven't got any more seats.'

Aggie and Hannah were sitting with him on the bench-type front seat.

'They could sit on the boxes in the back,' said Hannah.

'I'm sure Mr Bates wouldn't want them sitting in the back where he can't see them.' said Aggie, unwilling to share her good fortune with the village idiot.

'Oh, that wouldn't worry me,' said Fred.

'Old Ma Wilson is as honest as the day is long and I'm sure she wouldn't nick any of my vegetables but it wouldn't be very comfortable.'

'Would it be all right with you Aggie?'

'It's your van Fred, it's not for me to say,' she replied ungraciously.

So he stopped and offered them a lift home.

Old Ma Wilson was glad of the offer, for although she could stand the cold she didn't like the thought of Billy being cold and it was quite a while before the bus was due.

Billy was thrilled to bits at the thought of riding home with Hannah and he positioned two boxes so that they could look out of the little back window.

Hannah really enjoyed the ride, and in next to no time, it seemed, they arrived at the top of the lane where they lived.

Fred didn't take them right up to the house for it would have been difficult to turn the van around in the skiddy snow. Hannah skipped ahead of her mother, eager to give Betsy and Maureen their chips.

She burst into the kitchen where they were huddled round the little fire, which was almost out, and felt very angry at her father for not making it up.

They flung themselves at her before she had a chance to get through the doorway.

'Hannah, Hannah, did you get your new shoes? You've been gone a long while.' They jumped around her excitedly.

They didn't even ask where Aggie was, but they loved Hannah so much and missed her dreadfully if they were separated for any length of time and only felt secure when they were all together.

'What have you been doing? Your hands and faces are all black. Have you been playing with the fire?' she asked sternly.

'We haven't been playing with the fire, we've just been

poking it a little bit to make it get up. We've been very cold,' said Maureen.

'Where's Aunt Elsie, is she upstairs with Colin? I bet she's very cold as well. I'll make us all a nice hot cup of tea to warm us up.'

Just then Aggie came in and, with barely a glance at the children, went straight through and up the stairs to the bedroom.

'I can smell chips, have you had some chips, Hannah?' asked Betsy.

'Yes, I have and I've brought some home for you but you can't have them until you've had a wash.'

'Oh Hannah, please, can't we wash afterwards, they'll get cold,' said Betsy.

Hannah took the kettle off the fire and poured some water into a bowl, which she put in the sink.

'When you've had a wash you can have your chips,' she said, refilling the kettle and placing it back over the fire, 'and while you're washing I'll cut some bread and butter and make some tea. I'll put the chips in the hearth to warm up.'

They finished washing before she'd cut the bread. 'Let me see your hands,' she said.

They held out their hands gingerly toward her, clean palms, but dirty fingers.

She slapped their upturned palms and said, 'Wash your hands properly or no chips.' When she inspected them for the second time she was satisfied. 'Now, while we're waiting for the kettle to boil I'll tell you a little nursery rhyme.'

'What's it called, is it one we learnt at school?' asked Maureen.

'No, you won't know this one, its called *Mucky Meeces*. It's one I made up especially for you.'

She stood in the middle of the room and announced, as she was taught to do in class.

Mucky Meeces by Hannah Hardy.

They would not wash their faces,
and Mother used to say
if you don't wash the grime off
your skins will all turn grey

64

They laughed and called her silly
and went their merry way
skipping and trittity trotting
until the break of day

The farmer heard the scuffle
as he mowed the hay
but he could not see their faces
because they'd all turned grey

The mowing blade came closer
and made those meeces say
if we can leave this field alive
we'll be good every day

Good luck was with those rebels
as the farmer turned away
they ran back home to mother
to wash away the grey

So if you see some meeces
whose faces are all grey
tell them the little story
of the farmer and the hay.

When Hannah finished reciting they clapped their hands in glee and Betsy said, 'I did see them little meeces when we were down the fields with Daddy and they did have grey faces.'

'So did I,' said Maureen. 'I'll tell them that little story when I see them again, if they'll stop and listen,' she said in a serious voice.

Hannah couldn't help laughing at this, as she put the chips on the table.

'Get up on your stool now and have your dinner. I'll go and tell Mum and Aunt Elsie I've made some tea.'

They scrambled up the table and began hungrily tucking in to their nearly warm chips and a big plateful of thick slices of new bread and margarine.

Hannah took a slice as she went to fetch the grown-ups. I don't think there's anything in the world I like better then new bread, she thought.

When Aggie and Elsie came in they huddled round the fire and Hannah gave them a mug of steaming hot tea which they drank gratefully and quickly. She then filled their mugs again and this time they drank more slowly, savouring the sweet tea and little warmth from the fireside.

'What did you think of Colin today?' Aggie asked Elsie, 'do you think he's getting better?'

'He's a king to what he was last time I saw him,' replied Elsie. 'I can hardly believe he's turned the corner so suddenly. If anybody saw him today they'd never believe he'd been ill, but don't get carried away because he's not out of the woods yet. Let's just keep our fingers crossed he doesn't have a relapse.'

'Well you're a bloody pessimist and no mistake,' said Aggie. 'Anyone would think you didn't want him to get better.'

'That's a crazy wicked thing to say Aggie. Of course I want him to get better but I don't want you to get too carried away yet. Just hold your horses for a few more days and then if he continues to progress you'll know he's really on the road to recovery.'

'I know you're right Elsie, it's just that I've been really crazy with worry and now that he's getting better you've thrown cold water over me. I didn't mean to bark at you, you're the only real friend I've got and I seem to take my spite out on you, but you know I don't mean it.'

'Course I do Aggie, don't worry, I don't take it to heart, I know you don't mean it. We've been friends for too long to let a little argument come between us and you haven't been yourself since Colin's been ill, but thank God the others didn't catch it; they're tough little buggers,' she said, looking over to them, with a relieved smile. 'How did you get on at the doctor's?'

'Just as I thought. I am you know what,' she said, looking over to the children, as if to say, 'Don't say too much in front of them.' 'He's given me an iron tonic to buck me up. He said, I should have put on more weight than I have and I've got to take more care of myself or I'll have a hard time of it.'

'Well, now Colin's getting on you'll have to look after yourself better and you could start by cooking a good old stew or something every day. It don't cost a lot. You don't have to put a ton of meat in it as long as you put plenty of vegetables and onions in it. You wouldn't have to leave Colin for very long for once you've put everything in the pot you can leave it to simmer slowly on the front of the fire, and when was the last time you made any dumplings? I know things are tight but flour and water don't cost much.'

'Oh shut up Elsie, you're making me feel hungry,' said Aggie.

'Well that's a good sign, that means you're beginning to feel better. Have you had anything to eat today?'

'Yes, we had some chips in King's Lynn after I came out of the doctor's but I'm hungry again now.'

'Look here,' said Elsie, putting her hand in her shopping bag. 'I got two tins of stewing steak from the shop before I came here today so you take one of them and cook a big pan of potatoes and that'll make a tea for you all.'

'I can't take that off you,' Aggie protested weakly.

'Yes, you can, you're not robbing me for I was going to put one on the shelf anyway, so you can pay me back next week if you like.'

'I'll peel the potatoes, Mum,' said Hannah, thinking what a treat it would be to have something cooked.

'You'll have to go down to the shed to get some,' said Aggie.

'I'll walk out with you,' said Elsie. 'It's time to go for the bus anyway.'

'Thanks for everything Elsie,' said Aggie.

'You're welcome, I'll come and see you again next week. Take care of yourself.'

John came home early from the market. The prices had dipped so low that only the very desperate sold any of their poultry. Most, like him, brought them home in order to take them back again next week, the only drawback being that it would cost him corn to feed them until the next market day and he was almost counting the grains now. Still, he thought, the bloody daft chickens will peck around for a few more days even when there is nothing to peck at. He'd never known such stupid animals. The only good thing about them was that they didn't need much tending. He'd make up one big tub of mash and meal once a day for them, a handful of corn and a trough of water and they'd be happy. They didn't have to be mucked out like the pigs.

He banged the muck and snow off his boots outside the kitchen door and walked in. He sniffed in disbelief. 'Bloody wars' he thought. 'I do believe she's actually got off her arse and cooked something. Not before time either for he'd had to tighten his belt recently and there was no fear of his kids out growing their clothes this year, poor little sods.

'You're early,' said Aggie.

'Well, there's nothing doing at the market today so I'll try again next week. That stew smells good, I'd nearly forgotten what it's like to have a hot meal.'

She explained about Elsie's generosity and how good she'd been to sit with Colin while they went to town and joyfully told him how much better he seemed.

'Thank God,' he said, 'now perhaps we can get back to normality.'

For the first time in weeks they all went to bed feeling agreeably full. Aggie felt good and was quite kindly disposed towards John and forgave him his brutal drunken behaviour and when she'd checked that Colin was sleeping peacefully, she allowed him to make love to her, surprised to realise that now she was feeling better, her need was as great as his and they fell asleep in each other's arms' sleeping soundly until morning.

6

John awoke and stretched, thinking how good he felt after a good night's sleep. Both he and Aggie had slept like logs and they hadn't heard a peep from Colin, or the girls.

He quietly got out of bed and pulled on his trousers. Aggie stirred sleepily.

'You stay there and have another five minutes; it'll do you good and I'll bring you a cup of tea,' he said.

He went down to the kitchen and lit the fire and put the kettle on to boil for the tea. He had a quick rinse under the tap. The water was icy cold but after he'd rubbed his face and hands briskly with the rough towel he felt invigorated.

He put the potato peelings into a big black pot with some water which would stand on the fire to cook after he'd made the tea and by the time he'd drunk his tea they would be cooked and ready to mash with some meal for the chickens.

What the hell can I give the pigs? he thought. He didn't have to worry about them too much as a rule, for they would eat any household scraps, but they'd been so hard up lately there was rarely anything left over from the table to give them. Still, things had to get better, he thought optimistically. They'd come through the worst of the winter, hopefully; and when the snow disappeared the animals would be able to forage around for bits and pieces and there'd be vegetables aplenty for the kids.

Thank God Aggie was more like her old self. It did her good to get out of the house for a bit and Elsie always managed to buck her up, she's got a heart of gold, he thought. How many people would have given Aggie a tin of stewing beef? I know she said we could return it next week but I do know that when next week comes she'll say she doesn't want it and if that is the case I'll make it up to her by giving her some eggs next time I can collect a dozen.

He was half way up the stairs with Aggie's tea when from the bedroom came the most fearful scream he had ever heard in his life. It made his blood turn cold.

Aggie had tiptoed over to the baby's cot to reassure herself that he was well tucked up against the cold. He lay on his back, eyes staring at the ceiling.

'You've been a good boy all night,' she said, taking hold of his arm to put under the blankets. It was as cold as ice.

She felt his face, cold as marble. She shook him gently, but his eyes stayed staring fixedly at the ceiling with not a flicker of an eyelash.

'Colin,' she whispered, 'wake up baby,' and then, louder, 'Colin, it's me, Mummy, wake up.' No response.

'No,' she shouted. 'No.' And then the scream that could have been heard miles away.

John reached the bedroom door the same moment as Hannah and they rushed in to find Aggie standing, like a statue, staring into the cot.

'What is it Aggie?' But his instincts answered him before she could.

He went fearfully to the cot and looked in. At first his brain wouldn't connect with his eyes, for in the cot was a life-sized doll, and then the click, the connection.

'Oh no, please God, no it can't be, no it can't be' he repeated. 'He's a lot better, he can't be dead.'

But all the time he was rejecting the obvious, tears were gushing down his face and he crumpled to his knees beside the cot, taking the baby's little hands in his big rough ones.

Hannah crept, in terror, over to the cot. 'He's not dead is he Dad?' But neither John nor Aggie answered her. She looked in the cot at her baby brother and thought, How smooth and peaceful he looks, and she knew he was dead.

Maureen and Betsy had been standing in the doorway, rooted to the spot in terror, and they walked slowly over to Hannah. She put an arm around each of them and squeezed them tightly to her, to give them comfort and support as they looked at the doll-like little figure, and then all three of them cried and cried as if their little hearts would break, sobbing and clinging to each other.

John was in his own private world of grief and Aggie stood as if turned to stone, neither of them in any condition to afford any comfort to the girls.

After a very long time, exhausted from crying, the girls sat down on the bed, with little sobs coming from first one and then another of them.

John was quiet now, still kneeling, and gently rubbing the little arm as if to bring warmth to it. Eventually he put the little arm under the blanket and with a huge sigh of resignation, closed the baby's eyes. He pulled the blanket up to his chin. He knew he should cover the baby's face, as was the procedure when a person died. But he could not bring himself to carry out this last final action.

He got to his feet, went to Aggie and put his arms around her but since that first piercing scream she hadn't uttered a sound. She stayed rooted to the spot, eyes staring and glazed. She felt as cold and stiff as the little body in the cot.

'Come and sit down love,' he said, coaxing her toward the bed, 'I'll send for Elsie.'

The children moved to make room for her on the bed beside them. She allowed him to seat her on the bed without a sound.

She's in shock, he thought, and I haven't a drop of drink to give her. I hope Elsie has got a drop of brandy in her house.

'Hannah, get dressed and run down to the village as fast as you can. Go to Fred Bates and ask him to ring for the doctor and then go to Aunt Elsie's. Ask her if she can come over straight away. Tell her everything and ask her if she's got some brandy for your mother.'

'We want to come with you,' said Betsy, clinging to Hannah.

'No, you'll have to say here. Dad might need you, and I'll be able to run faster on my own.'

They followed her into their bedroom where she quickly dressed, and then down to the kitchen, still shaking with cold and fear. She poured them a mug of tea and sat them beside the fire. She gulped a couple of mouthfuls and then telling them to stay there until she got back, she set off for Heysham.

When she arrived at the village quite a lot of people were about, doing their weekend shopping in Fred's shop, as it was Saturday.

Pam was helping her father, weighing sugar and putting it into little blue bags. She loved helping in the shop and Fred always paid her a shilling a week, which she usually put in her savings account at school on Mondays.

Hannah rushed in but was so short of breath that at first all she could do was fling her arms around her friend.

The words she tried to utter came out all jumbled and nobody could understand what she was trying to say.

Pam's mother came into the shop and saw the dreadful state she was in.

'Whatever's the matter, Hannah, is somebody chasing you?'

Hannah looked up into the friendly face.

'It's Colin,' she gasped. 'please phone for the doctor.'

'Bring her through to the kitchen and make her a cup of tea,' said Peg to her daughter.

She sat her down and put her arms around her, 'Now, take your time and tell us what's wrong.'

Bit by bit the story unfolded and Pam tried to comfort her whilst Peg phoned the doctor.

'I've got to fetch Aunt Elsie,' said Hannah, trying to stand on her wobbly legs.

'You just stay where you are,' said Peg. 'Ken can run and fetch her.'

Ken had heard everything on coming into the kitchen and he felt quite ashamed recalling his uncharitable thoughts when he'd met her in the chip shop.

'Course, I will, don't you worry Hannah, I'll have her here in no time.'

Hannah lifted her tear stained face to him. 'Thank you very much Ken, I know you can run much faster than me,' she said, beginning to cry in gratitude for their kindness.

By the time she'd drunk two cups of hot sweet tea and calmed down, with the help of her friend, Ken returned, saying that Elsie was on her way. The doctor was out on a call when Peg phoned but his wife said he would come straight out again on his return.

Elsie arrived and took Hannah in her arms and for a minute or two they cried together. Then Hannah remembered the brandy.

'Oh, Aunt Elsie, I should have asked if you had any brandy and I forgot to tell Ken to ask you.'

'It's all right love,' said Elsie, patting her handbag. I've got some here. I knew there wouldn't be any at your house. Now we'd better be going, if you feel all right.'

Fred came in, and took off his big, white apron. 'I'll take you in the van,' he said.

'But what about your customers?' said Elsie.

'That's all right, I've got a very capable family, they'll be able to hold the fort for half an hour.'

His family readily agreed and with a final hug for Pam they set off.

Reaction was setting in now and Hannah began shaking from head to toe, dreading the thought of going home as the full horror swept over her again.

'Come on now lovie, buck up,' said Elsie, 'you've got to try to be strong to look after Maureen and Betsy and I'm here now, so don't you worry. Everything will be all right,' and she kept her arms tightly round her until the shaking subsided.

Fred drove them right up to the gate and with thanks from Elsie and Hannah, he drove off, telling Elsie to let him know if he could do anything at all to help.

Maureen and Betsy were sitting exactly where Hannah had left them and they began to cry when she walked in.

Elsie went to them and cuddled and comforted them as best she could. 'Now, you've got to be very good and do as Hannah tells you,' she said. 'I'll be upstairs with your mum if you want me.'

She went up to the bedroom, where John sat on the edge of the bed, looking as if he'd just taken a beating, with his arm around Aggie, who sat silent and staring as if hypnotised.

She went over to the cot and one look told her that the baby had indeed left this world. Why God? she thought. Why did you allow him to get better only to snatch him away so suddenly? The Lord certainly moves in mysterious ways, to take this baby that Aggie loved to distraction only to put another baby in her belly that she didn't want. There was no rhyme or reason, she thought, shaking her head in bewilderment.

'Are you all right John?' He nodded his head dumbly. She looked at Aggie. 'How long has she been like this?'

'She's been like this all the time,' he replied.

'Has she cried?'

'No, not one tear. She just gave one terrible scream and she's been like stone ever since.'

Elsie took the brandy from her bag and gave some to John.

'Drink this and then go down and have a cup of tea and a smoke. The girls are sitting down there terrified. Try and talk to them a bit. I'll see to Aggie. She looks as if she's in deep shock; I'll try and bring her round.'

She sat down and put her arms around her friend. 'Oh Aggie love, I don't know what to say. I can't believe it. He looked so well yesterday.' And she began crying and hugging Aggie. 'Have a good old cry love, don't hold it back, it won't do you any good.'

But no matter how much she coaxed and cajoled she just couldn't reach her. She got her to drink some of the brandy but she drank it like a robot with never a word or any indication that she was aware of the presence of Elsie, who was by now a bit out of her depth and praying that the doctor would arrive soon and take over.

Hannah tapped on the door and walked in with two mugs of tea. She handed one to Elsie and the other to her mother. 'I've brought you a nice cup of tea Mum,' but Aggie didn't bat an eyelash.

'What's the matter?' she asked Elsie, her eyes big with perplexity.

'Just put it down here, I'll give it to her in a minute. Don't worry, she'll be all right when the doctor gets here.'

But the doctor, when he came, got no more respone than Elsie. She'd held out her wrist while he took her pulse; she obeyed his instructions in everything he said whilst he examined her but she didn't say a word.

John came back into the bedroom and he and Elsie and the doctor started to make arrangements for the funeral. They couldn't penetrate Aggie's stupor so John took the reins and hoped and prayed that when she came out of shock he had done things to her liking. He knew that she would want the orthodox funeral and as there were no extenuating circumstances to the death the funeral was arranged for the following Friday.

Elsie helped John make out the list of relatives he'd need to contact and she offered to write to them all to alleviate the pain it would cause him. For this he was very grateful, especially as his reading and writing were very poor.

They did all that could be done at this stage and Doctor Lawson left to make arrangements with the undertakers, who would probably come after lunch.

John coaxed Aggie into the girls' bedroom and Elsie washed and prepared the little body.

I don't know why I do this, she thought, with tears rolling down her face. I'll never be able to do it without getting upset, even when it's somebody I don't know very well. If it was an elderly person she was attending it wasn't quite as bad but when it was a child it broke her heart. Even so, she knew how much her services were appreciated, so she would always be on hand to help out.

There wouldn't be a bus back to the village for about two hours so she went downstairs and made some sandwiches for the children and explained, as kindly as she could, about their little brother's death and briefly about the funeral. She didn't elaborate on the latter for it was improbable that they would be expected to attend and she didn't want to frighten them unnecessarily, but she also knew if she didn't explain things to them nobody would and they would be very bewildered by the events of the ensuing week. She filled their bellies with lots of sandwiches and by the time she left they were a lot more relaxed.

Thank God Hannah is a capable little girl, she thought, for her sisters would be leaning on her heavily; they'd get little comfort elsewhere.

The next few days passed by in a whirl of comings and goings. Friends and relatives conveying their condolences and taking a last look at the baby who was laid in his little coffin in the front room.

Aggie spent all of her waking hours sitting with him in the cold room, leaving only when John led her to bed. She had still not uttered a world and everybody was tut-tutting and worrying about her state of mind. Each one who came wanted to be the one to break through her mental block, but no matter how much they cried, coaxed, comforted, it was all to no avail. She remained as if turned to stone, obeying instructions but making no responses.

John was very worried for her sanity but he tried not to dwell on it too much, just hoping that he could get her through the day of the funeral before she erupted, which she was bound to do eventually.

Elsie spent the whole of the day before the funeral cleaning the house and preparing for family and friends who would be coming back to the house after the funeral service. She was, as John had said of her, worth her weight in gold in times of crisis and he didn't know how he could have maanged without her. She had done the necessary shopping, buying the milk, sugar, bread and ham in order to offer refreshments to the mourners, as was the custom, and in her generosity had brought her best tea set from her own house for them to use for she knew Aggie hadn't got a whole set of decent cups.

John was very touched at this final gesture, for he'd heard Aggie laugh about Elsie's best tea set which had never been used but just looked at in its place of honour on her dresser.

I'll be very relieved when it's wrapped up and returned, he thought. It would be really dreadful if anyone had an accident and broke anything.

Elsie wouldn't be attending the funeral but would stay behind at the house to prepare the food and drinks and take care of the children.

The morning of the funeral arrived, along with the close relatives who would follow the coffin to the church.

Hannah and her sisters were very pleased to see Aunt Lil and Uncle Bill for they'd had a very miserable week and badly needed the hugs and kisses that were showered on them, for their parents had virtually forgotton their existence since Colin's death and they were very frightened and bewildered by Aggie's strange, silent behaviour. Hannah wondered what would become of them if their mother didn't get better.

She'd been having terrible, jumbled nightmares about the funeral, for although she'd never attended one she'd been told many scary stories about dead people and how they haunted you.

One night she dreamed she was going to the funeral, wearing her new shoes and a little hat that belonged to Colin. She was in the church and Colin came galloping in on his little dog on wheels that he'd got for Christmas and snatched the hat from her head and called her a wicked thief, in a horrible high-pitched voice. Then her mother was wheeled in, in a big cage, screaming and shouting at the vicar, saying that if he buried Colin she would send the police after him because Colin wasn't dead.

She'd felt very ashamed at her mother's outburst because the church was filled with people all wearing their best clothes, so they'd have to bury him, otherwise they'd all put their best clothes on for nothing.

Aggie was stretching her arms through the bars of the cage towards John. 'You've got to stop them she begged,' but John just shrugged his shoulders and said 'It's too late Aggie, love, they're all here now.' And all the people in the church began waving their arms at Aggie, shouting, 'Shame on you, be quiet you crazy woman, go home and stop spoiling our fun.'

Hannah had woken feeling very frightened, and hoped that she wouldn't have to go to the funeral, and as it turned out, Elsie had suggested to John that Hannah stay at home to look after Betsy and Maureen.

In complete contrast to Hannah's nightmare the funeral service passed very quietly and they had all now returned to the house for the customary refreshments. But for the first time in her life Hannah couldn't eat anything.

The ham sandwiches that Elsie had prepared looked lovely and appetising but although she tried she just couldn't swallow anything. It was as if her throat was closed.

The visitors were trying to act as normal but she just wanted to go somewhere and cry, which had been almost impossible to do until now, for she'd tried to hold back the tears for fear of upsetting Betsy and Maureen.

By early evening the mourners had all left, except Elsie and her husband Tom—Big Tom as he was called, to distinguish him from his son.

Elsie had done the washing up and had carefully wrapped her tea-set in newspaper and put it in a cardboard box for safe travelling.

John walked over to her and put his big arms around her. 'You've been bloody marvellous Elsie,' he said. 'I don't know what we'd have done without you.'

'Oh, go on with you,' she said gruffly, 'anybody would have done the same.' She moved away from him and over to Aggie.

'Is there anything I can do for you before I go?' Aggie didn't answer but her face crumpled as if in pain. 'What is it Aggie love, what's wrong?'

In reply Aggie clutched her stomach and doubled up in pain.

'Oh my God.' said Elsie, 'John, come quick, help me to get

her on the couch.'

'What's up with her,' he asked.

'I hope I'm wrong but I think she's about to miscarry. Hannah, take your sisters into the kitchen, and you two,' she said to Tom and John, make sure there's plenty of hot water and see if you can find me some clean rags.'

When they'd supplied Elsie with her requirements they gladly sped back to the kitchen with orders to stay there unless they were called.

Some time later she emerged looking and feeling very tired. The men stood up as she entered the room but she motioned with her hands for them to sit down again.

'I'm sorry John, there was nothing I could do.'

'Perhaps it was for the best,' he replied, unable to feel any grief over something that had barely crossed his mind.

'Should we send for the doctor?'

'There's no urgency, I've done all that needs to be done for the moment but I'll contact him when we get back. I should think he'll come out tomorrow. Meanwhile, just try to keep her warm and quiet.'

She turned to Hannah, 'You've been a good help this week and I know that you're eager to go back to school but I think you should stay at home for another week to help look after your mother and sisters. I'll pop in as much as I can but she'll need you here until she's on her feet again.'

Hannah could have cried at this for she was looking forward to going back to school and seeing her friends.

Elsie put her arms around here. 'I know it's hard on you love, but it won't be for long, so try and bear up a little longer.'

7

Aggie did not improve with time, and although doctors, family and friends did everything possible to aid her recovery nothing helped. She remained locked up in her own private, silent world and never uttered a word. Things fell very heavily on to Hannah's shoulders and at the tender age of fourteen she had become mother, housekeeper and nurse to her mother.

Elsie came one day a week to help with the washing and ironing and to give Aggie a bath, for she'd become incapable of washing herself. She found this last task very trying but she knew if she didn't do it nobody would.

John had given up on her and since she'd become so dirty he sought his bodily pleasures with a widow who lived in King's Lynn.

He had become very surly and uncommunicative and the children were very afraid of him. He never had a kind word for them and they only felt relaxed when he was out of the house. This was most of the time, for as soon as he finished his chores he'd have a quick wash and then go off to Lynn to spend the evenings swilling beer with his mates and then, quite often, share a bed for the night with his woman friend, Gladys Butcher.

Her neighbours couldn't understand her relationship with John for they found him big, coarse and uncouth, the very opposite of her late husband, who had been the kindest, most gentle man you could ever wish to meet. But while some tutted, others realised how very lonely she was and were happy for her.

She knew John's situation at home and Aggie's condition and never asked more of him than he could give, which was very little. In return, she moulded her very existence around his visits and he always went to a clean, warm house and a hearty meal. Her late husband, Peter, had been killed the previous year on 13 March, when the docks had been bombed.

He had been working the Bentinck coal hoist, which received a hit, and although only one side of the hoist was fractured Peter caught the full brunt of it and was killed instantly.

It had been a very bad year for air-raids with hits on the Boal Quay and nearby Norfolk Street where explosive bombs were dropped, killing four soldiers.

There had been a night raid on the City of Norwich when three people were killed and two hundred injured. Two more raids were carried out on the city in the next few days and three enemy aircraft were shot down by night-fighters from Coltishall under the command of Max Aitken, the son of Lord Beaverbrook. The biggest raid of that year had taken place on 12 June when the Boal Quay was completely destroyed and the adjacent Bridge Street badly hit.

The smell around that area had been terrible for the sewers had been broken.

Two little boys had been killed on this occasion but it was doubtful if they knew anything about it because they were in bed and had probably been killed whilst asleep.

The Ship Inn had been demolished, killing many people inside. John had thanked his lucky stars for at one time he used to drink there, but now he was a regular at The Eagle.

In February of that year anti-aircraft fire had shot down a Heinkel HE111 which crashed at Ovington near Swaffham, just a few miles from King's Lynn and the five man crew had been taken prisoner. So far this year, things had been pretty quiet but nobody became complacent. They had become very wary and spoke in whispers as 'Walls Have Ears' was proclaimed on posters.

The country people fared better than the townspeople for they were more self-sufficient and lived quite well off the land in spite of the rationing.

The Minister of Agriculture had suggested that farmers leave their potato crops as late as possible in order for them to grow bigger.

There was much sense in this but John grumbled, 'It's all very well for him, in his big house, living in luxury, to say, leave the potatoes as late as possible. When you've got hungry kids you can't tell them to wait for the potatoes to grow bigger.' So, subsequently, when most people started their potato picking his potatoes had almost gone and he was quite envious of their big ones they were now lifting. But they knew of his position and very often gave him a feed for his kids, so one way and another he survived.

Hannah had left school and although she had so been looking forward to getting a job and bringing home a pay-packet she was needed at home, so it was out of the question.

There had been a terrible scene between Hannah and her father when he'd told her she'd have to stay home to take care of her sisters and her mother.

She had screamed and cried in disappointment but had to submit when John said if she insisted on going out to work he'd have Aggie commited to a mental home and put the children in an orphanage, for she knew this was no idle threat. He didn't give a fig for any of them. He fed them grudgingly with no more thought than throwing a bone to the dog and as far as he was concerned that was all he was obliged to do for them.

He had long since ceased caring for them as his family, his only interest now being the widow in Lynn.

Apart from the baker and Elsie's weekly visits she hardly ever saw anyone.

Pam had a job in an office and was learning typing and shorthand, so she saw very little of her.

Her family had taken in an evacuee whose name was Norma. Norma's parents kept a pub in St Johns Wood, London, called The Crown. They'd sent her away with great reluctance but they knew she'd be safer in the country. London was no place for children, with all the bombings.

At first Norma nearly went out of her mind. The quiet of the village was almost unbearable after the noise and bustle of the city, but gradually she settled in. She attended the school that Hannah and Pam used to go to. Although a year younger than Hannah she looked older than her years. She had thick, black curly hair like a gypsy, rosy cheeks and although a little on the plump side she was very attractive. She had a quick wit and took great delight in laughing at the local yokels who, she'd written, in a letter to her mother, were 'too slow to catch a cold!'

She especially liked to poke fun at Billy Wilson who she jokingly called 'Quassi Modo' after the hunchback of Notre Dame, but it didn't bother him. He was fascinated by her; he'd never met anyone as glamorous as her.

On one occasion, when Hannah had gone to visit Pam, Norma spotted Billy and said, 'Come on, let's have a bit of fun with him.' and had run up to him, dancing around him chanting, 'Billy, Billy, show us your willy.'

'Leave him alone,' said Hannah, dragging her away.

'Well, well,' said Norma, 'what 'ave we 'ere? Is 'e your boyfriend Hannah? As 'e got a big willy?' And she started to chant again, 'Billy, Billy, wiv a great big willy, stick it in Hannah, to give 'er a frilly.'

'Pack it up you're disgusting,' said Hannah, 'If you upset him I'll scratch your bloody eyes out.'

'Cor blimey, you're only little but you can't 'arf fly. Calm down, its only a bit 'o fun. I didn't mean any 'arm. I didn't upset you, did I Billy?'

Billy just grinned and dribbled. She hadn't upset him, he'd quite enjoyed the little pantomime.

Just then Ken came on the scene. 'What's going on?'

'We're just 'aving a bit of fun with Billy, but 'e don't mind, do you 'andsome?' she said to Billy.

She tucked her arm through Ken's. 'Come on big bruver, I'll let you take me for a walk and give me a nature lesson.' she said, looking up into his eyes suggestively.

'No thanks,' he said, unlinking her arm, 'I don't like cheeky cockney kids.'

'Take me for a walk and I'll show you I ain't no kid,' she said, putting her arm through his again.

He again released her arm, saying, 'Well, you're a kid to me, do you want me to get had up for cradle-snatching? Come and see me when you're grown up.'

He smiled at her, as a father would to a favourite daughter and Hannah's heart plunged.

Oh please Ken, she thought, don't fall in love with Norma.

If only he would smile at her in that way, but he just nodded in her direction and walked away, with Norma skipping and chattering at his side.

She must have said something very funny to him for he threw back his head and laughed, giving her a brotherly hug. Hannah thought she would die with jealousy and had to stop herself from thinking of all the time they could laugh and talk together, living under the same roof.

Pam saw the look and thought, I wish he would take a bit of notice of her. I know she's carrying a torch for him, but he doesn't know she's around and grudgingly, she had to admit that next to Norma, Hannah faded into insignificance. Poor old Hannah, she doesn't seem to get any luck, she thought. I wish her mother would snap out of it so that she could lead a normal life and spend some time brightening herself up and going out with her friends, for I know, if she hadn't got all those responsibilities on her shoulders she could look very pretty with a little help and then, perhaps, Ken would notice her.

She gave Hannah a hug. 'Cheer up, don't break your heart over him, he's not worth it and I should know, I live with him.'

'I don't know what you're talking about, Pam,' said Hannah, blushing to the very roots of her hair.

She turned to Billy in embarrassment. 'Do you want to walk home with me? We can look for mushrooms on the way,' and although she knew her leg would be pulled if she were seen with Billy she thought it worth the risk for, if ever a German plane flew overhead it frightened the life out of her and she wouldn't be so afraid with the big lummox beside her.

She reluctantly said goodbye to Pam for she didn't know when she would next be able to visit her.

Today, when Elsie had come over she'd persuaded Hannah to take a break and go and see her friend while she took care of her sisters and she'd jumped at the chance to get away from the house for a while.

When they reached the field where the mushrooms grew Billy announced that he wanted a pee.

'Go behind the hedge,' she said, 'I'll start looking for mushrooms.'

A few seconds later she heard a drone and looking up she saw a German plane approaching. Without thinking she rushed behind the hedge where, Billy, having heard the plane was pretending to shoot it down with his cock.

Her mouth fell open in astonishment. It was huge. She'd never seen anything like it, not even on animals.

'Duck down Hannah, I'll get the German bastard,' he said.

'Billy,' she shouted, 'do your trousers up.'

'But I gotta shoot him down,' he said. 'He's heading for Lynn.'

'There are soldiers there, with guns; they'll get him, don't you worry Billy; now, do your trousers up,' she said, this time more sharply.

He obeyed her this time, noticing the sharpness in her voice. 'Shall we look for mushrooms now?' he asked.

Hannah was so scared after the plane had gone that all she wanted to do was run home but she knew he would be bitterly disappointed if she did and it was most unlikely that the plane would come back again, so they collected some mushrooms.

It didn't take very long, for the mushrooms were as big as dinner plates and they didn't need many.

They set off, carrying the mushrooms carefully, trying very hard not to break them. She especially loved to get them in and out of the frying pan and onto the plate in one piece and if there were some bacon in the house they would have a feast tomorrow; they could only eat one mushroom each for the large ones were very strong and would make you feel sick if you ate any more.

'I got something to show you Hannah,' Billy said, carefully placing his mushrooms on the ground.

He delved in his pocket and took out a white rabbit's foot which he gently rubbed on his face. 'It's lovely and soft,' he said.

'Where did you get it from Billy?'

His eyes filled with tears and his big lips started to quiver.

'My Wally wabbit died,' he said, 'but Mum wouldn't let me keep all of it, only one of his feet, for luck. I had to put the rest in a box and bury it in the garden.'

'I'm sorry Billy, but I tell you what; when our rabbits have some more babies I'll let you have one.'

She knew he'd take care of it for he'd had his other one a very long time. It must have died from old age.

'Can I have a white one please, Hannah, like my Wally,' he begged.

'If there are any white ones you can have one but, if not, will you have a black one?'

'I don't mind Hannah, I don't mind if I have a black one or a white one,' he said, cheering up instantly.

All too soon they arrived at the gateway leading to the house and reluctantly, with sinking spirits, she walked towards it.

Hannah had had a lovely day, perfected by the bonus of seeing Ken, and wondering when she'd be able to get away again. Perhaps Elsie would mind her sisters so she could go again next week. She didn't like to take advantage of her good nature but Ken would be going off to college soon and while the weather was good she wanted to take every opportunity of going to the village.

Before I go next week, she planned, I'll wash my hair and put some of Mum's dinkey curlers in, and (thinking of Norma's luxuriant hair) I'll put a few drops of vinegar in the rinse water to make it shine.

'I'll wait here,' said Billy, hanging back in the gateway.

'Don't be silly, come and see Maureen and Betsy and you never know, we might get a bit of bread and butter and a cup of tea off Auntie Elsie.'

He was tempted but kept looking nervously down the field, where a distant figure was working.

She followed his gaze. 'That's only Dad, he won't bite you. Let's go and show him our mushrooms.'

He still hung back for he was afraid of John and knew he wouldn't be welcome on his land.

'Come on Billy, I'll tell him how you protected me from the Jerry Planes, my hero,' she said dramatically, holding her hands crossways over her heart and fluttering her eyes at him, as she'd seen the heroine do at the pictures when she was being rescued from the baddies.

'I'll always 'tect you Hannah, nobody will hurt you when I'm around 'cos you're my best friend and I'd kill any one who tried 'cos I'm strong,' he said, sticking out his chest.

'Dont' be daft, 'nobody's going to hurt me, you big dope,' she said laughingly.

'Well, they'd just better not try, cos you're my girl.'

'I'm NOT your girl Billy, I'm not anybody's girl, I'm your friend.'

'Yeah, well,' he began.

'Oh come on, these mushrooms will start to cook if we don't get them indoors soon.' So reluctantly he followed her down to the fields to where John was mucking out the pigs.

Hannah walked up to her father and Billy stayed at the far side of the sty where there were some baby piglets with their mother and as Billy drew closer she turned towards him and snorted, warning him to keep away from her babies.

It made him jump and then, laughingly, he snorted back at

85

her.

Another snort from the pig and one in reply from Billy, who was enjoying himself now, swapping snort for snort.

John turned round. 'What's that bloody idiot doing here?' he snarled.

'Leave him alone, Dad, he walked home with me and I'm glad he did. Did you see that Jerry plane?' We were in the field and it frightened the life out of me. Thank goodness Billy was with me.'

'What the hell were you doing in the field with him? If you let that bloody imbecile touch you I'll knock your head off your shoulders.'

'Da'ad,' she squirmed in embarrassment. 'We weren't doing anything wrong, we were just picking mushrooms. Look,' she held them out for him to see. 'Have you ever seen such big ones?' she asked proudly.

'It's a pity you've got nothing better to do than piss about picking mushrooms with the village idiot. What do you think people would say about that? Haven't you got any normal friends? Or are you too stupid for them?'

She tried to make light of his surliness, aware of Billy watching suspiciously.

'Just look at this one Dad; I'll cook this one for you, if you like, it's the biggest one I've ever seen.'

'Piss off, girl, and take your mushrooms and that idiot with you and don't let me see him about here again.'

'But, Dad,' she began.

He swung his big hand towards her and caught her a stinging blow around her head, lifting her off her feet and smashing the precious mushroom.

'Don't you dare answer me back, now get home.'

This was too much for Billy. With a roar he flew to the other side of the sty, picking up the shovel that John had been using, and brought it down on his head with a mighty blow.

There was a ringing thud as metal met skull and pig shit flew in all directions as John fell, face down on the heap he'd just cleaned out of the sty.

Hannah picked herself up. 'Oh Billy, you shouldn't have done that, you might have killed him.'

'I hope I have killed him. The old bastard, he shouldn't have hit you. Don't you worry Hannah, I'll see he don't hit you again, I told you I'd 'tect you didn't I and I have.'

Some time later, when they reached the field adjacent to the house, Betsy and Maureen came running towards them, flinging themselves at Hannah.

'Are you all right?' they asked tearfully. 'We heard the Jerry plane go out and we were frightened in case you'd got bombed.'

'Yes of course I'm all right, I had Billy looking after me. Anyway, you'd have heard it if I'd got bombed, they make a lot of noise you know,' she said, smiling at their innocence.

'It's all right Aunt Elsie, she's here, she's not bombed,' shouted Betsy.

Elsie met them at the kitchen door.

'Oh, I'm that glad to see you, I was beginning to worry about you. I heard that plane go over earlier, I don't know what would happen to your sisters if anything happened to you. Not that that's the only reason,' she added, hastily giving Hannah a big hug in relief.

'Hello Billy, you're quiet, are you all right?'

'Yes, he's all right,' broke in Hannah quickly. 'I think he's wondering if he'll get a cup of tea before he goes home.'

'You can both have a cup of tea, then I must get off home. It's starting to cloud up. Did you see your father?' she asked, and went on before they could reply. 'I expect he'll come charging in like a bull at a gate and then go off to Lynn, to see his fancy woman. I don't know how long this state of affairs can go on' she sniffed, 'it ain't right, it just ain't right, to stay out nights leaving you kids on your own. Oh, I knew all about it,' she said, catching Hannah's gaze. 'It's not a secret, you know, the whole bloody town is talking about it. Thank goodness your mother's not in any state to understand.' She looked at Aggie, who sat like a little child, washed and dressed, waiting to go to a party, looking at them with eyes that didn't see.

'I do feel sorry for your dad,' she said, looking at Hannah. 'I know he's got his needs like any average, healthy man but when a woman has got troubles "down below" or, in your mother's case, "up top" they should just put up with it. But not your father, he's too bloody selfish. I dread to think what'll happen when the welfare people hear about the goings on and they will sooner or later. Some busybody will tittle tattle and then you'll all be in the cart. Its a wonder they haven't rumbled before now but I suppose they've got more important things to worry about with the war and everything. I don't know what's going to happen' she said, shaking her head worriedly, 'I wish you all lived a bit closer so I could do more for you, but as it is I've got my own family to see after and they've got to come first.'

'Oh well' she said with a big unhappy sigh, 'I must get off now. Take care of yourselves and I'll see you next week, all being well.'.

'Goodby Aggie, love, I'll be praying for you.' She gave her a hug and kiss. 'Come on, you big lummox,' to Billy, you can walk back to the village with me, it's many a year since I walked down the lanes with a bloke.' She winked at Hannah.

As they set off Billy turned as if to say something but Hannah held her fingers to her lips in a silent command of secrecy.

It had been a lovely day, this day, Friday 12 June but now the clouds were rolling across the sky and Hannah hoped Billy and Aunt Elsie would get home before it rained.

She took in the linen horse which was standing outside the back door airing the washing which Elsie had done earlier; pathetic little frocks and underwear that had seen better days. A lump came to her throat seeing how carefully they had been washed and ironed when they were little more than rags. She had planned to mend some socks tonight but when she took them off the horse she saw that they had all been neatly darned with no signs of the 'big potatoes' in the heels.

'God bless you Aunt Elsie,' she thought, for she hated mending. It was such a thankless task for they were so thin they'd be in holes again by next to no time.

The sky had darkened ominously and a stiff breeze blew up, causing her to shiver, and quite suddenly she felt depressed and very alone.

It's not fair, she thought, having an unusual attack of self-pity. I can't do any of the things my friends do, I've got Mum to look after and Betsy and Maureen. I don't want to spend all my life like this.

She gave herself a mental shake. Come on Hannah Hardy, you'll only make yourself feel bad. Don't let the others know how afraid and miserable you are, it will rub off on them. I'll be all right tomorrow. There's just so much happened today and nobody to talk to and then, unwillingly, tears rolled down her face. Oh Dad, why did you have to hit me? Billy didn't mean to do what he did, he doesn't know any better, he was just protecting me.

'What's the matter Hannah, are you crying?' asked Maureen tremulously.

'I'm all right,' she replied, putting on a brave face. 'I've got a headache, that's all. I'll have an early night tonight, that'll put me right. Now who wants some tea?'

She cut a big plateful of bread and spread it with jam. Aggie had some, as well as the children.

Nowadays Hannah regarded her as one of the children. She ate and drank whatever she was given, went to bed and got up when told. She was no trouble but sometimes her very silence was unnerving. Her eyes would follow Hannah about as she carried out the daily tasks and she appeared to be listening when she was spoken to but when you looked into her eyes it was like looking into an empty pit; there was nothing there. Her very soul had disappeared, buried with her baby two years ago.

She had become very thin and her hair had greyed prematurely. A stranger coming into the house would think it was an old grandmother sitting on the little stool by the fireplace. She was a pathetic sight and Hannah had great compassion for her, although she hadn't been much of a mother. She was now just someone else who needed her as much as the children.

After tea Betsy and Maureen washed their hands and faces and Hannah washed Aggie's.

'We haven't got to go to bed yet, have we Hannah?' asked Maureen.

'Yes, we'll all have an early night, it won't do us any harm.'

'But it's too early, Dad's not even home for his tea yet.'

'Well,' said Hannah. 'We're going, aren't we Betsy? You can stay down here on your own if you like.'

'No, I'm not. I'm coming with you, but will you tell us a story before we go to sleep?'

'Just one 'cos I'm very tired and I have got a headache.'

So, on the inducement of a story they quickly ran up the stairs and jumped onto bed. 'Come on Mum, bed-time,' said

Hannah, gently leading Aggie out. 'It won't hurt you to go to bed early.'

It was a very muggy night and the little bedroom was very stuffy. Although the window was open and a breeze was blowing through, it was a warm wind and afforded little comfort.

Maureen and Betsy lay on top of the bed, wearing only their knickers, but Hannah, although very warm, left her vest on as well. Her little breasts were beginning to bud and while, secretly, she felt very proud and grown-up, she would have been very embarrassed if her sisters noticed and remarked on them. Other subtle little changes were taking place on her body. She had a few silky fine hairs under her arms and a very fine, soft down between her legs.

She had been watching and waiting for these developments for her friend Pam and other of the school friends had had these signs of womanhood ages ago and she had felt very left out. Now she was very happy to join the ranks.

She told her eager little audience the story of *The Three Bears* which was the shortest one she could think of, but because it was so short they begged for another one.

'Just one more please Hannah,' said Betsy.

'I'm too tired, I'll tell you a longer one tomorrow.'

'Just one nursery rhyme then,' she wheedled.

'Oh, all right,' said Hannah, resignedly 'and then please go to sleep for my head aches quite badly. Which one do you want to hear?'

'*Five naughty bunnies*', please,' said Betsy snuggling, up to Hannah, sucking her thumb and closing here eyes in happy anticipation as Hannah began;

> *Five naughty bunnies who would not obey*
> *till mother bun said you must not go to play*
> *but they all ran off to have some fun*
> *and didn't heed the farmers gun*
> *Bang, bang, how dreadful, one bunny lay dead*
> *the shots from the gun had gone right through his head*
> *The others scampered off back to their nest*
> *and all own now that mother knows best.*

Aggie used to tell this little rhyme to Hannah when she was

tiny but she couldn't remember all of it and it was no good asking Aggie now. But Betsy didn't appear to notice the shortened version and to Hannah's relief, quickly fell asleep. Hannah slipped into a troubled sleep and a nightmare.

John was dead in the heap of pig-shit and the pigs were eating him and he said to Hannah, 'I told you them greedy buggers would eat anything,' and then, Billy's dead rabbit came hopping in on one foot, (Billy, had chopped one off for luck), and the pigs began eating him as well.

Hannah yelled to Billy, 'Stop them Billy.'

'I can't do that Hannah, I can't 'tect everyone, I can only 'tect you.'

She tried to pull the pigs away but by now they'd half eaten John and he was still swearing at them and calling them 'greedy buggers' until they ate his tongue and then all she could hear was the snorting of the pigs and a thump, as Billy fell off the gate he was swinging on.

She woke up, covered in perspiration, thanking God it was all a dream but her relief was short-lived. The air-raid siren began to wail as if an extension to her nightmare, but this was no nightmare, it was the real thing.

She roused Maureen and Betsy and sent them downstairs to the kitchen while she got Aggie up. Aggie yawned sleepily and allowed her to lead her out, completely oblivious of the air-raid warning.

John had drilled them, in case of an air-raid and she grabbed some pillows and a blanket and made a temporary bed up, under the kitchen table.

By now they could hear the monotonous drone of the German planes going overhead and it filled their hearts with dread.

Aggie sat, quite undisturbed, while the children cried and hugged each other in terror. The noise from the planes died away as they headed toward the town and the children dried their tears and gradually calmed down.

Then another wave of planes came over. This time the children screamed in terror, certain they would drop some bombs on them this time. But, once again they flew towards King's Lynn.

After a very long time, when they were sure no more planes were coming, Hannah crawled a few paces to the little fireplace where the kettle was still hot and made them all a cup of cocoa.

'Where's Dad? Why's he not here looking after us? I bet he's in King's Lynn looking after his fancy woman,' said Maureen. 'He should be here with us.'

'What are you talking about, fancy woman?' said Hannah.

'I know all about her, I'm not a baby you know,' said Maureen, who was now eight years old, 'I've heard Aunt Elsie talking about her and it's not fair. Just because her daddy got killed she's pinched ours.'

'Don't say things like that in front of Mum.'

'Why not? She don't understand, she's a dummy.'

Hannah gave her a slap. 'Don't you dare say that, she's not a dummy.'

'Yes, she is, 'cos everybody at school says my mum is "tetched" and they tease me and call me names,' she replied, bursting into tears, 'and you're as bad. Now, she don't hit us any more, I suppose you're going to start aren't you?'

'No, I'm not, I'm sorry, but you musn't talk like that about Mum. She's ill, she's not "tetched", she'll be better one day, you'll see, and then your so-called friends can laugh on the other side of their faces.'

Betsy had been looking on in silence and now she sidled up to her mother and put her arms around her protectively, kissing her sunken cheeks. 'Don't worry 'bout what they say, I'll look after you lovie,' she said, using the endearment she'd heard Elsie use when talking to Aggie. 'You just drink your nice cocoa, there's a good girl.'

Tears sprang to Hannah's eyes. Bless her heart she thought, she's had very little love from Mum, but she's full of love and pity for her.

They finished their cocoa, and shortly afterwards the siren sounded the 'all clear'. Maureen and Betsy dragged the pillows and blankets upstairs and Hannah led Aggie back to bed.

There were no more raids that night and they all fell, gratefully, into a deep sleep.

8

The sun that blazed through the little window and onto the girls' bed was quite hot and Hannah, on waking, felt the warmth and thought, it must be quite late and we've overslept. Then she remembered it was Saturday and they didn't have to rush about.

She stretched, enjoying the warmth, then sat bolt upright as memories of the day before came rushing in.

Her heart pounded heavily against her chest, as if it would burst and her head thumped painfully as she recalled the horrors.

Ken and Norma who, she felt sure, would wind up falling in love with each other, Billy's enormous cock shooting at the German plane, the sickening scene in the pig-sties, the sound of the air-raid. No wonder they'd over-slept. She felt quite exhausted reliving the day before's events.

A wave of fear, panic and depression engulfed her, causing her to break down in an onslaught of tears. 'Oh, Mum, Dad, oh God please help me, I can't go through another day like that. I'll run away, but how and where and even if a miracle happened and I did get away, what would happen to Betsy and Maureen'?

It must feel like this when you're in prison she thought helplessly, 'but at least when you're in prison you don't have to worry about other people, you get fed and exercised and go to bed early'. It seemed quite inviting in comparison to her existence.

Maureen opened her eyes and saw Hannah crying.

'Does your head still hurt Hannah? Do you want me to get you a drink of water?'

'Yes please, I'm sure a nice cup of cold water will make me feel better and then I'll get up and make breakfast.'

By the time Maureen returned with the water she had given

93

her nose a good old blow and dried her tears and dressed Betsy.

'I can't see Dad about anywhere. Do you think he stayed in Lynn last night Hannah?' she said.

'Perhaps,' she replied, and quickly went on, 'as you're up and dressed take the bowl and see if the chickens have laid. If they have, we'll have boiled eggs for breakfast.'

'How do you know that Dad hasn't got orders for the eggs? He'll wallop us if they were booked for one of his customers.'

'Well, he's not here, is he? So he won't know, and by the time he gets back they'll be gone so he won't be none the wiser, so jump to it and I'll be cutting some bread and boiling some water.'

Maureen ran off down to the chicken runs, nervously excited at the prospects of hood-winking John. Although the chickens were laying very well right now that didn't mean the children would have any, for John would sell every last one if he could. The children only had them if he had no customers for them.

She returned triumphantly, carrying the bowl filled with at least a dozen eggs. Hannah's eyes lit up when she saw the lovely big brown eggs, still warm, with bits of feathers sticking to them. 'We're all going to have two each for breakfast and egg sandwiches for tea,' she announced bravely.

The younger children looked at her in amazement at her daring and quickly climbed onto their stool at the table before she changed her mind.

Aggie sat happily on her little stool near the fireplace and ate her eggs which Hannah had cooked until they were firm. Otherwise Aggie would plunge her bread soldiers in and lose all the yolk down the side of the egg cup.

There was an almost full jug of milk, which Hannah shared between them. It would go off before the end of the day in this sort of heat so she thought they might as well drink it up once and for all. There was no point in saving any for already the flies were starting their invasion and she had a tin of milk they would use for their tea.

Due to the fact that Elsie went through the house like a train on Fridays, doing washing, ironing and any other jobs she could squeeze in, Hannah was able to enjoy a comparatively easy day on Saturdays. As John was not about she decided to feed the animals and then just relax with her book in the sunshine. She knew that before this hot day drew to a close

Betsy and Maureen would be bored, tired and a little fractious so she sought to occupy them with an easy chore to help fill in a part of the day and armed with an empty sack they set off to the fields to collect rabbit food, dandelions, clover, sou'thistle and the like. Aggie watched them set off with never a flicker of comprehension.

'Come on mum,' said Hannah, 'You can come for a walk as well. You don't want to sit here on your own all day. The fresh air will do you good, you can help me feed the chickens.'

She gave Aggie a full bucket of corn to carry while she filled another bucket with water.

It was already too hot to move very quickly so they just dawdled down to the chicken runs, stopping every once in a while to set the buckets down, have a little rest and then continue, alternating the buckets from one hand to the other.

She shivered apprehensively, recalling the Jerry plane that had flown over while they were picking mushrooms, but she knew, from listening to the grown-ups, that it was highly unlikely any planes would approach on a clear day like today. They liked to plan their raids in poor visibility whenever possible.

I wonder if they had another go at the docks last night, she thought. For although they'd had one attempt, people were of the opinion that insufficient damage was caused on that occasion and they would be back for another try.

They fed the chickens and then she supervised the feeding of the rabbits. She daren't leave it to her sisters for if they gave them too much green they might contract diarrhoea, and if that happened they would almost certainly die, as they'd learnt from past experience.

She was thrilled to notice one of the does was pulling her fur out from under her chin and making a nest in the corner of the hutch. This meant that there would be babies born within the next twenty four hours but she wouldn't tell Billy about them until they were old enough to leave their mother because a few weeks would seem like a lifetime to him and he would probably want to make camp there and she'd never get rid of him.

Nevertheless, she was very happy and excited at the thought of the babies. She could spend hours watching them in their early days.

John had made a little enclosure with wire-netting where

they could run and frolic during the day. She smiled to herself, remembering the last litter and their first day in the enclosure, eating grass for the first time, tugging at what were to them enormous blades and toppling over backwards in the attempt. They were absolutely enchanting in their first weeks.

She avoided the pig-pens. She couldn't face them after the drama of the day before, and anyway, she thought, there were no scraps to give them so there was no point in going there.

The chores over, they all settled down on the grass for a lazy afternoon. Betsy and Maureen made daisy-chains and searched for 'lucky' four leaved clovers.

The last time they'd found some, people gladly paid them threepence each for them which they then pressed in their favourite book or bible, convinced they would ensure them of good fortune, fen people being very superstitious.

Aggie sat with some women's weekly magazines on her lap, which Elsie had brought her.

Sometimes she turned the pages but mostly she just looked at the top cover and Hannah turned them over for her.

There was a serial called *The Silver Birch*, which Hannah looked forward to every week. It was very sad and romantic and she, being very sentimental, often had a little cry whilst reading it.

Her friends used to laugh at her for being so 'soft-hearted' so she tried to curb her feelings but there were times when she just couldn't, especially where sad songs were concerned. Music moved her very deeply and would reduce her to tears and tingles.

A very popular song that Vera Lynn could be heard singing on the wireless recently was called *We'll meet again* and where-ever Hannah happened to be or with whom, the tears rolled down her face whenever she heard it. She thought Vera Lynn had the loveliest, saddest voice in the world and would often sing her songs to her sisters who, in turn, thought their Hannah had the loveliest voice in the world. In actual fact she did have a lovely, clear, emotional voice and had always been chosen to sing at school concerts.

The music teacher, a Welsh lady called Miss Bertha Williams, had been very impressed with Hannah's natural talent and had tried to persuade Aggie to allow her to take music lessons but as these would cost money it was ruled out of the question, much to the disappointment of Miss Bertha William's who was convinced that, with training, she could have had a musical career.

Hannah wasn't particularly perturbed over this as she had little idea of the God-given talent she possessed.

She had a quick ear for music and only had to hear a song a couple of times to remember it and she derived great pleasure from singing to her sisters or to herself.

Another of Vera Lynn's songs she particularly liked was called *Yours* and began, 'Yours till the stars lose their glory, Yours till the birds fail to sing' and whenever she sang it she secretly dedicated it to Ken and used to imagine she was older and very glamorous, like a film star, sitting at a table, singing across to him, and he'd be enraptured and fall in love with her and beg her to marry him.

They spent a pleasant, lazy afternoon and when they became hungry and thirsty, reluctantly decided to return home. Maureen had put daisy chains in Betsy's hair and round her ankles and wrists and Betsy stood up very carefully so as not to break them.

They had been unlucky in their search for four-leaved clovers so there'd be no threepenny bits for sweets.

It made little difference to them that sweets had been rationed for they very rarely had the money to accompany their coupons anyway.

On occasions, Pam would use all her month's sweet coupons in the first couple of weeks and would give Hannah sixpence for some of hers, thus enabling them to buy some sweets.

They were about half-way back to the house when Billy came lumbering across the fields towards them, almost tripping over his own feet in his excitement.

'Hannah, Hannah, you should have been in Lynn today, you just oughta see what the Jerry bombs done, they flattened half the town, dead bodies everywhere.'

'Calm down, Billy, tell us the truth. What did you really see? You didn't see any dead bodies, did you?'

'I did Hannah, honest, no fibbing, the Eagle has been bombed flat and they brought hundreds of bodies out in sacks and the cattle market was bombed as well but I didn't see any bodies there, but, guess what they missed?'

'I don't know, I hope they missed a lot of things. They

couldn't have flattened the whole town.'

'Well, I'll tell ya, they missed the chip shop, ha ha, they're not that bloody clever.'

'Oh Hannah, do you think Dad was in the Eagle? He always goes in there for a drink. Do you think the Jerries got him? I bet they did, I bet he's dead' said Maureen and she and Betsy began to cry uncontrollably. 'What are we going to do? What'll happen to us?'

'No, he wouldn't have been in the Eagle, would he Hannah,' said Billy.

'Shut up Billy, just be quiet and stop frightening them. I don't believe you saw hundreds of bodies. You don't know the difference between five and five hundred.'

'I'm not telling fibs Hannah, honest. I really did see them bringing bodies outa the Eagle,' said Billy, dancing about, agitatedly, grabbing his cock nervously.

'All right, all right, calm down, I believe you. So stop dancing about playing with yourself.'

She found out later that there was an element of truth in what Billy had said. There were actually forty-two people killed. The Eagle had received a direct hit and had been packed with customers at the time, including service-men celebrating a colleague's twenty first birthday.

Rescue work had gone on all through the night and day, by police, home-guard and civil defence.

The Eagle had been completely demolished and shops on both sides of it badly damaged. The bodies had been brought out in sacks and taken to nearby Tower Street, where a temporary mortuary had been set up.

Aggie looked from one to the other of her younger daughters and Hannah thought she detected a slight flicker of concern, but it went as quickly as it came.

It would be strange, she thought, if one tragedy drove her out of her mind and another one brought her back again. She had heard that shock did things like that to people, but Aggie was now looking as vacant as ever.

By the time they reached the house she had managed to calm the children down but they were still very frightened.

'Come on in Billy,' she said, 'I'll make you a cup of tea before you go home.'

She made them all a cup of tea and egg sandwiches but the

girls were too upset to eat them.

Aggie munched through two 'doorsteps' and Billy polished off the rest in record time, as if he hadn't eaten for a month.

'They were lovely Hannah,' he said, wiping his large wet mouth with the back of his hands and belching loudly.

'Can we put the wireless on now? You get some lovely stories on the wireless.'

'That's a good idea, it might cheer us all up,' said Hannah, switching it on and twiddling with the knobs until she located the Home Service, but it did little to cheer them up as they'd tuned in just in time for the news, which was all war talk.

The announcer briefly mentioned that there was no trace of Amy Johnson, the brave flying lady who had flown her plane thousands of miles on dangerous missions for her country. He didn't add that they no longer expected to find her or her plane, for it was over a year since her disappearance and everyone knew she just had to be dead, but her poor family still lived in hopes and would do so until any evidence was found.

He went on to say how the 'American Army Air Force' were settling in in East Anglia since their peaceful invasion, following the Japanese attack on Pearl Harbour and although, in the early days they were resented (especially by the local young men), they were now beginning to accept each others' customs.

The local girls found the Americans very glamorous and exciting, for there was little excitement in the sleepy little town and villages.

They would breeze into the pubs and cafes, looking very smart in their uniforms, which were heaps better than the British ones, smelling deliciously of the Old Spice after-shave lotion, which the girls found irresistable.

They were always chewing gum and before long all the girls were chewing all day, much to the annoyance of their parents, who thought it made them look common.

Whenever an American walked down the streets there was always a gang of children dogging their footsteps chanting 'Have you got any gum, chum?' And they were nearly always given a stick of gum, for the soldiers were very generous and most of them loved children.

The locals in the pubs were very hostile toward the Americans.

They resented the fact that they were so much better off than them, for while they would be sitting over their solitary pint, making it last as long as possible, the Americans would sail in and order whiskies one after another but, although they noticed the locals' resentment they tried very hard not to show it and gradually won them over with their natural generosity. They could afford to be generous for they earned about four times as much as the local people, so it was little wonder that before long they were snapping up all the local girls, who were given nylons and candy and if, and when, they were invited to the girls' homes they were lavish with their gifts to the mothers.

They would take them such things as tinned fruit, salmon, cakes and cartons of cigarettes for the men. It was like Christmas every week and it was as if there were no war on. Little wonder that the local boys disliked them for they just couldn't compete and they used to say there were only three things wrong with Yanks, 'They were over-paid, over-sexed and over here'.

The girls who started courting them were frowned upon at first and considered cheap by narrow-minded people, especially as they began to adopt American mannerisms, like eating their food with just a fork, instead of a knife and fork and they would wear their boyfriend's dog-tags wound two or three times round their wrists and thick anklesocks which came from the stores of the American bases, and which branded them as Yankie Molls.

But, as time went on, all things were cautiously accepted. There was a war on, the Yanks were here and they just had to get on with their lives in these strange times.

The announcer finished the broadcast by reminding everyone to throw nothing away but to keep things such as rags, boxes, scrap metal, paper and cardboard in separate bundles for collection by the dustmen, and lastly and most importantly to observe the black-out by curtaining the windows before switching on the lights.

Most of the broadcast went over Billy's head but he did understand the last bit and sprang up, offering to close the little scrappy kitchen curtains. These John had appreciated were inadequate to conceal the light and a large square of cardboard had to be stood on the window-sill, close to the window in front of the curtains.

'Not yet Billy, it's not dark enough to switch on the lights yet. Anyway, don't you think you ought to be getting on home?'

'Not yet Hannah, let me stay and hear the play on the wireless, there's a murder tonight.'

'Oh all right, but then you must go, before it gets dark or your mother will be worrying about you and you'll get a ding round the lug for being late.'

'You're right there Hannah,' he replied, 'she in't very big but she can reach my lugs all right'.

'Maureen, Betsy, get yourselves washed, then you can listen to the play before you go to bed,' said Hannah.

They began crying again, 'Please, let us stay up until Dad comes home, we're frightened,' said Maureen.

'That's no good you blahing, if he's dead, he's dead,' said Billy, making them cry even louder.

'Shut up Billy,' said Hannah, sharply, 'if you can't keep quiet you can go home now.'

'Can't Billy go and get Aunt Elsie? She'll know what to do. Please Hannah, please,' begged Maureen.

'Come on now, pull yourself together and stop all that noise. You'll upset Betsy and Mum. It's not as though we haven't been alone nights before.'

'That was different. We knew where Dad was then. We don't now. He might have been killed in the Eagle. Please, get Aunt Elsie.'

'Look,' said Hannah, 'if he's not home by tomorrow we'll fetch her. She won't be able to come out here tonight and leave little Tom, but, I promise, tomorrow, if he's not here we'll fetch her. In fact, if it's fine, we'll all walk down to the village and we'll go and see Pam and Norma as well.'

This pacified them and they washed and settled down to listen to the wireless.

By the time the play was over the younger children were half asleep and after seeing Billy off Hannah ushered them to bed with no more protests. The sleepless night before was taking its toll.

'I'm sure if there were a raid tonight, I'd sleep right through it, I'm so tired,' thought Hannah, nevertheless crossing her fingers, just in case she'd tempted providence.

The night passed peacefully and uneventfully and they all enjoyed a dreamless sleep.

Hannah awoke to find Betsy sitting up beside her.

'Are you awake Hannah?' she asked, as soon as she'd opened her eyes.

'What's the matter Betsy? Aren't you well?'

'Yes, I'm all right. I've been awake a long while, waiting for you to wake up. Can I go and see if Dad's home?'

'It's very early, and I think we would have heard him if he'd come in.'

'Can I just creep into Mum's room and see? I'll be very quiet, I won't wake anyone up.'

'All right but do be quiet.'

Betsy crept out of the room like a little mouse and returned sniffing tremulously. 'He's not there. Can we go and tell Aunt Elsie? You said we could if he hadn't come back by this morning.'

She got back into bed, wrapping her arms around Hannah's neck, who, in turn hugged her, tears silently running down her face, crying not so much for her father or herself but for the unhappiness her darling little Betsy was suffering.

'Don't cry love, I'll look after you, don't be frightened. We'll go and see Aunt Elsie a bit later. We can't go yet, it's Sunday and I know she enjoys a lie-in on Sundays, so come and snuggle up for a little while and then, when we've had something to eat we'll go.'

On hearing their voices Maureen awoke.

'What's the matter? Why are you two whispering? Has Dad come home? I'm hungry.'

'One thing at a time. No, Dad has not come home and if you're hungry we might as well get up and have some breakfast. You can go and get Mum up. Betsy, you can dress yourself and I'll go and put the kettle on.'

They each sprang to their various tasks, glad to do something to calm their pent up nerves.

Hannah prepared their breakfast of bread and margarine and big mugs of hot, sweet tea. I must remember to take a ration book with me when we go to the village she thought. We're nearly out of sugar and marg and the last slither of Lifebuoy soap had been used.

The soap no longer came in its familiar packet, as a national ecomony measure, but it still cost threepence, which she thought was a bit of a cheek; they should knock a ha'penny off the price as they didn't have to buy the paper.

Tonight, she planned, I'll get the bath in, if I can lift it down from the shed, where it hung on a nail, and we'll all have a lovely bath.

They usually had a bath on Sundays. Betsy first, then Maureen and lastly Hannah.

They didn't change the water each time but started off with a shallow bath for Betsy, then added some more hot water for Maureen and yet more for Hannah. It was a good system for this way the kettle had time to reheat over the fire for each tot-up.

John usually emptied the bath but as he wasn't there she would have to scoop the water out with the bowl and tip it down the sink. Then she'd be able to drag it back to the shed.

They quickly demolished their breakfasts, eager to go to the village.

'Can we go now Hannah?' asked Betsy, jumping down from the stool where she'd been sitting, knocking her mug over in her haste.

'No, we can't. We're not going until you've cleaned your teeth and then I'll brush your hair and put it in pig-tails with a nice clean piece of ribbon, and tonight, when you've had a bath I'm going to wash your hair and do it with the dicky comb.'

'Oh no, please don't Hannah, that hurt ever so much.'

'I can't help that. You were scratching your head half the night and if you haven't got nits I'll eat my hat.'

'It's them 'vacuees fault, everyone at school has got nits since they came down from London. They must've brought them with them.'

'You don't know that, it's not fair to blame them, we could have given them nits.'

'No we couldn't, it's their fault. You should see the one I have to sit next to at school. She picks the fleas out of her head and cracks them between her finger-nails, *and*, she wet herself *and* she smells, and she's always crying for her mother.'

'Well wouldn't you cry if you had to leave your family and go a hundred miles away and live with someone you didn't know and go to a school where nobody liked you?'

'Yes, I suppose I would,' said Betsy quietly.

'Then, perhaps you'll think of that next time she cries or

103

wets herself. She only does that because she's sad to be away from her mummy, so you try to be kind to her. If somebody made friends with her she wouldn't be so miserable and then, perhaps, she wouldn't wet herself.'

'I will be kind to her, Hannah, I promise. I'll try anyway, but if she don't want to be friends that won't be my fault.'

'No, it won't, but it'll please me if I know you've tried. Now, come on get a move on.'

'What about Mum? Who's going to look after her?' asked Maureen.

'We'll have to take her with us,' replied Hannah.

'No, it'll take us all day. You know how slow she walks.'

'Well, you stay here with her while me and Betsy go.'

'No, I'm not staying here with her on my own, I'm frightened.'

'You're not frightened of Mum are you?'

'No, but what if there's an air raid?'

'Well, you know what to do. Get Mum under the table with you and stay there until you hear the "All Clear".'

'No,' she whined, 'I don't want to stay here on my own.'

'All right, we'll all go together then,' said Hannah, 'but first I want to go and look at the rabbits. I think there might be some babies today.'

'How do you know that?' asked Betsy.

'Didn't you see one of the bunnies pulling her fur out yesterday? Well, she was pulling it out to make a nice warm nest for her babies.'

'We'll leave Mum here while we go and look. She won't hurt being on her own for a little while. We can run there and back, she'll hardly notice we're gone if we're quick.'

She gave Aggie a book to look at and they sprinted out, eager to see if there were any babies.

It was just as Hannah had predicted. Right up the corner of the hutch was a big fluffy nest. You had to be very still and quiet to notice a very slight movement caused by the babies gently breathing.

'Can we look at them?' asked Betsy.

'No, you can't, you must never disturb the nest, for if the mother bunnie sees you or smells your scent on the babies she might abandon them or at the very worst, it has been known for them to eat the babies, so you'll just have to wait until they're a bit older.'

'Ugh, how horrible,' said Maureen, shuddering, 'how long will we have to wait then?'

'If the weather stays nice and hot you might catch a glimpse of them in about a week but if it turns cold she'll keep them covered up longer.'

'Won't Billy be happy when we tell him?' said Betsy.

'Yes, he will,' replied Hannah smilingly, thinking of his big ugly face and the pleasure it would reveal. 'He was very unhappy when his rabbit died, but we'll have to keep it a secret for a few weeks, for if we tell him now he'll want to take a baby straight away and then it would die. We'll tell him only when it's old enough to leave its mother and then he can come and pick one out himself. I hope there's a white one for they're his favourites.'

'We'll give the mother some water for she'll be very dry after washing all her babies, then we'll go to Heysham to see Aunt Elsie.'

They walked back to the house, more slowly now, as it was getting very warm.

Aggie sat exactly where she'd been left earlier, apparently oblivious of their absence.

'Come on Mum, we're going to see Aunt Elsie,' said Hannah, getting her to her feet.

They set off for the village and by the time they'd gone about half way they were all very hot and thirsty. The sun was beating down on them fiercely and there was hardly a hint of a breeze.

'Why did we have to bring Mum?' grumbled Maureen. 'It'll take us all day at this speed.'

'We're all tired, so stop moaning. You had a choice, you could have stayed at home,' replied Hannah.

'What do you think Aunt Elsie will do when she knows that Dad hasn't come home? Do you think she'll come and look after us?' asked Betsy.

'How can she? She's got Big Tom and Little Tom to take care of, she can't just leave them to come and look after us,' replied Hannah.

'Well, who's going to look after us? We can't live alone with no mummy or daddy.'

'I know what they'll do, they'll put us in an orphanage and

dress us in rags and make us sleep on the floor with rats. Oh Hannah, I'm frightened. Let's go home and not tell anybody about Dad,' she said, beginning to cry.

'Come on, don't be a big baby. They won't put us in a home. I wouldn't let them do that, and anyway we can't just carry on as though nothing's happened. We've hardly any money and somebody has to look after the crops and the animals.'

'Why can't we pick the vegetables ourselves and sell them and then we'll get some money?' said Maureen.

'And what happens when the vegetables run out? Who's going to look after the animals and take them to market and do all the other work that Dad does? And even if we were strong enough you have to go to school so don't talk such rubbish.'

'What'll they do with us then? Betsy's right, they will put us in a home. Oh Hannah, I'm scared,' and she promptly burst into tears and joined her little sister who had sat down by the side of the lane, rubbing her eyes with hot grubby little fists.

Aggie looked at her daughters with a hint of perplexity in her eyes.

'It's all right Mum,' said Hannah, 'we're just having a little rest. There's nothing to worry about. You sit down for a little while. I'm sure your feet must ache. You haven't walked this far for ages.'

Nothing to worry about, she thought, if only that were so, for she was beginning to feel afraid now, but she tried not to let it show.

After a few minutes Hannah stood up and brushed the grass from her skirt. 'Come on, upsadaisy, let's get going, now.'

They slowly arose, with great reluctance.

'Lets go home, Hannah, I'm too hot to walk to Heysham,' said Betsy.

'I'll give you a piggy-back for a little while. There's no point in going home. We're halfway there now, and whether we like it or not we've got to let Aunt Elsie know about Dad.'

They set off once again but it took them much longer to travel the second half of the journey.

The sun was beating down on them mercilessly and the closer they got to the village, the slower their footsteps became, fear and apprehension sapping their strength.

Hannah felt quite faint, not so much from the heat, which was almost unbearable, but from worrying about her sisters.

When Betsy had voiced her terrors concerning an orphan-age, she had made Hannah face a possibility she had thrust to the back of her mind, but now, as they neared the village the threat loomed larger than ever.

Hannah Hardy, she remonstrated sternly, pull yourself together. Fancy letting the children worry you like that. You're not a baby, so stop thinking like one. You've got to be strong for them. If they see you're frightened they'll go to pieces and anyway, Aunt Elsie won't let anything nasty happen to us. It's 1942 not 1842, children aren't starved or beaten nowadays, and anyway, we're not orphans; we've got a mother, even if she is ill. She has been looking a bit better lately. Perhaps she'll snap out of it and then we won't have to worry about orphanages.

Then there's Aunt Lil and Uncle Bill. They're family and if Aunt Elsie can't think of what to do I'll write to them.

The approach to the village was flanked by hedgerows and running streams and the children thankfully dropped to their knees to drink the lovely clear cold water.

They drank their fill, washed their hands and faces and then sat down and dangled their feet into the iciness.

Hannah guided Aggie to the water's edge and helped her to cup her hands and drink and then seated her and took off her shoes, enabling her to cool her feet.

They dallied there for about half an hour until they felt cool and comfortable and then set off through the village to Elsie's house, feeling much happier now they were refreshed.

To the people coming out of church, the sight of the little family filled their hearts with pity. They were well acquainted with the family's circumstances – Aggie's simple-mindedness since losing the baby, Hannah having to stay at home to look after her instead of taking a job like her friends and worst of all, John's carryings-on with the widow in King's Lynn.

The parson, shaking hands with his parishioners as they left the church, gave up a silent prayer for Aggie and her family, asking the Lord to look upon them with favour, especially little Hannah, who had too heavy a load on her frail shoulders.

Pam spotted her friend and ran towards her, throwing her arms around her and hugging her tightly.

'Oh Hannah, are you all right? I was that worried about you Friday night. Did you hear the planes flying over to Lynn?

I was scared out of my wits. What are you all doing here on a Sunday? Is anything wrong? You don't usually bring the whole family with you?'

'It's Dad,' burst out Maureen. 'Billy told us the Eagle got bombed and we think Dad might have been in there.'

'Oh my God, is this true Hannah?'

'Well, he hasn't been home since the bombings. That's why we've come to see Aunt Elsie. I don't know what to do,' Hannah replied tearfully.

Norma had followed Pam and on hearing the exchange between the two friends said, 'Gawd, don't say your old man's been killed. You poor little bleeders, whatever are you gonna do?'

'NORMA your LANGUAGE! It is Sunday and anyway it might just be a coincidence. He's stayed out all night before, hasn't he Hannah?'

'Yes, but he's always come home early the next day in time to give the animals their morning feed and it's been two days now.'

Some of the villagers had heard snatches of their conversation and the word soon spread that John had been killed and they started to cluck and fuss around Hannah, stifling her with their well-intentioned sympathy, so much so that she wanted to scream and run.

Pam's parents, noticing her distress, broke through the crowd and guided her and her family away.

'Come on Hannah, you come back to our house. Perhaps your mum would like to rest a while before you go to see Elsie.'

'Yes please,' said Hannah, gratefully, 'and do you think we could buy some sugar and soap from your shop? I've brought a ration book. I know it's Sunday but we're right out or I wouldn't trouble you.'

'As long as you don't expect me to put my apron on to serve you,' said Pam's dad, good naturedly.

At the shop he put the sugar and soap in bags.

'Have you any sweet coupons?' he asked.

'Oh yes, we've plenty of coupons but we haven't any money for sweets.'

'Well, as I'm feeling generous, I'll treat you, come on,' he said to the younger girls, 'thre'pence each, what would you like?'

Their eyes told him they'd already chosen. They were almost dribbling at the sight of the jar full of sticks of barley sugar that stood on the counter.

'A sensible choice,' he said, 'it should last you all day if you suck it. Now what about you Hannah?'

'If you don't mind I'd rather have liquorice-wood,' said Hannah, 'I like that much better than sweets.'

'Ugh, I think that's like sucking rope, but, if that's what you'd like. Does your mum like sweets?'

'She used to like toffees but I don't think she's had any for years.'

'Well it's high time she did. Here you are Aggie, we're never too old for a bag of toffees are we?' He smilingly handed them to her, diplomatically avoiding her blank expression.

'Come on through to the front room, Ken, turn that gramophone down, we've got company.'

Hannah hastily smoothed her hair and skirt, having forgotten that Ken might be there, and blushing with embarrassment at the thought that he hadn't seen Aggie since her illness. What would he think?

He carefully took the needle off the record and turned round.

'Hello Hannah, Mrs Hardy, this is a surprise,' he said politely. 'Have you walked all the way in this heat? There's nothing wrong I hope.'

Pam saved Hannah the job of reciting their story yet again by explaining their plight to him.

'Have you heard anything from the police?' he asked. She looked at him in terror.

'No, why should we?'

'In that case I shouldn't worry too much. If your father had been killed in the Eagle he would have been identified by now and they would have informed you.'

'That's true,' said Fred, 'but just to make sure I'll ring the King's Lynn Police Station to see if they can tell us the names of the people killed.'

He went out of the room and returned a couple of minutes later.

'The police were very helpful,' he said. 'They have identified forty people killed there but there were also two others they couldn't identify. They had caught the direct blast

109

making it impossible for identification. They can't even say if they were men or women, so I shouldn't worry too much, Hannah, it's a million to one chance that your dad was one of them.'

'It could have been Dad and his fancy woman,' said Maureen.

Pam's parents looked at each other and then at Hannah in surprise.

'Oh, it's no secret, she knows all about it,' said Hannah.

'If you're talking about Mrs Butcher,' said Ken, 'I saw her in town yesterday and I assure you she's alive and kicking.'

'Now that the police know your dad is missing they'll make some enquiries and they'll more than likely want to speak to her, so we'll at least find out if she was with him on Friday night. They said they'd ring me if they have any news, so that's all we can do for the moment, and remember, no news is good news,' said Fred, trying to make light of it.

'What are you having for your dinner?' Peg asked Hannah.

'Oh we'll have a picnic with some sandwiches I should think.'

'You'll do no such thing. When you've been to see Elsie you can all come back here for dinner.'

'You won't have enough meat for all of us,' protested Hannah weakly, mentally drooling at the thought of a proper cooked Sunday dinner.

'Don't you worry about that. A few sausages will help stretch the joint. Now not another word.'

Hannah glanced at Ken, who smiled at her, making her heart turn over.

'Yes, do stay Hannah and I'll let you hear my new records.'

She couldn't resist this last offer, so it was agreed.

'Come on Maureen, Betsy, let's go and see Aunt Elsie now, then we'll be back in good time for dinner.'

'Why don't you leave your mum here,' said Peg, 'she can sit in the kitchen while I do the cooking. There's no point in dragging her to Elsie's in this heat.'

'I thought she might like to see Aunt Elsie but I don't suppose she'd even know her, so if you're sure it's no trouble,' said Hannah and they set off.

They reached Elsie's little house where whoops of laughter could be heard coming from the enclosed backyard where little

Tom was being pushed high in the air on a swing.

On hearing the gate click Big Tom turned.

'Hello younguns, what you doing out here on a Sunday? Is Aggie all right?'

'Yes, thank you, we've come to see Aunt Elsie. Is she here?'

'Yes, she's in the kitchen, cooking my dinner, I hope. Go right in, the door's open.'

Elsie was indeed in the kitchen, which was as hot as an oven.

She turned away from the cooker to wipe her brow on the bottom of her pinny, her face as red as a turkey cock's rear.

'Hello, my little lovies, what are you doing traipsing around in this heat? Is anything wrong?'

The girls looked at each other, each waiting for the other to relate their story yet again.

She sensed something was amiss so she said, 'Maureen, Betsy, go out the back and see my Little Tom and in a minute I'll bring out some lemonade. Sit on that chair near the door Hannah, you'll get a bit of breeze there. Now what's up?' She said, seating her ample bottom on a chair the other side of the doorway.

Hannah told her of John's disappearance and that Fred Bates had contacted the police.

Elsie looked very concerned. 'I don't want to frighten you but I think we have every reason to worry. I know I've sworn about the old bugger, for the way he neglected you lot but I wouldn't want to think he'd come to any harm. But two days,' she shook her head, 'I don't like the smell of it. Still, now that the police know they'll do their job and make enquiries, so we'll just have to sit back and wait.'

'Now buck up, I'm sure he'll turn up, like a bad penny. Come and help me make some lemonade. I've got a new packet of lemonade crystals.'

Hannah stirred the crystals into a big jug of water and when they'd dissolved they all enjoyed the lovely sharp refreshment.

'As you've come all this way you might as well have a bit of dinner with us, I can soon do some more potatoes.'

'Thanks Aunt Elsie, but Pam's mum has asked us to have dinner there and Ken's going to let me hear his new records.'

'Well, I can't compete with that. A handsome son and his music, I know how you love music and I know you're a little bit partial to Ken.'

'Aunt ELSIE,' said Hannah, blushing furiously. 'I'm friends with Pam, not him, and anyway Norma's got her hooks into him.'

'I hope he's got more sense than to be trucked up with her, she's too bloody cocky for my liking. Still he's off to college soon, so we don't have to worry on that score.' They finished their lemonade and made their way back to Pam's.

Elsie worriedly watched them walking away, wondering what would happen to them if, indeed, John had been killed.

Her heart ached for them and she wished, not for the first time, that she lived a bit closer to them so that she could lighten Hannah's load.

Pam opened the door to them, on their arrival.

'You timed it just right, Mum is about to serve up,' she said, slipping her arm through Hannah's. 'I hope you're hungry. Mum has cooked about a ton of new potatoes.' The smell of mint wafted out tantalisingly.

They enjoyed a sumptious meal of roast pork, Yorkshire pudding, as light as a feather, dishes full of fresh vegetables, gravy, rich and thick, and just when they thought they would explode, a hot apple pie appeared, shining with sugar topping and to complete the dreamy meal a glass of lemonade, not the home-made variety this time but equally delicious.

'Can I help you to wash up?' asked Hannah, as the dishes were being cleared away.

'Bless your heart, no,' said Peg, 'I'm sure you have enough of that to do at home. Take your mum through to the front room and I'll make her a cup of tea and you can listen to Ken's records while your dinner is going down.'

The two younger girls skipped off to play with some children in the street and Hannah, Pam and Norma spent a lovely afternoon chatting, with Ken popping in and out to put on records.

Hannah thought, How clean and fresh he looks. He was wearing a crisp white shirt with the sleeves rolled up to reveal lightly tanned arms with little golden hairs showing his early manhood and soft, brown corduroy trousers, worn thin with numerous washings, comfortably hugging his lean hips.

He sought her eyes for approval each time he put one of his favourite records on the gramophone, aware that she enjoyed and appreciated his music more than Pam or Norma and she felt an affinity to him through it.

If only we were alone, she thought but, on reflection, it's just as well we're not for I'd be nervous and tongue-tied; I couldn't flirt and tease like Norma, I'd just want to sit close to him, breathing in the very air he exhaled. And she shivered deliciously as the very idea, with strange, warm feelings causing her to moisten between her legs and a terrible longing for she knew not what.

'Are you all right Hannah?' asked Pam. 'You look a bit pale.'

'I'm a bit hot and thirsty, I'll go and get a drink of water to cool me down.'

'I think she's in love,' said Norma, winking at Ken, 'I think she's gone off Billy and is thinking about a REAL man.'

Hannah blushed furiously, thankful that she was halfway out of the room.

Trust Norma to spoil my day, she thought, I must try to be more matter-of-fact when he's about; not that there were likely to be many of these occasions, she sighed.

She was ill at ease now and was glad when it was time to go home, the lovely warm feeling being replaced by her old anxieties. But, as they bade their goodbyes, with many thanks to Peg for the lovely dinner and were given an apple pie to take home with them, her spirits lifted somewhat.

9

Lil, happily humming a tune, wrapped a soft white towelling robe around herself on leaving the bathroom and made her way to the kitchen, where a delicious smell of bacon met her.

He really is a good old sort, she thought to herself, as Bill placed her breakfast on the table. They didn't usually have time for a cooked breakfast before leaving for work but this week they had taken time off to decorate the flat.

It was Thursday, and although they'd expected it to take all week a couple of hours today should just about finish it.

'This looks lovely Bill, you really do spoil me at times but with the war and everything I feel quite guilty living as well as we do. How do you manage to get meat with the rationing so tight?'

'It's not what you know, it's who you know,' he replied, tapping his nose meaningfully with his fore-finger. 'I did a good deal for a bloke on a bit of property. A butcher he is and he was very grateful, and so he should be, I saved him a lot of money. Anyway, I wouldn't take a back-hander so he slips me a bit of meat now and then to show his gratitude.'

'I thought you were on a diet,' said Lil. 'I don't begrudge you anything darling and it doesn't matter to me how fat you are but I do worry about your health, you get very short of breath at times.'

'And we all know what times you're talking about don't we?' he replied, planting a kiss on her cheek. 'But I promise you, next week, I'll start to cut down but don't nag me this week while we're on holiday, I'll go on to salads next week.'

He then sat down beside her to a plateful of bacon, eggs, fried bread and tomatoes and finished off with toast and marmalade and two cups of tea to wash it down.

He knew he spoiled her at times but she was a good old girl and well worth spoiling and he'd been very worried about her

114

since her problem didn't seem to be abating

For the past two years she's been visiting doctors and hospitals in an attempt to find the cause of her frequent bleedings, to no avail. If things didn't improve they feared it would mean an operation to remove her womb, but if that's what it takes to put things right he thought, the sooner the better; then they could get back to living a normal life. As it was now he was only having sex about one week in four and although he knew in no way was it Lil's fault, he was a full-blooded man with a big appetite. In spite of this he had stayed faithful, but he doubted his ability to remain so if things continued in this way.

Lil knew that he was, like herself, very worried but they tried to make light of it in order to save each other from worrying unduly. She also knew deep down that things would not magically right themselves and she was almost resigned to having an operation. She had all but given up hope of having a baby but even so she knew that once the hysterectomy had been performed she had absolutely no chance of becoming a mother and it seemed a terrible, final acceptance of being a not quite complete woman.

They had lightly touched on the subject of adoption. While there was hope they hadn't gone into it in depth but she knew that if it were to be considered seriously it would have to be put into motion within the next few years, as they weren't getting any younger. She was now thirty seven and Bill forty seven and she'd heard that the adoption society didn't consider a woman eligible after she'd reached the age of forty.

'Shall we take a little ride out to the country this afternoon? We've all but finished in here and a breath of fresh air will do us good. We've been cooped up here all week working, and I'm very pleased with all we've accomplished without having to employ experts. We've saved quite a lot of money doing it ourselves. Now, I think, we deserve a little rest. What do you say, Lil?'

'I'd like to go and see Aggie and the kids, I feel quite guilty for neglecting them so long.'

'Well, I was thinking more of Hampstead Heath than Norfolk. We'd be like a couple of lobsters driving all that way in this heat. Don't you think we ought to leave it until the weather is a bit cooler, love? And you've no reason to feel guilty, there is a war on and you know what a job it is getting hold of petrol. I've got a full tank now but I don't know how long it will be before I come by any more.'

'Perhaps you're right, but there are times when I wish they didn't live a hundred miles away, especially with Aggie being the way she is and poor little Hannah having to do for them all. I don't know what I'll do when I see John again. I'll probably throttle him with my own hands for the way he carries on and neglects them poor little sods. Thank God my poor sister don't know what's going on.'

'Now, now, don't get yourself all upset, you do the best you can for them as you always have and you know as well as I do that John wouldn't carry on the way he does if Aggie was all right, but a man has his needs and he has to get his relief from somewhere.'

'You sound as though you condonc what he's doing. I suppose if it had happened to me you'd be dipping YOUR wick somewhere else as well. Men are nothing more than animals at times.'

'No of course I wouldn't. You should know me better than that. How could you say such a thing? I'd never dream of touching another woman,' said Bill, looking very hurt.

'I'm sorry, I didn't mean it, I know you'd never do anything like that. It's just that I worry so about them all and I feel so helpless.'

'It's a sad state of affairs, I admit, but you shouldn't reproach yourself. You're a good sister to Aggie and we do have our own jobs and lives to consider.'

Their conversation was interrupted by the banging of the door-knocker.

'I'll go,' said Bill, relieved to leave the table.

He did not return immediately and Lil, on hearing murmering, called out 'Who is it Bill? Is anything wrong?' She made her way to the front-door where, standing just inside, was a policeman, hat in hand, talking to her husband.

'What is it? What's wrong? Is it Aggie?' she asked, feeling quite faint with foreboding.

'Now, now, don't upset yourself Mrs Huggins, it may be nothing to worry about but the King's Lynn police asked us to contact you in respect of your brother-in-law, John Hardy, you being the closest family.'

116

They invited the constable into the living room and poured him a cup of tea while he told them of the probability of John's death in the Eagle.

They were concerned as to who would take care of the family in the event of their fears being justified, Aggie being incapable and Hannah too young to legally fend for them.

'We were wondering, you being her sister, if you could take care of them for a while until the authorities sort something out.'

'I'm afraid that is out of the question,' said Bill, answering for Lil, who was sitting down, looking quite pale.

'My wife has a business to run and there's nobody capable of running it in her absence. They're managing this week while we're having a few days off to do some decorating but they're incapable of carrying on indefinitely, they just haven't the experience.'

'I do see your point, Sir, but we really don't know who else to approach. Usually, in cases like these the families sort something out between them.'

'Well, this is a bit of a bombshell, if you'll pardon the expression,' said Bill.

'I think the best thing we can do for the moment is to go down to Norfolk and talk things over with the local police there. They know the family and their friends personally and they might be able to come up with something.'

'That's a good idea, Sir,' said the constable, putting on his helmet. 'With your permission I'll ring them from the station to inform them of your impending visit.' To Lil he said 'I'm sorry to be the bearer of bad news ma'am, but perhaps things aren't as bad as they appear, I'm sure the Lynn police will do everything in their power to assist you.'

'Yes, I'm sure they will,' said Lil, regaining a little of her composure. 'Thank you for letting us know, you haven't got a very nice job these days.' She saw him to the door.

The journey to Norfolk seemed interminable and unbearably hot and the closer they got to King's Lynn, the heavier the traffic became, with everybody who had managed to aquire petrol rushing like lemmings to the beach, a few miles the other side of the town.

Lil's early morning feelings of well-being had disappeared and her head pounded painfully as they drove into the police station courtyard.

The police told them that although all the evidence was circumstantial it was too strong to be dismissed and they could only logically conclude that John had been killed. They had visited his family, who could throw no light on the matter, his daughters having not seen him since two days prior to the bombing of the Eagle.

They spent about an hour at the police station but could reach no decision as to the fate of the 'bereaved' family.

Certain suggestions had been tossed around but not accepted by Lil who decided to visit Elsie Watson to see if she could come up with any ideas, assuring the police they would be informed if any descision was reached.

After numerous cups of tea and hours of wracking their brains they reluctantly reached the only possible conclusion and Elsie offered to ride out with them to inform the police and then to break the news to Hannah of their decision.

The two women were both crying freely, terribly unhappy at the only solution that had to be miserably accepted and Bill was at a loss as to how to comfort them.

He had never had to face anything as serious as this and was completely out of his depth, silently wishing the next few hours to pass quickly so they could get back to their home and away from this misery.

The children heard the car approach and ran to meet it, hurling themselves at the occupants before they were half out of the doors, excitedly jumped up and down, hugging and kissing them until they were quite breathless. Lil's heart was near to breaking, knowing that before long their happiness would turn to horror and disbelief when their future was laid before them.

Aggie sat on her stool in the stuffy little kitchen and Lil went to her, wrapping her arms around her sister, crying.

'Oh Aggie love, I know you won't understand what's about to happen to you but I promise with all my heart that things will change at the first possible moment. It won't be for long.'

'What do you mean, Aunt Lil?' asked Hannah, fear clutching her heart. 'What's going to happen to Mum? What are you talking about, you're frightening me?'

Her fear relayed itself to her sisters, who stood, wide-eyed and silent, waiting for Lil's reply.

118

Elsie went to the younger girls. 'Come and sit down with me my little lovies, there's nothing to be afraid of. You know your Aunt Lil and I wouldn't let anything hurt you. Just come and listen quietly while she tells you what we have to do, but, remember, it's not forever, just for the time being.'

She sank her large frame on the stool with the two younger girls either side of her, her big, fat arms holding them to her bosom protectively.

Bill went over to Hannah, taking her little hand in his, squeezing it comfortingly and for once Hannah wasn't averse to his touch, some inner instinct telling her she would need the reassurance of it before long.

'Now'' said Lil, 'before I tell you what must be done I want you to understand it's only temporary until your dad turns up.' (She'd decided it would be kinder to act as if John was only missing and would turn up one day, thus helping them to believe it was only a short-term measure.)

'The police came to tell us that your dad was missing and we've had a little meeting, Aunt Elsie as well, to decide the best thing to do until he turns up and this is what we've decided. You must understand that if we don't carry out these plans you will all be taken into care and probably placed with foster parents but because there are so many war-orphans the authorities have agreed to comply to our wishes.

'As you know, neither Aunt Elsie or I, have enough room to take you all in so we've decided, for the time being,' she added, 'that Maureen and Betsy will go to live with Aunt Elsie. She has a pretty little spare room, which I'm sure you'll love and you'll be closer to the bus route for school so you won't have that long walk every day.'

At this, Elsie gave them a rib-crushing hug, to convince them of their welcome.

'Hannah will come to London with us and stay in our spare room and perhaps we will be able to get you a proper job.' she said, smiling at her.

'No, no' shrieked Betsy, jumping up and running to Hannah, flinging her arms around her legs. 'You can't take my Hannah to London, she's got to stay with us. Don't go Hannah, tell her you won't go and leave us, please don't leave us, PLEASE, Hannah, PLEASE,' she cried, bordering on hysteria.

Hannah bent down, hugging her and kissing the little hot, tear-soaked face.

'Please don't cry Betsy, it's only for a little while. Just pretend you're going on a holiday, it'll be really lovely. You've seen Aunt Elsie's little bedroom where you'll be staying. It's got pretty flowered wall-paper. Do you remember how pretty you said it was once and how you wished you had a bedroom like that?'

But Betsy was unconvinced, crying all the louder. 'I'm not going without you and that's that, and you can't make me, I won't go, I WON'T, I'll run away and look for Dad, he won't make me go.'

By now Maureen had come and joined her sisters and the pathetic little trio hugged each other and cried and cried until they were quite exhausted.

Eventually their cries died down to dry, racking little sobs and Lil and Elsie stood silently by, tears streaming down their own faces, allowing the children to get it out of their systems.

Hannah was talking, between sobs, to her sisters, trying to convince them that it would only be for a little while and gradually they quietened.

'What about Mum?' asked Maureen. 'Where's she going? Is she coming with us?'

'No I'm afraid not,' answered Elsie. 'We've only the one spare room and it's far too small for two children and a grown-up.'

'Well, where's she going then?' chipped in Betsy, going over to her mother and idly toying with her fingers.

'Well, once again, it's only for a little while but we think its best for your mum to go into a hospital in Norwich where they can help people with head-sickness.'

'No, no!' screamed Betsy, hugging her mother to her. 'You can't, that's not a hospital, it's a loony bin, I know cos one of the girls at school has an uncle there and he's been there for years and years and they never let you out. You can't put her there, you can't. Nobody will be friends with me if they find out I've got a mother in the loony bin. She's coming with us.'

'Don't you worry, Mum.' She kissed Aggie gently on the cheek. 'I won't let them take you.'

My God, thought Lil, this is like a nightmare and I can't see any way out. She went over to her sister and stroked her hair.

'Leave her alone, she's my mum, not yours.'

'Betsy, I wouldn't hurt your mum for the world. I love her as much as you do, you know. She is my sister, like Hannah is yours and I wouldn't hurt her any more than you would hurt Hannah, Please trust me, love, I promise you nobody will hurt her and I'll go and visit her every chance I get to make sure they're looking after her all right.

'They run a bus out to the hospital every month so I'll be able to go and see her as well' backed up Elsie 'and you can be sure I'll see to it that she's looked after all right and I'll write to Hannah in London to tell her how she's getting on and remember, it's only for a little while till your dad comes back.'

'What if he don't come back? Will she have to stay there forever and ever?' asked Betsy.

'No, of course not. Don't you worry, your dad will turn up like a bad penny and even if he doesn't she won't have to stay there forever, only until she's better. And I'm sure that won't be long because she's only a little bit sick. I'm sure they'll soon fix her up and she'll be out in no time, then you can all come back home again. So, no more of this nonsense, we've got a lot of work to do sorting your clothes and things out and packing them up. I'll see if Fred Bates will give us a lift in his van so we can take your things all at once.'

'Uncle Bill and I will stay here tonight,' said Lil, 'and get everything sorted out tomorrow.'

Bill took Elsie back to Heysham where they visited Doctor Lawson, who made the arrangements for Aggie to go into the hospital the next day.

Fortunately, it was his day for visiting the hospital and he explained to his colleagues that Aggie was a personal friend. So they bent the rules a little by agreeing to allow him to drive her in his car; not a normal practice but these were not normal times and they were reluctant to send an ambulance for just one person as it might be needed for emergencies if there were an air-raid.

He watched them drive away with a heavy heart. He had been afraid of something like this happening. 'The Lord moves in mysterious ways' he thought, thinking of how yet another heartache had been laid at Hannah's feet. But she was a strong little body and he knew she would come through it all eventually and be a much better person for it.

He had recently acquired a long-awaited new car and it pleased him to think that at least Aggie would have a comfortable ride.

Friday morning, very early, Bill was up with the lark. He'd spent the most uncomfortable night of his life on the hard couch in the front room. The night had been very humid and every time he'd moved the imitation leather had stuck to him. He couldn't get away and back to London soon enough. Even the journey back seemed inviting in comparison to the night he'd just spent.

He moved around the little kitchen distastefully, wondering how people could live in such conditions. But, what you never had you never missed, he thought.

He made a pot of tea and after he'd had two cups he took upstairs one each for Lil and Aggie, who were sharing the main bedroom.

His nose wrinkled in disgust at the awful smell that hung around the bedrooms and when he walked in, even Lil looked a bit embarrassed as their eyes met.

They had quite a few things to sort out but Bill wouldn't stay in the bedroom, it made him feel quite queasy.

'When you've had your tea come down to the kitchen before the kids wake up and we'll try to decide what to do about the animals.'

Lil slipped out of bed, telling Aggie to stay and sleep for a little while longer.

Thankfully, the children were still sleeping. She knew they must be exhausted from the traumas of the day before. She would have liked to allow them to sleep all the morning but it was out of the question because they had a lot to get through before setting off back to London, but she'd allow them another hour while she and Bill talked privately. For after today their privacy would be limited, with the presence of Hannah.

They decided that Bill should go to see a farmer friend of John's, who lived just a few miles away, for advice about the animals.

He turned out to be very helpful, offering to take them to market as soon as possible, with the exception of the rabbit with the babies, which he would feed until they were old enough to leave their mother.

As some of the farmer's men had joined the armed forces he had a gang of Italian prisoners of war working on his land and with their help he would put John's in order at the first opportunity.

Even though the day had began early it was mid-afternoon before everything had been arranged.

Elsie came over mid-morning to give a hand and she gave Aggie a bath, for which Lil was very grateful, for although she could do most things she couldn't face this task and Elsie, in her wisdom, had forseen this and offered her services.

The younger children were very quiet, doing everything without argument but never leaving Hannah's side for longer than necessary, as if treasuring every minute of this day before they were separated.

Doctor Lawson and Fred Bates arrived almost simultaneously, which made things a little easier. For while the children's things were being loaded into Fred's van, Aggie and her few belongings were put into the doctor's car.

Pam had come over with her father, to say goodbye to Hannah and as soon as the two friends met they wrapped their arms around each other, crying bitterly and promising to write every week.

'Ken and Norma send their love,' said Pam between sniffs, 'and Ken says that when he starts college, if you're still in London, he will come to see you.'

Hannah hugged this thought to her heart, praying that he would keep his word.

It was a sad little procession that set off. Betsy and Maureen begged to be allowed to travel with Hannah as far the village, from whence they would go their separate ways, but Lil, knowing that they would think her heartless, refused. If she consented there would be another tearful farewell and this time it would be witnessed by the villagers and would only prolong the inevitable parting.

They had said their goodbyes at the house with much hugging and crying and Lil felt she just could not suffer another such scene.

News of the Hardy's separation had reached the locals and they stood in solemn little groups, watching their departure.

They had to drive through the middle of the village and many hands waved a sad goodbye to Hannah and her sisters and a few of the elders peered into Doctor Lawson's car to have a last – as they feared – look at Aggie.

Hannah was, by now, a quivering bundle of nerves, her chest and throat so dry and tight from the misery of the parting that she thought she would choke and the most terrible feelings of panic causing her to perspire so much that she could smell her own fears. The intensity of her misery terrified her and she thought she would most certainly die. On the one hand she hoped she would die but on the other she knew she just couldn't, for what would happen to her sisters if she did? She wasn't particularly religious but right now she thought the only person able to help her was God, so she closed her eyes and prayed that He would help her regain control of her senses to enable her to live through this agonising ordeal. She felt that if she could live through this experience she would be able to tackle anything the future might hold.

Her panic subsided a little, leaving her feeling utterly drained and more tired than she had ever felt in her whole life.

The times between the dry, quiet little sobs lengthened and she fell into an uncomfortable sleep on the back seat of the car with her few possessions squashed beside her – a change of clothes, a book, a bottle of lemonade that Elsie had made up for her for the journey and last of all, her gas-mask.

She and her sisters had worn their gas-masks for fun, their voices sounding strange and muffled as they talked to each other and looking quite horrible, like monsters, but even though they'd only worn them in fun she was always glad to take hers off for it smelt awful and made her feel as if she couldn't breathe properly. But at least it made them familiar with the feel of them so that if the time came when they would have to wear them it wouldn't be such a fearful experience.

She awoke much later and sat bolt upright in the car. She had never heard so much noise, it quite terrified her.

'Where are we? What's happening? Are we being bombed?'

Lil sitting beside Bill in the front of the car, turned her head to smile at Hannah, patting her arm reassuringly. 'Calm down, it's all right, we're in the middle of London traffic, there's nothing to be afraid of.'

'London, London,' said Hannah, disbelieving. 'We can't be, we've only been driving a few minutes.'

'We've been driving for over three hours, you've been

sleeping like a log.'

'I thought we were being bombed. I've never heard so much noise. Is it always like this? It's terrible.'

'Is it? Yes, I suppose it must sound pretty terrible to you. You went to sleep in a quiet little village and woke up to Bedlam. But no, it's not always like this, we're in the middle of the rush-hour traffic. It will get better as we get away from the city centre. We'll be home in about ten minutes.'

But it was a good half-hour later before the car came to a halt outside the flat and although much quieter now it still sounded pretty noisy to Hannah.

Her eyes filled with tears as she thought of her sisters and her mother and a terrible feeling of hopelessness engulfed her. She felt almost ashamed of her inadequacy.

How could this be happening? How could she have allowed the family to be split up? She wanted to run back to Norfolk, so achingly did she feel the need of her sisters' arms around her.

She followed her Aunt Lil into the flat as if in a trance. Her head felt as if it were stuffed with cotton-wool and she seemed to be walking on air as if in a dream. I must sit down she thought, my legs feel like jelly. Under different circumstances she would have been very impressed by the luxurious surroundings.

They entered the front door, the top half being made from coloured glass, giving it a church-like appearance. The hall was long and narrow and had been decorated with delicate floral paper and on a little table mid-way was a telephone and a vase of flowers. You smelt the flowers as you walked in, giving the illusion of walking through a perfumed garden.

Lil casually pointed out the various rooms as they made their way to the kitchen. Hannah looked a little bewildered.
'Don't worry, you'll soon learn the lay of the land but right now we're going to sit down and have a nice cup of tea. Then I'll show you your room.'

Hannah sank down gratefully on a chair by the kitchen table while Lil busied herself making the tea and Bill unloaded the car.

She felt considerably better after two cups of hot, sweet tea and when Lil enquired if she were hungry she was surprised to realise that she was indeed very hungry.

Her aunt led her to the bathroom and suggested that she

wash the travel-weariness away and then they would have tea.

The beauty of the little bathroom quite took her breath away. Everything was pink, dusty pink tiles and mats and big, soft pink towels.

Hannah felt a little alarmed. Everything was so clean, she was afraid to touch anything.

'Oh Aunt Lil, I can't wash in here, let me wash in the kitchen.'

'Don't be silly,' smiled Lil, 'you just go ahead and spoil yourself and don't worry about a thing. These towels are for you alone to use, Bill and I have our own. Go on,' she urged, 'there's no hurry. Have a bath if you like, you can use my talcum powder. I rather fancy it's going to be hard to come by in the future, with the war going on. Nearly everything we took for granted is going to be rationed but I've got enough for a year and the war will be over by then.'

So, on her urging, Hannah entered and took off her socks and shoes and filled the wash basin with hot water from the tap. She was far too overawed to run water into the shiny pink bath. Instead, she washed herself all over and put some talcum powder under her arms and between her toes.

She caught sight of herself in the full-length mirror and blushed at her nakedness. They had no big mirror at home so she rarely saw herself absolutely bare.

Her little breasts were firm and proud and her nipples hardened as she looked at herself. The triangle of hair between her legs shone like a raven's wing and she wished the hair on her head was as beautiful instead, it was dull and mousy by comparison.

She wondered if Ken would think her pretty, if he could see her now, all clean and smelling so nice. She blushed again at her thoughts. Whatever's come over me? I would never, never let anybody see me with no clothes on, least of all Ken. But even so, a delicious feeling crept over her and she ran her fingers gently over her body, enjoying the sensuality.

'That's better,' said Bill, as she re-entered the kitchen. 'You look like a different person now, it's amazing what a bath does for you.'

'Oh, I didn't have a bath,' said Hannah quickly, 'just a wash.'

'Oh well, whatever, you look a lot better anyway. You can

have a bath in the morning.'

Whatever for? thought Hannah. I've just washed myself all over, I'm sure I won't get dirty again by the morning, not in this house anyway.

Bill twiddled with the knobs of the wireless until he got the station he wanted and they all listened to the news, which was nearly all war news nowadays.

Lil had made some delicious, thin cucumber sandwiches for tea and there was also a plate full of thin bread and butter to be spread with jam, if they were still hungry.

Hannah felt a little ill-at-ease having someone waiting on her like this. Usually, she was the one preparing the food for her family.

Lil sensed her unease and went over to her and gently put her arms around her.

'I know you feel strange, love, but don't worry about it, you'll feel better after a few days when you've settled in. Just try and relax and enjoy having things done for you for a change.'

And strangely enough she did relax and enjoy her tea but afterwards felt guilty at having done so. Were Betsy and Maureen all right? Were they enjoying their tea? But of course they were, Aunt Elsie would see to that. They may not be having wafer-thin sandwiches (more like door-steps) and they may not be drinking sweet tea from delicate cups, but whatever they were eating and drinking would be served with lashings of love, so why was she worrying so? She had only been away from them a few hours and was missing them dreadfully already. And what of poor old Mum. She just dare not dwell on this for if she tried to imagine her surroundings she knew her imagination would run riot and blow everything up out of all proportion. Just believe what you've been told, she said to herself, Doctor Lawson will keep a close check on her and Aunt Elsie said she would go to see her, so I'll have to be content with this.

It could have been a lot worse, she reasoned with herself. If Aunt Lil and Aunt Elsie had washed their hands of them her sisters could have been put in an orphanage and Hannah could never have accepted that.

She insisted on helping Lil clear away the tea things and wash up. It was against her nature to sit back and let somebody else do the work so Lil allowed her to help, knowing that it would be better for her to be occupied as much as possible for a while, thus leaving less time to fret and worry about her family.

She was then shown to her bedroom, which was such pure delight that she could have cried from the sheer beauty of it.

The little bed was covered with a patchwork quilt made from scraps of material of every colour imaginable and the sunlight shining through the window danced on it, bringing all the glorious colours of life.

Standing against the wall was a glass topped dressing table with a mirror and around the bottom of it hung a pretty gingham curtain, matching the curtains at the window.

On the shiny canvas-covered floor beside the bed was a little rug, once again made from scraps of material and it looked so cosy and inviting that Hannah wanted to take off her shoes and wriggle her toes in it.

'Oh, Aunt Lil, it's so beautiful I hardly dare walk in. I'm afraid I'll never want to leave it.'

'Well, there's no need to be afraid, it's yours for as long as you need it. Put your things away and then, when you're ready, come to the living room and we'll listen to the wireless for a while. It's too early for bed yet and tomorrow I'll take you to the city and show you some of the sights you've read about in school and we'll have tea at Lyons.'

'Will Uncle Bill come with us?'

'No, I think we'll make this a girls' day out and that will give him a chance to finish the decorating.'

This was the answer Hannah hoped for and she felt the first stirrings of excitement at being in the Big City.

10

There were many bombings and casualties over the next two years but thankfully the flat was still intact.

Hannah soon became accustomed to city life and even began to take the frequent air-raids in her stride.

True to his word, Ken paid her a visit a year after she'd moved in with her aunt and uncle and he took her out to tea, to the very popular Lyons Tea Rooms. But it was not the exciting experience she had dreamed about and she had the feeling that he'd only carried out this mission because of the promise to his sister. The afternoon was fraught with tension and discomfort and he only began to loosen up as the parting time drew near.

He took her back to the flat and only then did they begin to feel comfortable with each other.

He kissed her lightly on the cheek on parting, with the promise that he would visit her again before long, but Hannah knew he was only being polite and although she loved him for saying it she didn't really expect him to come again.

Initially Lil had taken Hannah to the flower shop to help out until another job came along but as naturally as breathing she had fitted in, with a real feel for the business and before long was an important member of the team.

The little business had grown in spite of the war and it was not just a charitable act on Lil's part that allowed Hannah to stay on there; her nimble little hands had become much needed and appreciated.

Lil was more than pleased with her natural aptitude for the business and always introduced 'my niece' proudly to customers when they asked to thank her personally for work she'd done exceptionally well. Lil paid her a very good wage and treated her like a daughter, often buying her little gifts for the sheer pleasure of giving. On Hannah's sixteenth birthday she had paid for her to have her hair permed and she now looked a proper city girl.

She was still very thin but with good quality clothes and Lil's guidance she was slowly emerging like a butterfly, still shy and sensitive but acquiring Lil's composure naturally, from living with her every day.

Somehow, Bill always managed to get hold of some petrol whenever he needed it and took them to Norfolk to visit her sisters whenever they could all arrange a day off together.

She lived for these visits but it tore her apart every time she had to leave them. Maureen was still a skinny, mousy child but Betsy was filling out to near-fatness from Elsie's loving care.

They rarely mentioned their mother nowadays and Hannah found their very resilience quite hurtful, but she realised that this was the way of nature and children's wounds healed very readily.

She managed to spend some time with Pam on their visits and guessed, from her friend's off-handedness when speaking of Norma and Ken, that things were developing much as she'd feared and no wonder. Ken was a very handsome young man and Norma was turning out to be a real beauty.

When Hannah looked at her she knew she didn't stand a chance against her wit and charm but she also knew, young as she was, that what she felt for Ken wasn't just infatuation. She was sure she could never feel such intensity for another man and although she knew it was a hopeless love she would always carry him next to her heart.

He had not been at home on her recent visits so it was now about a year since she'd last seen him and according to Pam he was thinking of leaving the college and joining the Air Force. So far, his parents had managed to dissuade him, praying that the war would end before he could carry out his threat.

The idea of Ken going to war filled her heart with dread and if she had to choose between him going to war or marrying Norma she would choose the latter. Even though it would break her heart, at least he would be alive and, like millions of others, prayed more fervently that the war would end soon.

Always, after her visits to Norfolk, she was very depressed and unsettled for a few days but then she would settle down again to her new life.

Elsie, keeping her promise, visited Aggie every month and always wrote to Hannah, assuring her of her mother's well-being. There was very little to report; Aggie was still in the same mental state but with tender, loving care, regular meals and baths, she looked much better than when she was first admitted.

Hannah had wanted to visit her mother but Elsie suggested she wait a while longer, for although she, Elsie, didn't mind in the least going to see Aggie, she knew that mental hospitals unnerved some people. God knows why, it was just like any other hospital, with sick people either in bed or sauntering around the wards. The only difference, as far as she was concerned, was the lack of conversation. But, nevertheless a lot of people were afraid to go there.

The staff, if it were possible, were even more caring and loving than in a general hospital and to Elsie's mind, were worth their weight in gold for their dedication.

The war carried on, life carried on and a few months after her last visit, a letter from Pam informed Hannah that Ken had signed up for the Air Force. Assuming that he passed the medical – and according to Pam, anybody who was under forty with two arms, legs and eyes passed – he would be in uniform within weeks.

She added that he and Norma had gone all soppy and decided to get engaged before he went but, she added (Hannah knew, for her benefit), it wouldn't last; they were just being dramatic, copying other couples who were to be separated. She said it wouldn't be long before Norma was tagging along with someone else, and although Hannah would have liked to believe this, she thought it most unlikely. There wasn't a man for miles around who was a patch on Ken.

The next few months found Hannah sunk in a deep depression. She had thought, after the split-up of her family, that she would never ever feel such pain again but this was a different kind of agony. One half of her feared for Ken's life, the other feared for his coming home and marrying Norma.

She became quiet and withdrawn and began to lose weight.

Lil was very concerned and tried to get her to tell her what was worrying her but she insisted there was nothing wrong, so her aunt concluded that the war was getting her down, as it was millions of others.

She seemed to have no interest in boys, although more than one young man had tried to encourage a relationship, so Lil

131

had no worries on that score. She wished that Hannah would take a boyfriend and although that would give her something else to worry about it would at least be more natural than moping about in this fashion. I'll have to take her out a bit more, to places where she can meet more young people of her own age, she thought, for although I dearly love her company it's selfish to keep her to myself so much.

One day on hearing the familiar flop, flop of the letters being thrust through the letterbox Bill, knowing that Lil and Hannah would be flying around doing their last minute titivations before leaving for work, called out, 'I'll get it.'

He walked back down the hall into the kitchen. 'Br'r'r' it's brass-monkey weather today all right, I shouldn't be surprised if we have a White Christmas. One for you Hannah,' he said, giving her hand an over-familiar squeeze, 'and one for you love,' handing Lil a long brown envelope.

Hannah recognised the hand-writing on hers as that of her friend Pam's, and decided to put it in her handbag and read it at her leisure, during her lunch-break.

Lil, realising there was little time now, also put her letter into her handbag to read later and, putting on warm coats, they left for work.

The day turned out to be very busy. It was two weeks before Christmas and the orders were coming in thick and fast – holly wreaths for graves and doors, table decorations, personal flowers from lovers as well as the regular day to day trade.

There was no time for a proper lunch-break for any of them; they had to make do with a quick sandwich and a cup of tea. Consequently it wasn't until after they'd had dinner and listened to the evening news that they were able to read their letters.

Hannah's was, as she had guessed, from Pam. She brought Hannah up to date with the local gossip and said that Ken was fit and well and thoroughly enjoying his life in the Air Force. He was so full of exuberence that his parents felt he had made the right decision after all. His training camp was only two hours' journey away so with luck he might just MIGHT get home, for a little while over the Christmas holidays and if he did, he was bringing a friend called Dennis (Denny to his friends) with him, whom Pam had met briefly once before and was looking forward to seeing again.

132

She concluded by saying that she and her family would be more than happy if she could spend Christmas with them (if she didn't mind sharing a bedroom with Pam).

If I didn't mind sharing a bedroom with Pam, thought Hannah. She couldn't think of a better way to spend the holiday than with her very good friend and the possibility of seeing Ken. She felt happier than she'd felt in a long while and blessed Pam for the invitation.

Smiling to herself she glanced over to where Lil was reading her letter, Bill looking over her shoulder. Her aunt's face, drained of colour, looked up at her husband who, in turn, wrapped an arm around her shoulder to comfort her.

'What's wrong?' asked Hannah, going over to them.

'It's from the hospital' said Lil. 'There will be a bed available for me in two weeks' time. They've decided that I must have a hysterectomy; well, not *must* but in my own interests they strongly advise it.

'I don't know why I'm so surprised. I've been half-expecting it but I've also been hoping that it wouldn't come to that.' She began to cry quietly as Bill lowered her to a chair.

'You'll be all right love, dozens of women have that operation every day. They don't even regard it as a serious operation nowadays.'

'It's not the thought of going into hospital or the operation that worries me, it's just, just,' and she couldn't go on.

'I know, I know,' said Bill, taking her hands in his. 'I know exactly what you're thinking but there's always adoption. We have talked about it haven't we? When you come out of hospital we'll set the wheels in motion. Don't you worry love, we'll have a baby one way or another. I know it's not the same as having our own child but I think, deep down, we've always known it wasn't to be.'

'But there was always a chance,' said Lil, blowing her nose. 'This makes it so final.'

'I'll make a cup of tea,' said Hannah, as an excuse to leave them alone for a while.

It was at least fifteen minutes later that she re-entered the room with the tea, and to her relief her aunt and uncle were talking quite calmly to each other. She knew there would be further upsets during the weeks before Lil's admission to hospital but at least the first shock was over and they were now

133

quietly making plans.

For the rest of the evening they all tried very hard to talk and act normally but when they finally went to bed Hannah could hear the soft murmur of their voices long into the night and her heart was very heavy, knowing how badly her aunt had yearned for a baby.

'It's not fair, she thought to herself, all the poor families in the world have lots of babies they don't want and can't afford and poor Aunt Lil would give her right arm for one. I just don't understand how God works things out and she slipped into a fitful sleep. The happiness she'd felt on reading Pam's letter had quickly disappeared and she wondered if her aunt's going into hospital would affect her prospects of going to Norfolk for Christmas.

The following morning her aunt and uncle were, on the surface, their usual cheerful selves; apart from the fact that Lil was a little pale, everything seemed to be as normal.

'I know it's nothing to be ashamed of,' Lil said to Hannah, 'but I don't want anyone to know that I have to have a hysterectomy. When the time comes I'll say that I'm having an operation to remove a cyst. I don't like telling lies but I'm just so terribly embarrassed and I'd hate it if people knew I couldn't have any children, I don't think I could take their sympathy. So, please, let's keep this between the three of us.'

She looked imploringly at Hannah.

'Of course I won't tell anybody outside of this room, nobody will ever know,' said Hannah, going over to her aunt and giving her a big hug.

Lil's eyes filled with tears. 'You see what I mean.' she said, 'I'm just no good at taking sympathy but thank God I have you and Bill to talk to. I don't think I could bear it alone.'

'You don't have to, I'll be here to take care of you for as long as you need me and when you come out of hospital, after Christmas, I'll take my two-week holiday so you'll be able to have a good rest. I know what you're going to say,' she added quickly, 'we can't both be away from the shop at the same time, but you know as well as I do there's a slack period straight after Christmas so they'll be able to manage. I know there's no good time for going into hospital but if you had to choose a time you would have chosen this time for it's about the only slack period we ever get so you won't have to worry yourself sick over the business.'

'Yes, you're right, of course, but what a prospect, Christmas in hospital.'

'It won't be too bad,' chipped in Bill. 'The nursing staff are wonderful at Christmas, they decorate the wards and Father Christmas visits the children. I know it's not like being at home but they do their darndest to make your stay as happy as possible in the circumstances and we will spend all the visiting time allowed with you, you'll see, it won't be too bad at all.'

We, we, thought Hannah, I won't be here, I'm going to Pam's for Christmas.... But of course I won't, she thought on reflection, if they're not going down to Norfolk I won't be able to; Uncle Bill won't want to drive all that way just to take me, he'll want to spend all his time with Aunt Lil.

'I'm so sorry Hannah,' said Lil, as if reading her thoughts, 'I know you've been looking forward to seeing your sisters but, unless anything unforseen happens, like a heavy air-raid, heaven forbid, and they need all the hospital beds, we won't be going down to Norfolk as usual, but I promise you, as soon as I'm up and about, we'll make the trip and celebrate our Christmas a bit late.'

'That's all right,' said Hannah, swallowing her crashing disappointment, thankful that she hadn't mentioned her invitation from Pam. Perhaps it's just as well, she thought, for it would be unbearable if Ken were there and he and Norma were slopping about. Even so her heart was very heavy.

'Never mind,' she said brightly, 'we'll make up for it afterwards.'

They were, if possible even busier at the shop than the day before so she had little time to dwell on her disappointment.

The little bell on the door tinkled non-stop as customers tripped in and out incessantly. They were so busy serving in the shop that orders waiting to be made up were filling the back workroom.

Hannah was getting a bit worried about one very special arrangement that had been ordered and was to be collected in about an hour's time when as yet again the bell summoned her to the shop.

She put on a smile to greet a rather nervous looking young man who was glancing around at the arrangements on display. He gave a little cough, cleared his throat and fingered the inside of his collar as if suddenly very hot.

Hannah judged him to be about twenty years old and middle-class, by the looks of his well-cut suit.

'Can I help you?' she asked pleasantly.

'Oh um, yes, I'd like some flowers please.'

Hannah's sense of humour bubbled to the surface. 'Well, you've come to the right shop, that's a good start,' she said, smiling, to put him at his ease.

But instead he blushed furiously.

'If I pay for some flowers, can you deliver them?'

'Are they to be delivered locally?'

'Oh yes,' and he named an area that Hannah was acquainted with.

'I'm not very good at this sort of thing,' he said.

'Would you like me to help you choose something?'

'I'd appreciate it,' he said gratefully.

So after he named the approximate amount of money he wished to spend she suggested a certain flower arrangement, one of her own especially delicate creations.

'That's absolutely perfect,' he said, 'I'm sure she'll be delighted with that.'

Lucky girl, thought Hannah, she must be very special for it had taken a great deal of courage for him to come into a flower shop.

He gave her the name and address:

> Mrs John Hodiak
> 5 King Charles Street, Islington.

'Any message?' she enquired.

'Um, just put Happy Birthday, Love from John.'

'Thank you very much for your help Miss.......?'

'Hannah,' she volunteered. Well, she thought, as he left the shop, looks are certainly deceiving; I had him down for about twenty but if he's married he's probably older, I bet he's a very considerate husband.

The rest of the week appeared to fly away on wings. There were just not enough hours in the day and as Saturday drew to a close Hannah felt like going home and sleeping until Monday, but tonight was Bill's Company Annual Dinner and Dance and as he'd bought tickets for both Lil and Hannah they had to rush around again as soon as they got in.

Fortunately Hannah had managed to go out for an hour at lunch-time to get her hair washed and set and when she'd bathed and put on her new blue taffeta dress, she looked and felt like a new woman.

The dress was an early Christmas box from Lil who knew that Hannah didn't own a dress suitable for a posh do but Hannah knew there'd still be a little something from her aunt when Christmas day arrived.

Bill's eyes lit up in admiration as she walked into the room and he let out a loud wolf-whistle.

'Just look at our little Hannah,' he addressed Lil, ogling Hannah's cleavage.

Hannah blushed furiously, wishing she'd put a flower where his eyes were burning her breasts, instead of on her waist-band.

Lil didn't notice the lecherous looks in her husband's eyes as she replied, 'You look like a film star, love, all the boys will be queuing up to dance with you.'

'I hope not. I'm not a very good dancer,' said Hannah.

'You'll be fine,' said Lil, 'you love music, I know, and if you dance half as good as you sing you'll have nothing to worry about. Oh, I've heard you singing in the bath' she said at Hannah's look. 'You've got a beautiful voice, as good as Vera Lynn's. If you'd had her chances you'd be entertaining the troops now as well.'

Hannah was glad when it was time to leave. All this flattery was making her uncomfortable; she didn't know how to handle it.

It was a bitterly cold night and already freezing hard. The roads were like glass and they were very relieved to reach the dance-hall safely. Inside, it was lovely and warm with everybody jostling towards the bar in order to get a drink before going in to dinner. Bill got a large whisky for himself and a gin and orange for Lil and Hannah with lots of orange in Hannah's drink.

She didn't particularly like the taste of it but had to admit that by the time they went in to dinner she certainly felt much warmer.

The tables looked beautiful with flowers and candles upon snow-white table cloths. Everything shone and glittered, from the cutlery and the bottles of wine which were included in the ticket price, to the band's instruments, already assembled at the far end of the hall.

Everybody had a little ticket on the table with their names on and Hannah put hers in her little evening bag (lent to her by Lil) as a keepsake. There were even glasses on the tables containing cigarettes for the guests. Hannah didn't smoke herself but thought it a very generous gesture from the organisers, especially as they were sometimes hard to come by and knew that the men would find them more than welcome.

She marvelled at the whole scene, thinking to herself nobody would think it was war time as the evening went on everybody did their best to forget the war for one night.

After the dinner and speeches they all moved back to the bar to enable the waiting staff to clear and rearrange the tables.

Hannah refused another drink at the bar, already feeling a little tipsy from the pre-dinner gin and orange and glass of wine that accompanied the dinner but Bill brought her one anyway and although she tried to refuse it he insisted, saying that they might not be able to get back to the bar again for a very long time. So she took it but vowed to make it last for the rest of the evening. She was half-afraid to drink any more for already she was feeling a little peculiar. Her eyes were sparkling like diamonds and her face kept wanting to break into a grin every time she caught anyone's gaze.

The band was playing a quick-step as they returned to their table and already the dance floor was quite crowded, everybody intent on having a good time. For in times of conflict people responded by trying to enjoy every possible minute. Tomorrow, who knew if they would be alive to enjoy another dance?

Somehow some balloons had been acquired. Hannah hadn't seen any in the shops since the beginning of the war. They were suspended in a huge string bag high above the dance-floor, to be released at midnight, and she knew the people there would break their necks in order to retrieve one to take home for their children.

'Come on Lil, let's trip the light fantastic,' said Bill, pulling her to her feet.

'What about Hannah?' she replied, holding back a little.

'I'll be perfectly all right, you go ahead, I'm quite happy to sit here and watch the dancing.'

'Well, you're not sitting there all night' said Bill, 'I'll have you up next.' He whisked Lil onto the floor.

They really are very good dancers, thought Hannah. Although they're quite large people they're very light on their feet.

On returning Bill sank to his feet, taking a large white handkerchief from his pocket to mop his sweaty brow.

'Phew, I knew I was out of condition but I didn't realise how much. After Christmas it's diet and exercise for me,' he said.

Lil looked sideways at him saying. 'Yes, I've heard that before somewhere.'

'Ladies and Gentlemen,' announced the MC, 'please take your partners for an excuse me waltz.'

'Come on Hannah, this one's yours,' said Bill, pulling Hannah to her feet.

'No really I'd rather not. Please dance with Aunt Lil again. Honestly, I'm quite happy to watch, you know I can't dance very well.'

'Rubbish,' he said, 'anyone can do a waltz, just lean on me and I'll guide you.'

She looked at Lil for support but her aunt said. 'You go ahead, love, I don't think you'll break any bones if you tread on his feet.'

She could see that unless she made a big fuss she couldn't get out of it and she didn't want to upset her aunt, so, with great reluctance, she allowed him to take her hand in his sweaty palm and lead her onto the dance floor.

It was far worse than she'd imagined for he held her rib-crushingly closer and closer until she could feel his aroused manhood hard against her stomach.

She tried to pull away but he said, 'Loosen up and enjoy yourself Hannah, you're a big girl now.'

'Please Uncle Bill,' she began.

'Please what, Uncle Bill?' he said mockingly. 'Please come closer, like this.'

And he pressed even closer to her, making suggestive little movements.

She glanced around her but the floor was so crowded nobody noticed her distress until 'Excuse me, can I cut in?' said a voice and a hand was placed lightly on Bill's shoulder.

'Well, it is an excuse me,' he said grudgingly, walking off the floor back to Lil.

'Hello again. I hope you don't mind but you looked as though you needed rescuing. I didn't like the way that bloke was mauling you. Who is he?'

She looked up in relief into the face of the young man who'd brought flowers for his wife.

'Oh, he didn't mean anything, he's my uncle actually.'

'He wasn't behaving like an uncle. Where's your boy-friend?'

'I haven't got one, I'm here with my aunt and uncle, but it's all right really,' she protested weakly.

'Well, it didn't look all right from where I stood. Anyway, let's enjoy the rest of the dance before somebody cuts in. You're shaking, are you sure you're all right? Would you rather sit this one out?'

'No I'm all right, honestly,' she said, and slowly she began to relax and enjoy the dance.

Strangely enough, dancing with him, she forgot she was a poor dancer. Their rhythms matched perfectly and she was beginning to feel quite proud of herself, when all too soon the dance ended.

'Thank you very much,' he said, as he led her back to her seat. 'Perhaps you will dance with me again later.'

'Who was that?' asked Bill.

'Oh just somebody who came to the shop to buy flowers.'

'Well, I think he had a cheek, cutting in like that when you haven't been introduced.'

'We introduced ourselves, at the shop,' said Hannah. 'His name's John Hodiak and he works for the same agency as you but at a different branch.' She was amazed at her uncle's scorn for John's 'according to him' bad manners. You could hardly call what her uncle was doing to her on the dance floor good manners.

'I think he looked very nice,' said Lil, 'you should have asked him to join us.'

'Oh no,' said Hannah, 'he's married, he bought flowers for his wife.'

'Really,' said Bill.

'Oh don't be so pompous. He only danced with her, that's not against the law, even if he is married. I'm glad he danced with her, she doesn't mix with enough young people,' said Lil.

140

Her aunt and uncle danced some more and when Bill offered to dance with Hannah again she refused and this time he noticed the firmness in her voice and didn't insist.

She thoroughly enjoyed the rest of the evening and was perfectly happy just watching the dancing and listening to the music.

She didn't see John any more and supposed he'd left early and to her surprise, found herself a little disappointed.

As the MC announced the last waltz Hannah slipped out to the powder room so as not to look conspicuously alone and returned as the dance was ending, with the balloons cascading down amid much shrieking and pushing to obtain one.

The band ended the proceedings by playing the national anthem with everybody in the hall singing along seriously, the men standing straight and proud and the ladies with tears of emotion in their eyes. They then filed out soberly, to collect their coats.

The drive home was very quiet and a little eerie after the noise and jollity of the evening.

'Do you think there will be a raid tonight? It seems too quiet, like the lull before the storm,' said Lil, shivering in apprehension and wrapping her coat closer around herself.

'No it's much too clear a night, they'd be spotted too easily. Have no fear, we'll rest easy tonight. Look at the star-filled sky, it's almost as light as day,' said Bill.

His common sense calmed her and they reached the flat safely, in spite of the glassy roads and the fact that Bill had downed quite a few whiskies. He, like most of the men, sobered up quickly on reaching his car.

It was close to 1 am when they eventually climbed into their beds and Hannah fell asleep the minute her head touched the pillow.

The next morning when she awoke, her nose and ears, being the only parts of her above the blanklets, were as cold as ice but the rest of her, tucked firmly under the blankets was quite warm. She jumped out of the bed to open the curtains and smartly jumped back in again. The air was absolutely freezing.

Her little clock told her that it was almost 9.30 but as it was Sunday there was no rush. She smiled contentedly, looking around the little room. The sun shone through the sparkling, clean windows and a wintry shaft lay across her bed. She looked at her slightly crumpled dance dress hanging on the wardrobe door and thought back to the previous evening. To think, she hadn't really felt like going but it had turned out to be most enjoyable.

The band had been very good and she had enjoyed every foot-tapping tune they'd played. She thought it was a hundred times better than listening to the wireless.

She thought how nice it had felt dancing with John; she had never ever been in such close contact with a boy before and felt a little guilty at having enjoyed it so much. Remembering her love for Ken, she felt, somehow, that she had betrayed that love.

'Don't be silly,' she told herself, 'it was only a dance. I'll probably never see him again.'

She then shivered in disgust, remembering the dance with her uncle. Why do men behave like that when they've got lovely wives? she thought, and do all men behave like that? She hoped that they didn't, but no, even though she'd known John for such a short time she could never imagine him behaving like that. Although he was married and had danced with her, it had been very proper. He'd held her at a respectable distance. Even his wife couldn't have taken offence; at least, she hoped not for he hadn't come back for another dance. Oh dear, she thought, I do so hope she didn't get upset, but no she would know John better than that, he was an honourable man. Of that she felt sure.

I wonder what Maureen and Betsy are doing now, she thought and as always when her thoughts turned to her sisters, she felt a terrible pang of home-sickness. Although she was now living in comparative luxury, if she could turn the clock back a few years she would do so, in spite of the poverty and hardship they'd endured together. She missed her sisters dreadfully and she especially missed their need of her. She knew she ought not to worry about them for they would be loved and cared for by Aunt Elsie like her own children, and yet again she thought how strange fate was, for if Elsie had had a much longed for daughter she would have been unable to take them in and if Aunt Lil had had her wish there would have been no room for Hannah at the flat.

I shouldn't feel ungrateful, she thought, guiltily thinking how readily she had been welcomed with open arms by Bill and Lil. She couldn't have been treated better if she were their own daughter, but she wasn't and she would give anything to go back to her life as it used to be. Even if her mother was still like a dummy, she would put up with that just so long as they could all be together again. Her thoughts then returned to her father and the episode at the pig-sties but she forced her thoughts away from him. What was done was done. Poor Billy couldn't have helped himself, his love for Hannah had goaded his actions.

In a funny sort of way she missed Billy as well. He was a part of her life and there had been times when she'd been glad of his company. 'I hope he's all right and not being teased' she thought, remembering how Norma had teased him. But in all fairness, although her teasing had upset Hannah, it didn't appear to have worried Billy. She only did it in fun, she wouldn't really upset him.

From Norma her thoughts turned, naturally, to Ken and as she imagined them kissing and cuddling she felt a huge pang of jealousy. She groaned aloud. What wouldn't she give to be in Norma's shoes? A terrible longing overtook her and she went quite weak, her breath quickening and strange, wonderful, moist feelings arising from between her legs. Her hands went down to the strangeness and she touched herself gently, imagining it was Ken touching her.

'Hannah,' came Lil's voice through the door, 'are you awake, love? Do you want a cup of tea?'

She shot up in the bed, jolted out of her reverie.

'Yes I'm awake, I'll be out in a few minutes, I'll just have a quick bath and then I'll come and have a cup of tea,' she replied breathlessly.

'Are you all right, you sound a bit strange?'

'Yes, I'm all right,' she replied, blushing guiltily. 'I jumped out of bed too quickly, that's all.'

'Well, there's no need to break your neck. It is Sunday, remember. Come through when you're ready, there's no rush.'

Hannah bathed and put on her slippers and thick dressing-gown, which buttoned up to the neck with a warm woolly collar and went into the kitchen where a lovely smell of hot buttered toast assailed her nostrils.

Bill was making the toast and his eyes raked her from head to toe, mentally stripping her of her dressing gown.

143

She felt herself flush, remembering the dance with him.

He noticed the flush and thought to himself. She enjoyed it, the little minx. She may have protested and even though she wouldn't admit it, she enjoyed it.

They reminisced over the dance whilst eating their breakfast and Lil said again how nice she thought John was, and wasn't it a pity he was married? So young as well. Still there'd be other dances and other young men.

'What have you got planned for today, Bill?'

'Well, as it's such a lovely day I thought I'd take you two lovely ladies for a drive around the city. They don't tell us much on the wireless or in the papers about the bombings for fear of it getting back to Jerry but there's nothing to stop us going and looking for ourselves.'

'But the roads are like glass,' answered Lil, 'I don't think it's stopped freezing for days. Do you think it's wise to go driving?'

'We'll be all right, there'll be hardly any traffic about for that reason and we can take it nice and slow. There's no rush, we've got all day, but I do think we ought to see what's been going on around us. Thank God we've had no shelling on our doorstep, but thousands of other poor blighters haven't been so lucky.'

So they all dressed in warm heavy coats and Lil and Hannah put on fur snow-boots and thick scarves, for although they'd be in the car most of the time they wouldn't be going fast enough to generate much heat.

He took them first of all to the East End where they were horrified to see rows of terraced Jerry-built houses which had been devastated years before, on 9 September 1940 to be exact. But it would be many years later, probably after the war had ended, before pictures and figures would be published. Shortly after the bombings a communal rest and feeding centre had been established for the homeless people.

They saw sites of bombings and devastation they could never have imagined that day. Although they'd heard of the many raids carried out on the city it was incomprehensible how much of it had been reduced to piles of rubble and to think that they were living in the city but were relatively unaware of the vastness of the atrocities!

Everywhere were posters, Save Coal, Walk To Save Petrol, Grow More Vegetables, Loose Talk Costs Lives, and one quite frightening one which announced, WARNING LOOTING. Looting of premises which have been damaged by or vacated by reason of War Operations is punishable by Death or Penal Servitude for Life.

'Would they really kill a person if they were caught looting?' asked Hannah in horror.

'Well, the warning is loud and clear. If they want to risk their necks pinching from the dead, for that's what it amounts to, they deserve to be killed,' answered Bill and to back up his statement of the seriousness of the offence, at yet another part of the city that had been recently bombed, a soldier was guarding tinned provisions and soap that had been salvaged from a shop and lined up against a wall close by.

There were quite a few people like themselves, who wanted to see the sites of the bombings they had heard about. At one particular site a little group of people were standing, crying openly on a heap of rubble that had once been a school.

A lump came to Hannah's throat as she watched and she wondered if the people had lost a child there.

Hyde Park looked most unlike Hyde Park, with wreckage dumped all over it and amongst the things salvaged was a row of baths.

In yet another part of London they saw American MPs patrolling. To Hannah, they looked like giants, very big and fearsome and very smart. Beside them, Bill seemed to be a dwarf.

'Just look at them,' said Lil, 'don't they look handsome in their uniforms? It's no wonder they turn the girls heads. Our boys' uniforms look very rough next to theirs.'

'Humph,' snorted Bill, 'that may be so but they'll be glad to go back to the British boys when the Yanks have gone home, if they'll take them back,' he added.

Lil pulled a face at Hannah as if to say. Say no more, methinks he's a bit jealous.

He next took them to the famous Elephant and Castle and although there was much damage around the six-traffic arteries the emblem of the cockney world still looked down proudly as if to say, 'I'm still here me old cock-sparrers, keep your chins up' and they knew it must give the cockneys pride and hope to see the good old landmark standing firm against the odds.

Another famous landmark they visited was St Paul's

Cathedral.

On 29 December 1940, just over a year after the outbreak of war there had been a bad attack on the City. At that time the Thames had been at a particularly low ebb and there had been a great shortage of water. The fires had raged for days but somehow, in spite of flames licking all around it, St Paul's had emerged unscathed.

On their journey homeward, Hannah and Lil were by now quite tired from the traumatic sights they had seen. Bill pointed over to an air-raid shelter that was now being used as a night club.

'I'd like the Jerry bastards to see that,' he said, 'it'll take more than they've got to dampen the Londoners' spirits. They are standing up tremendously in the face of war. You've got to hand it to them, nothing keeps them down for long.'

It was with great relief that they arrived back at the flat.

They had seen sights that would go with them to their graves and further, if they were related to the next generation as they hoped they would be, if only as a deterrent against more wars. And they hoped and prayed that this would be the war to end all wars.

11

Hannah had, in reply to her friend's letter, refused with great reluctance the invitation for Christmas, explaining that her aunt had to go into hospital for a few days, though she had not disclosed that she was to have a hysterectomy.

Pam had replied post-haste, unable to accept Hannah's refusal. 'Please, please come Hannah,' she'd begged, 'if only for a few days. I'm sure your Aunt wouldn't mind, you could get on the train at Liverpool Street Station and my dad could pick you up at this end, at King's Lynn Station. I've made such plans for us all and Ken will be home and it will all be perfectly lovely. I can't bear the thought of you spending Christmas alone with your Uncle Bill. Please, please, Hannah do try.'

Her face, on reading the letter must have registered her sadness for Lil asked 'What's wrong Hannah? You look so miserable.'

'Oh, it's nothing really. Pam is just disappointed that we're not going to be able to see them at Christmas.'

'I feel like the wicked witch, preventing you from seeing your family and friends but it's too far for Bill to drive you down there and then to turn around and come straight back, that's assuming the weather is OK.'

'I wouldn't dream of letting Uncle Bill go all that way just for me, especially when he could be spending that time with you. Pam suggested that I go down by train just for a couple of days. But I can't go, you might need me, it's out of the question,' she said firmly, putting her letter back in its envelope as if to seal her decision.

'I think it's a good idea for you to go down by train for a couple of days. There's nothing you can do for me whilst I'm in hospital, it's when I come home that I'll need you more and I doubt that you'll be able to visit me straight after the operation. I should think Bill will be the only one allowed to visit me

147

for the first few days, so you'd only be twiddling your thumbs alone in the flat. I'd be happier knowing you were with your family and friends for Christmas, really I would.'

'What about Uncle Bill?' asked Hannah, hesitantly, hardly daring to let herself get excited.

'He'll be all right, he'll spend most of the time at the hospital and he's quite capable of cooking for himself. But I'd appreciate it if you would wash and iron his shirts. You know he likes a fresh one every day.'

'Of course I would, you didn't have to ask, I would have done them anyway. Oh thank you,' she said, wrapping her arms around her aunt and kissing her on the cheek.

The next week flew by, with Hannah and Lil working like Trojans to get through as much as possible before Lil was due to go into hospital.

Hannah felt as if she had wings on her heels, so happy she was at the prospect of spending Christmas with her friends and seeing Betsy and Maureen.

Saturday afternoon arrived and she could hardly believe a week had passed since the dinner and dance and her thoughts turned to John and she wondered why he hadn't come back for another dance. He hadn't seemed the type to say things he didn't mean just for the sake of making small talk. She thought how nice he'd looked at the dance. Although nobody could call him handsome, he was a bit too thin and pale, he had a nice open friendly face that denoted a beautiful person inside. She smiled to herself, remembering how easily their steps had fallen into place as though they'd been dancing together for years.

Ding-a-ling! The shop door-bell startled her and she jumped out of her reverie and looked, open-mouthed in amazement, as the person in her thoughts materialised.

'Oh hello, sorry, did I make you jump?' said John.

'Oh, no, it's all right, I was daydreaming, it's not your fault,' she said blushing in embarrassment, feeling as if she'd been caught red-handed doing something wrong.

'I haven't come to buy anything,' he said, 'but I felt I owed you an apology for leaving without saying goodbye or coming back for the dance.'

'That's all right, you don't owe me an explanation. I guessed that probably your wife wanted to leave early because of the icy roads or something. Really, it's quite all right.'

'Wife, wife?' he said, his brows furrowing in astonishment. 'I haven't got a wife. Whatever made you think I was married?'

'The flowers you sent, weren't they for your wife?' asked Hannah.

He threw back his head and roared with laughter. 'Oh, so you thought they were for my wife. No, they were for my mother, it was her birthday. My father's name was John, before me, hence my mother being Mrs John Hodiak. Do I look married?'

'Well, actually, no, I didn't think you looked old enough, but looks are deceiving.'

'The fact is, I'm not married. I don't even have a girlfriend but I couldn't go to the firm's dance on my own and I really wanted to go, so I took my mother along with me. But, unfortunately, shortly after I'd danced with you I thought she looked a bit peaky; she suffers with angina,' he added, 'and although she denied feeling unwell, for fear of spoiling my evening, I knew she was trying to stick it out for my sake so I feigned tiredness and boredom and suggested we go home before the end to avoid the crush and she thankfully agreed. I would have liked to come over to explain why I was leaving but I was so worried about my mother I just wanted to get her home as quickly as possible. In my eagerness to leave for the dance I'd forgotten to check that she had her heart tablets with her, and, she'd left them at home, so I felt the sooner I got her home and tucked up in bed, with a couple of her pills, the better. I hope that you will accept my apology, I'm sorry it's taken a week to get to see you but it's the first chance I've had to get away from work. Perhaps you'll let me make it up to you by taking you to another dance over Christmas.'

'No really, that's not necessary anyway I won't be here for Christmas, I'm going home to Norfolk for a couple of days.'

'Oh,' he said, looking very disappointed. 'Well then, will you perhaps come to the pictures with me one night before you go? I'd really like to take you, not just by way of an apology. I would have asked you out anyway eventually, when I plucked up courage.'

'Yes thank you, that would be very nice. There's a picture on at the Regent next week that I'd like to see called *That Uncertain Feeling*. Merle Oberon is in it and it's supposed to be

149

very good, if that's your kind of picture. But I suppose you'd rather see something a bit more exciting, like a war picture.'

'No not really, there's enough of the real thing going on without going to the pictures to see it. I don't mind going to see a sloppy picture, at least it takes your mind off the war for a little while.'

So they arranged to meet the following Wednesday.

Lil was scheduled to go into hospital on the Thursday so Hannah arranged it thus to enable her aunt and uncle to spend the evening before alone.

'Right, see you on Wednesday,' he said, leaving the shop as Lil entered.

'What's all this then, see you Wednesday?' she said.

'I'm going to the pictures with him to see that film I told you about,' said Hannah, colouring slightly.

'But I thought you said −'

'I know, but I was wrong, he's not married, he was buying flowers for his mother.'

'Is that what he told you?'

'Yes, and I believe him.'

'I'm only joking Hannah, I'm pleased you're going out with him. You spend far too much time alone, it'll do you good to go out and enjoy yourself.'

Bill, on being told of Hannah's date, tried to throw cold water on her excitement.

'I don't think it's right, going out with a perfect stranger. What do we know about him? He could be a murderer or worse, I don't like it.'

'What's the matter with you Bill, you sound like the heavy father. You've met the young man and he works for your company. If anything untoward happened we'd soon be able to track him down. He doesn't live a hundred miles away, and I thought he seemed a very nice young man.'

'You women are all the same, you see a man with a nice face and that's as far as your budgie brains go.'

'I don't understand you, Bill, you seem prejudiced against him. At least give him a chance.'

A chance to do what? thought Bill. A chance to kiss and cuddle and maul her and who knows what else? And he was filled with an uncontrollable jealous rage.

'Well, don't say I didn't warn you,' he said, stomping out.

150

'Don't take any notice of him,' said Lil to Hannah 'he's just being over-protective, you can't really blame him for that for over these past few years he's come to think of you as his daughter and he feels responsible for you. I should think he's behaving just like any father whose daughter is going out on her first date. Just ignore him, he'll come round.'

Hannah had her own ideas as to why he was so unreasonable and it was nothing to do with his feeling paternal but of course her aunt was the last person in the world she could voice her thoughts to.

Wednesday evening arrived and Hannah had only an hour to get ready for her date so she had little time to notice Bill, morosely pretending to read his newspaper and glaring jealously at her each time she passed. Lil, on the other hand, did everything possible to ensure that she enjoyed her first date.

She gave her a lovely lace-edged handkerchief sprayed with scent to put in her bag.

It's funny, thought Hannah, I still get an enormous amount of pleasure from having a pretty hankie. Perhaps that's because when we were little we had only rag to wipe our noses on. Not that I'd blow my nose on this one; it's just for show, I've got a plain one in my coat pocket if I want to wipe my nose; and joy of joys, a pair of real nylons! They were so sheer that Hannah was afraid to touch them, let alone pull them onto her legs.

'Oh no Aunt Lil, I daren't wear them, I might ladder them, I know you've been saving them for a special occasion, I just couldn't,' she said, at the same time touching them lovingly.

'Oh yes you can, and this is a special occasion. It's your first real date and whether it turns out good or bad you'll always remember it. If you ladder them we'll mend them and anyway Bill always manages to get me a pair when I need them. I don't really know from where but I think he knows a bloke down the market and they do a swap with a couple of chops or something. I don't ask any questions but it always seems that when I need a pair he has to acquire some meat for the transaction, so not another word; you go and have a lovely time and ignore your uncle. He'll come around the next time you have a date, he probably won't even bat an eyelash.'

A gentle tap on the door announced John's arrival.

'Go and let him in, love,' said Lil to her husband, but he pretended not to hear, buried deep in his paper.

Lil smiled at Hannah, as if to say, 'silly old fool,' as she went down the hall to greet John.

On entering, he very carefully wiped his feet. His shoes shone like glass. He was wearing a mac, with a scarf tucked around his neck, for it was a bitterly cold night.

His eyes lit up as Hannah approached and she was very glad her aunt had persuaded her to wear the nylons for she thought he looked as smart as a carrot and she wanted him to be proud of her. Although they'd be in the dark for most of the time at the picture-house, she knew that when the lights went up at the interval everybody would gape around to see who was with who and what they were wearing and she wanted to look her best for him.

'Is it all right if we go for a bit of supper after the pictures?' John asked Lil, 'or will that be too late?'

'No, that's perfectly all right. It's good of you to mention it, so I won't worry if you're a bit late. Anyway, we're on holiday now so you go out and enjoy yourselves.'

'Goodbye Uncle Bill, we won't be too late,' said Hannah and he grudgingly held up a hand in acknowledgement, pretending to be deeply engrossed in his paper and quite oblivious of the young couple.

There was a queue at the Regent and by the time they got inside, half an hour later, they were thoroughly frozen.

On the bill-board outside the theatre was a notice suggesting that patrons retain their admission tickets in case they had to leave before the end of the performance due to bombings; thus, they would be allowed in for another performance, at no extra charge.

Hannah shivered, as much in apprehension as with the cold. Please, she prayed silently, don't let there be an air-raid tonight, on my first date and not with Aunt Lil booked to go into hospital tomorrow. For, although it would mean a re-prieve for her if the hospital beds were needed for casualties, she would only have to suffer another nerve-wracking week all over again and she didn't want that to happen. Much as she hated the thought of her going into hospital, she knew it had to be, so the sooner the better, to get it over with.

Once seated inside, they took off their gloves and rubbed life back into their hands and slowly thawed out as the picture began.

John had brought a bag of hard fruit gums which they happily sucked through the first half of the performance.

When the lights went up at the interval there was a great deal of shuffling and combs and lipsticks appeared as the courting couples tried to disguise the fact that they had seen very little of the picture.

At the end of the show, after the national anthem, John took her to a fish restaurant where they had large plates of cod and chips and a pot of tea.

Hannah had thought that she would be too nervous to eat in front of John but she felt so at ease with him that she happily tucked in, whilst they swapped life-stories. In her case she didn't fill in all the details, just bare essentials. She was too ashamed to tell him of her father's affair and of her Uncle Bill's strange behaviour towards her since she was a little girl. She told him, with great embarrassment, of her mother's commitment to the mental hospital but after he'd heard of the events leading up to it he was very compassionate and understanding and on hearing about Billy Wilson they had a good old laugh together, he saying he hoped he'd meet him one day, he sounded such a character.

All too soon it was time to go home and by the time they'd slowly walked to her front door it was after midnight.

In spite of the bitterly cold night they were reluctant to say goodbye and although they were both at heart very shy, there had been no signs of it for the past few hours; they had got on like a house on fire. But after a few minutes the cold was too much to bear so they parted, with Hannah promising to go out with him again after Christmas.

He kissed her gently on the cheek. 'Thank you so much for a lovely evening, I look forward to seeing you after Christmas. In fact, I wish I could wave a wand and it was all over. Oh, I'm sorry,' he added, 'I'm being selfish, I know how much you're looking forward to seeing your sisters and your friend. I just wish I could share it with you.'

Strangely enough, so did Hannah. Although she was aching to see Ken, she was also sorry at not being able to see John who, she knew, would be having a very quiet Christmas, with just his mother for company. He really was very nice and although he didn't set her pulses racing the way Ken did, she enjoyed his company very much and as she could never have Ken she would make do with his friendship with gratitude.

As she walked into the living-room she was surprised to see the lights on and even more surprised when her uncle sprang up out of his chair, stubbing out a cigarette into an overflowing ashtray.

'Where the hell have you been? It's after midnight and I know the picture finished at 10.30,' he said angrily.

'You know where I've been, you must have heard us say we were going to have supper afterwards.'

'You mean to tell me it's taken you an hour and a half to eat supper?'

'Well no, but we didn't hurry and then we had to walk home. You didn't have to wait up for me Uncle Bill, I'm perfectly all right. You should be in bed with Aunt Lil, she must be very jittery tonight, with going into hospital tomorrow.'

'She is, that's why the doctor gave her a couple of sleeping pills for tonight. She'd been dead to the world since eleven o-clock; she should sleep soundly until about five or six in the morning.'

'That's good, well good night then and thank you for waiting up, but there was no need,' she said.

'Don't be in such a hurry,' he said, grabbing her arm as she was about to leave.

'Tell me about Mr Nice Guy, did he try anything on?' he said, fixing her with a glassy gaze, which told her he had been drinking.

'I don't know what you mean, I'll tell you and Aunt Lil all about it tomorrow, it's late now,' she said, trying to loosen his hold on her arm.

But he tightened his clasp on her, drawing her towards the couch and pulling her down on to it beside him, his fingers digging into her flesh painfully.

'What are you doing? Let me go, you've been drinking, you don't know what you're doing.'

'Of course, I've been drinking, I've been going crazy thinking of you with that little squirt.'

'We only went to the pictures, we didn't do anything wrong.'

'That's what you say. Anyway it won't hurt you to come and sit with me for a minute,' he said, putting his arm around

154

her and breathing his foul breath over her.

She averted her head in distaste, thinking. If only people realised what beer and tobacco did to their breath they wouldn't touch either one.

'Can you remember when you last sat on a couch with me, Hannah?' he asked.

'No, I can't, please let me go to bed, you'll wake Aunt Lil up.'

'No, I don't think so. If there were an air-raid tonight she wouldn't wake up, she's out like a light. Can't you remember' he went on, 'that Christmas before little Colin died, when there was just you and me in the front room and we had a game of hunt the thimble? You were only a skinny little kid then but by God, you lit my flame even then. I'll never forget how soft your little Mary-Ann felt. I bet it's even lovelier now, all soft and fluffy,' and he began to put his hand up her skirt.

'Stop that,' she screamed, 'you're disgusting, let me go.'

But he held on to her even tighter, his hand now inside her knickers.

By now, she was really frightened and began to struggle and push his hand away with all her strength but she was no match for him and he pulled her down to a lying position.

There was nothing for it now but to fight for all she was worth. She kicked and scratched and yelled 'Aunt Lil!' at the top of her voice.

'Be quiet, you little fool, I told you it would take more than a bomb to wake her up so don't waste your energy.'

She knew she was no match for him physically, so she tried a different approach, trying very hard to sound calm and collected. She said 'Uncle Bill, let's stop this now, there's no harm done and if you let me get up and go to bed I swear I'll never mention it to Aunt Lil. I know it's the drink making you behave like this and tomorrow you'll thank me for stopping you doing something so foolish.'

'Foolish is it?' he said, 'Yes, I suppose it is foolish for a silly old bugger like me to want his niece but you know I've never looked on you as a niece, or a daughter, as Lil mistakenly surmises. I've waited for years for this opportunity and nothing you say or do will make any difference,' and he tightened his hold on her with one hand and with the other fumbled to unbutton his trousers.

155

Hannah was by now crying uncontrollably and struggling for her life. Please God help me, don't let this happen to me.

'It's no good you begging for help, there's nobody here but you and me and I'm not giving you anything you haven't had before so just be quiet and enjoy it and stop making noises like a virgin.'

'Please, please don't Uncle Bill, I AM a virgin, I'll die if you do anything, please. I'll do anything else you say but not this,' she sobbed. She knew it was absolutely futile struggling, she was no match for him. He was a big man and the drink and his passion for her only added to his strength.

She screamed again, in the vain hope that she could rouse her aunt from her drug-induced sleep, but to no avail.

He brutally forced her legs apart and thrust himself inside her, with a loud groan of satisfaction.

She screamed again, this time in pain and by the third or fourth thrust fainted and sank into dark oblivion.

She gained conciousness and looked down to where she was bleeding profusely.

At first she thought she'd awoken to a period but as she moved the pain reminded her of what had occurred and tears gushed down her face as she realised she'd lost her virginity and would never again feel clean.

Bill came into the room, carrying a bowl of water and a towel, looking amazingly sober and docile, not a bit like the animal that had attacked her such a short time ago.

'You really were a virgin,' he said incredulously. 'I can't believe my luck, I'll never forget it. You were a thousand times better than I'd ever imagined. Lay still and I'll clean you up my little love.'

'If you come near me again I'll kill you, you vile beast, and as soon as Aunt Lil is in hospital I'm going to the police; they'll make sure you never get the chance to attack anybody else.'

'Come on, now, be realistic, who do you think would believe I attacked you, with my wife asleep in the next room? What they will believe is that you let your new boyfriend go a bit too far and then got scared when you couldn't stop him from going all the way after you'd led him on. There'll be witnesses from the pictures and the cafe who saw you two together but there won't be one witness to say that I waited up for you and Lil will swear that I went to bed early with her, which I did; but I got up again when the pills had taken effect.'

'Aunt Lil will believe me when I tell her exactly what happened. She knows I don't tell lies.'

'And she also knows that I don't tell lies. I'm her husband. Who do you think she'll believe? She knows I love you like a daughter and nothing in this world, not you, not anybody, would ever make her believe that I could do such a thing. If you say anything to her it'll break her heart to think how good she's been to you and you invent something wicked like this just as she's about to have an operation. It would do her untold harm to go under the anaesthetic with something like this on her mind. Just think about it. Do you want that on your conscience? I don't think so; if you have any love or loyalty for your aunt you'll keep quiet.'

'I wouldn't do anything to hurt her, I love her far too much, but I'll never understand how you got her to marry you, she's far too good for you. I'll keep quiet only until she's had her operation and is well on the road to recovery and then, even at the risk of her disbelief, I shall tell her the truth and let her make her own mind up, I promise you that,' she said, with tears of futility streaming down her face.

He was taken aback by her vehemence as he said, 'Look, neither of us wants to hurt her. Let's just forget it ever happened. I know I shouldn't have done it but some of the fault is yours. You must know I always had this terrible hunger for you and I'm only flesh and blood after all. What do you say? For your aunt's sake keep quiet and I promise I'll never lay a finger on you again.'

'You won't get the chance. I couldn't stay here now. I'll look for a flat whilst Aunt Lil is in hospital. I can't bear to be in the same house as you.'

'I thought you were going to take care of her for a couple of weeks when she comes out of hospital, that's a fine way to show your gratitude. She took you in when you needed a home and you pay her back by running out on her when she needs you most. That won't do much to aid her recovery will it?'

He was getting worried now and grasping at straws, but Hannah felt too drained to argue with him any more.

She made her way to the bathroom and he made no attempt to stop her. He knew he'd given her food for thought and was fairly confident that she couldn't destroy her aunt by relating what had happened. But he also knew that he must never try to touch her again. If necessary he'd have to go to a prostitute and pay for it, for it would be a long while before Lil could carry out her wifely duties.

He crept into bed, beside his wife who, he felt sure, had heard nothing of what had gone on that night and was fairly smug in the knowledge that if ever the worst come to the worst she would swear that he'd never left her side all night.

Hannah sat in the bath, feeling as if the bottom had fallen out of her world. It was hard to believe that just a few short hours ago she had been so happy with John. Now she felt she would never be able to face him again.

She let the water run until it was so hot that her skin was bright red and as it became unbearable she'd reluctantly turned it off and sat until she was sure she'd scalded off all traces of her harrowing ordeal.

When she eventually emerged she gently patted herself dry and indulged in some of Lil's precious talcum powder. She had been told to feel free to use it but as it was hard to obtain she only used it high days and holidays. But she felt this was an emergency and never would she feel a greater need for some comfort to her skin as she did now.

She quietly crept pass her aunt's bedroom and was amazed to hear the sound of Bill's heavy snoring. She couldn't believe, after what had happened, that he could crawl into bed and fall asleep as if nothing had happened. As for herself, day was breaking before she finally slipped into a fitful, sleep, still unresolved as to whether to tell her aunt or the police of what had occurred.

Very early next morning, she joined Lil, who was making a pot of tea, pretending it was just like any other day.

'Hello love,' she said, a little too brightly, 'You're up early. I hope I didn't wake you up, I didn't expect to see you so soon, after your late night. Did you enjoy yourselves? I didn't hear you come in, you must have been quite late. Do you want some tea?' She rambled on, obviously trying to hide the fact that she was terrified of the day ahead. She turned. 'Are you all right love? You look awful, didn't you get much sleep? You mustn't worry about me, I'll be all right,' and when Hannah didn't reply, she said, 'Is anything wrong? Here's me rambling on, not giving you a chance to get a word in edge-wise.'

She went over to Hannah, taking her face gently between her hands and kissing her on both cheeks, looked into her eyes searchingly.

Now, thought Hannah, tell her now. But the thought of bringing her aunt's world crashing about her ears was out of the question today.

So, she lost her chance for the moment saying, 'I'm quite all right, I had a late night, that's all. You know I'm not used to late nights, I must have been over-tired because I didn't sleep very well.'

'You certainly do look peaky. I hope you're not going down with a cold, especially as you're travelling down to Norfolk, and how did your date go, did you have a good time?'

'Yes, lovely, I thoroughly enjoyed the picture, though I did feel a bit sorry for the lady in the story; she suffered with uncontrollable hiccups. I suppose in a way it was quite funny but it must have made her very tired and then she had an affair with the pianist, it was very good.'

'So you'll be seeing the young man again then!'

'Oh, I don't know, we'll see,' said Hannah, leaving the kitchen with her cup of tea as Bill walked in.

'She seems a bit strange today,' said Lil, pouring a cup of tea for her husband. 'I hope you weren't right when you suggested that John might try something on. She was a bit vague when I asked her about last night. Do you think she's all right?'

'She's probably worried about you. Don't give it another thought, you just get yourself in and out of hospital as quickly as possible. I'll look after Hannah,' he said, giving her a big sloppy kiss.

At the chosen time they drove to the hospital via Liverpool Street Station, where Hannah was seen safely on to the train bound for King's Lynn, after much hugging and kissing and a few tears between the two women.

It would be about two hours before she reached her destination so she tried to get some sleep to make up for her restless night. But it was so cold in the carriage, which thankfully she had to herself, that she found it impossible, so she tried to lose herself in a book but for once could not do so. The events of the night before kept churning round and round in her head. If only there were someone else she could talk to. There was Pam but she didn't want to spoil the holiday by unburdening herself on her friend so she would just have to ride it out alone. And quite unwittingly the tears rolled down her face as she recalled the joy she'd anticipated of travelling to Lynn alone and how fate had stepped in yet again to dish her up another plateful of misery.

After a very cold journey the train shunted into the station and before it came to a stop she could see her friend running up and down and jumping up to peer inside the carriages, impatient to see Hannah.

The two girls, one either end of the platform, hurtled towards each other, their breath making vapour trails on the cold morning air. On impact they hugged and kissed and tears sprang to Hannah's eyes.

I really must learn to control my emotions, she thought. If I allow myself to cry so easily at every little thing I'll give the game away and then Pam will know there's something wrong, so she bravely put on a bright face for her friend.

On the drive to Heysham, with Fred Bates at the wheel, they chatted and giggled all the way, like two five year olds, so overjoyed at being reunited, so painfully aware of how much they missed each other.

The village, as they approached, looked to Hannah like a Christmas postcard and with the sun shining on the frost-bejewelled trees and bushes, it was a sight for sore eyes after months of looking at the big, ugly, grey buildings of London, and she took a big breath as if to inhale and store some of the fresh beauty of it all.

Outside Fred Bates' shop, patiently walking up and down, was the ugliest man Hannah was likely to come across in all of her lifetime and he gave a loud roar of delight as the van drew to a halt.

She had hardly stepped out before being swooped up into the air.

'Hannah, Hannah, I knew you'd come home, I knew you wouldn't stick it in London. Don't you ever go away again, stay here with us an' I'll tect ya like I allus do, an I kept my promise, I never tol' our secret to no-one so you're all right, no-one'll ever hurt you again, not when I'm around.'

'What are you talking about?' asked a bewildered Pam.

'Oh, take no notice of the big lug, he's as daft as a brush, aren't you Billy?' asked Hannah affectionately, struggling to get her feet onto the ground.

'Do you know,' said Pam, 'he's been waiting here since we left to pick you up from the station over an hour ago. He must be frozen stiff, the big daftie.'

'No, I'm not cold, I'm tough,' he said, thumping his chest like a gorilla, 'are you coming to play snowballs Hannah, and I'll make ya a big snowman?'

'No, not today Billy, I've got to go and see my sisters later on. Perhaps we'll play tomorrow. Anyway, it's dinner-time, your mother will be waiting for you.'

At the thought of food, he agreed to postpone the games and after one more long look to make sure that Hannah was really home he loped off, grinning like the Cheshire cat.

'Ain't love grand?' came a voice from the doorway, and there, looking very pretty and grownup, was Norma.

'Good gawd Hannah, I wouldn't av known ya, yer look like a real city girl, 'ow do ya like London? I expect you won't wanna come back down 'ere to live again will ya?'

'I'd come back tomorrow if I could, you can have the city, I'm a country girl; and I'd give my right arm to swap places with you!'

'It's a funny old world innit?' said Norma. 'There's you in London, when you'd rather be 'ere an there's me stuck in the country when me 'eart's in the "smoke". Never mind, it'll all come out in the wash' she added in her usual cheerful manner. 'Come in outa the cold, ya poor little bleeders, before ya freeze to death, it won't matter much where ya live then.'

Hannah and Pam smiled at each other, as if to say, There's been a lot of changes in the last few years, since the war began but Norma will never change; it will take more than a war to stifle her philsophical outlook.

12

During the Christmas festivities Hannah managed to force the memory of her uncle's brutal onslaught to the back of her mind. Pam's family made her feel so happy and welcome that it was beginning to seem like a bad dream and were it not for the soreness between her legs she could almost imagine it was just that.

Ken and his friend, Denny, had managed to get home for two days, Christmas Day and Boxing Day, and Hannah couldn't help noticing that Pam was quite smitten with her brother's friend. When they were close there was a kind of electricity present and she felt sure that love was developing. Although very happy for Pam it made her feel a little lonely; even though Pam made a point of spending the majority of her time with her it was apparent where her heart was.

When the boys returned to their squadron it seemed very quiet and even Norma was a little subdued, for a day at least, but then she was her old self again, keeping their spirits high with her cheeky cockney banter.

Ken had seemed much older and wiser and although he played around with his high-spirited fiancée, when caught off guard Hannah found him fixing her with a quizzical look as if seeing her through new eyes, and she would have had to be blind not to notice the open admiration there. They both shared a realisation that the new respect in which he held the neatly dressed woman was a far cry from the embarrassment with which he used to acknowledge his sister's scrawny friend, and aware of this, her heart swelled.

Ken, on leaving, had kissed his mother, Pam and Norma and he couldn't very well not kiss Hannah without making it obvious that she was not one of the family, so she received a quick peck on the cheek, which seemed to burn down to her very soul and which she would treasure for ever.

She visited her sisters, who seemed to be growing out of recognition with Elsie's good home-cooking. It wasn't quite so easy to swing Betsy up in the air now-a-days; although still on the chubby side it was plain that in a couple of years time her darling baby sister would be whittling down to a trim teenager and Hannah felt very sad at the thought, for the older she got the less she would rely on her, and Hannah needed to be needed. Damn and blast this war, she thought, for it allowed her sisters to grow up and away from her and out of childhood far too quickly and nothing would ever be the same again.

Elsie marvelled at the 'posh' young lady Hannah had become, teasing her and saying that the old country folk wouldn't be good enough for her any more after the war, but Hannah vehemently disagreed with her, hugging and kissing her lovingly in the same old way as she always had and always would.

Elsie wasn't a worldly-wise woman by a long shot but she had inner wisdom and foresight that couldn't be learnt from books and although Hannah seemed apparently well, there was something deep behind her eyes that told her something was amiss but when she asked if everything was all right, Hannah had hastily replied, 'Of course, you just don't get rosy cheeks in London.'

But Elsie wasn't convinced, she had a feeling in her water that something was worrying her.

'You would tell your old Auntie if anything was wrong wouldn't you, love?' she had said to her. 'You know you can tell me, or ask me anything in the world and it would never go any further. With your Mum being the way she is there must be times when you want to open your heart and I want you to know that I'm always here if you want me. Any little worries or troubles you have, don't bottle them up and make yourself ill. I've seen and heard all sorts in my life and it'd take a lot to shock me so I want you to promise me that you'll come to me if you ever want a shoulder to cry on.'

'Of course I will,' Hannah had replied, kissing her dear old face, 'but I hope I never have reason to.'

'So do I, lovie, so do I, but I'm afraid nobody goes through life without some ups and downs but if you share them with your nearest and dearest there's nothing that can't be overcome.'

Hannah would dearly have loved to confide in her but for one thing she didn't want to cast a cloud on the much cherished visit and for another, she knew that Elsie would erupt in indignation and try and prevent her from going back to London and much as the thought of not going back was inviting, she owed it to her Aunt Lil to be there for her, at least until she was on her feet, and then she would have to think up a convincing story for leaving. Meanwhile she would try and go on as usual, keeping her ears and eyes open for a flat or a room to rent elsewhere.

All too soon it was time for the return journey and even though the drive to the station was a scenic panorama, with the trees, bushes and rooftops covered in snow, looking like a winter wonderland, it did little to lift her spirits. Much as she was looking forward to seeing her aunt, she knew it would be quite a few months before she would be able to make a return trip to Norfolk and already she was missing her sisters and cursing the war all over again.

'Cheer up Hannah,' said Pam, brightly, 'I know what you're thinking but if you can't manage to come down again I'll try and get up to see you and don't forget, Ken will come to see you if he gets the chance of a twenty-four hour pass. It's hardly worth coming home for but at least he can visit you.'

Hannah bucked up a bit at his, for she felt that he wasn't just being polite when he'd said he'd try to visit her this time and she felt sure that the next time would be better than the last time. It surely couldn't be worse she thought, wryly.

Bill met her at Liverpool Street Station and she was surprised to notice how pale and worried he looked and she immediately panicked, thinking there was something wrong with Lil.

'Is anything wrong? Is Aunt Lil all right?'

'She's fine, there were a few problems at first but everything is all right now. The operation went like clockwork but it was afterwards that things kept going wrong one thing after another, infections etc. They've assured me everything is hunky-dory now.'

'Why didn't you telephone me at Pam's?'

'There was nothing you could do. There was no point in worrying you. Anyway, she's going to be all right now.'

'You look awful,' she said, trying but failing to not feel sorry for him.

'I'm OK, just tired, that's all. I didn't leave her bedside for two days and nights. My God, when I sat there all those hours, wondering if she was going to pull through, I took count of all my misdoings and I made a pledge that if only she'd come out of it all right, I'd devote the rest of my life to her, AND I mean it. I never want to go through anything like that again. It was bad enough losing my mother, I didn't think anything could be worse than that. But she was old and she'd had a good innings, not like my Lil, still in her prime. Still, the worst is over now, thank the Lord, so let's go and see her shall we? I know she's looking forward to seeing you. As soon as she started to feel better she started worrying about you. I know it'll be a tonic for her to see you.'

It was a short drive from the station to St Bartholomews Hospital, affectionately named 'Barts' by the cockneys, and on entering the ward Hannah would have walked past her if Bill hadn't stopped at her bedside. She looked very ill and had quite obviously lost a lot of weight.

She noticed Hannah's shocked look before she could disguise it.

'Come and give me a kiss and take that look off your face, I'm not dead yet,' she said with a glimmer of her old smile getting through.

'Oh, Aunt Lil, don't talk like that,' Hannah said, kissing her gently, tears spilling from her eyes.

'Oh come on, give me a big hug, I won't break, I'll be up and about in no time, you just see if I'm not; I wanted to lose some weight anyway,' she said.

So Hannah hugged and kissed her, her love for her aunt pouring out and thinking to herself. To think I was going to tell her about Uncle Bill. I could never hurt her, I love her far too much. And her ordeal paled into near insignificance in comparison to the thought of nearly losing her aunt.

She left a few minutes before the end of visiting time to enable them to spend the last few minutes alone and on looking back, as she left the ward, seeing Bill tenderly holding Lil's hands it seemed impossible that he was the same beast that had invaded her body and she prayed that he would keep his vows and mend his ways and strangely enough she believed he would. In almost losing Lil he had come to realise just how

165

lucky he was and she didn't think he'd dare break his pledge to God.

True to his word, Bill's behaviour towards Hannah was exemplary, so much so that she began to think his attack on her had been a bad dream.

He drove her to and from work and every evening they visited Lil who was improving steadily and was expected to go home in about two weeks' time; but it was, in fact another four weeks before the doctors were satisfied with her recovery and allowed her to leave.

Hannah arranged her holidays to coincide with Lil's discharge in order to nurse her, for which her aunt was very grateful, for although she was progressing satisfactorily she couldn't seem able to lift herself out of the doldrums and Hannah spent most of her time comforting her through her daily bouts of depression.

Bill couldn't understand why she kept crying. He'd talk to her constantly, reminding her that there was nothing to worry about. The operation was a success, everything was healing as it should, she was lavished with love and affection from Hannah and himself but when, after two weeks, she was still in the same depressive state he contacted her doctor, who reassured him by saying that many women went through this stage after a hysterectomy. It was nothing to worry about, they must just carry on comforting her until she came out of it but there was no hard and fast rule as to when this would be.

She wasn't well enough to be left alone yet so it was decided that Hannah take a few more weeks off (with pay) until such time as she was strong enough to take care of herself.

Bill would call in at Flower Corner every day and report to Lil so that she could keep her finger on the pulse.

The staff were wonderful, working very hard, keeping the flag flying until Lil's and Hannah's return.

They had no idea as to the reason for Lil's stay in hospital but as they were aware of her longing for a child they assumed that she'd had some treatment to enable her to conceive and prayed for its success.

They told Bill that 'that nice young man' who'd taken Hannah to the pictures had called at the shop to convey his best wishes for Lil's speedy recovery and would it be all right to call on Hannah?

166

Lil was very pleased to think that he'd called but Hannah appeared not to be very interested, which surprised Lil, who'd thought her niece had been quite smitten with him.

'Tell him he can call to see Hannah whenever he likes, she's been cooped up with me for far too long. It will do her good to get out for a bit, I'll be all right on my own for a few hours.'

'No,' said Hannah, sharply, 'really, I'd rather you didn't. I don't want to see him again, not yet anyway,' she added hastily, 'not until you're better.'

'Don't be silly, Hannah, I don't want you to make a martyr of yourself on my account. It's been over a month since you've been out for a breath of fresh air, we don't want you getting ill. Who'd look after me then?'

But she was adamant. 'Please Uncle Bill, tell him, if he calls again, that I'd rather he waited for a few more weeks, at least. I wouldn't be able to relax, leaving Aunt Lil on her own yet. He'll understand.'

'Just as you like,' said Bill readily, which surprised Lil, who thought he'd got over his over-protectiveness towards Hannah.

Although Hannah was feeling a little under the weather and quite honestly would have welcomed an outing, she had no intention of seeing John again. She felt sullied and unworthy of him and decided to give him the cold shoulder if she bumped into him. She knew he would be very hurt and a little bewildered but she felt that she must be cruel to be kind and in time he'd meet another girl who would be more worthy of him and she just hoped that their paths wouldn't cross again, for to see him with somebody else would hurt her and remind her of what might have been.

She need not have worried, for John, on receiving the message, respected her wishes and said he would wait until he heard from her before making an approach. Meanwhile, he'd pop into the shop from time to time to enquire after Lil's health, thus keeping in contact.

During the next two months Lil continued to improve slowly and gradually she emerged from the depressions and started to take an interest in things again.

She pottered around the flat doing light chores, but it would be a few months yet before she was able to go back to work.

As she grew stronger and stopped worrying about herself she became aware that Hannah was looking far from well. Although she'd put on a little weight and her figure was more rounded, she was very pale, with dark circles under her eyes, and she felt terribly guilty to think that she'd been so wrapped up in her own miseries that she'd failed to notice all was not well with her devoted nurse. When her doctor paid his routine visit she voiced her concern.

'The young lady certainly looks very pasty,' he said, 'but that's understandable. If she's been cooped up for months, you must try to talk her into going out for a daily walk or she may get agoraphobic. If you're still worried about her and she doesn't seem to improve before my next visit get her to make an appointment to come and see me at my surgery and I'll give her a check-up. She's probably a bit anaemic; if so, an iron tonic will perk her up.'

So, on Lil's insistence, Hannah began taking daily walks and when the weather improved slightly Lil accompanied her on short walks. Although it was nearing April, the winter was reluctant to release its hold and they both felt that with the better weather their health would benefit, but in Hannah's case this was not so.

Although Lil made sure that her niece got her proper rest, food and fresh air Hannah seemed to go downhill and had been physically sick on more than one occasion, and Lil persuaded her to make an appointment to visit the doctor, by now half-convinced that she had consumption.

With great trepidation Hannah entered the doctor's consulting room, her imagination running riot, sure that he would tell her that she must go to a sanatorium.

He examined her thoroughly, paying special attention to her heart and lungs, and although pretty certain that there was nothing wrong in that direction he decided to send her for X-rays for confirmation.

'Well Hannah, you've got me flummoxed,' he said, 'but to leave no stone unturned I'll give you an internal examination and if everything is all right there I'll give you a course of iron and see you again in a month's time.'

He gently carried out this final test in the examination room then told her to dress and return to the consulting room, where he sat, twiddling with a pencil, looking most serious.

'What is it, Doctor? Have I got consumption?'

'No, no my dear.'

'Thank God, I was sure I had, then why have I been so sick?'

'Harrumph.' The doctor cleared his throat and began asking her very personal questions. Did she have her periods regularly? When did she last have a period? Had she got a boyfriend, etc, etc?

The more questions he asked the more uncomfortable and embarrassed she became.

'You haven't got a boyfriend you say, but you have had one?'

'Not exactly, I did go out once with a boy to the pictures, before Aunt Lil went into hospital.'

'And you don't see him anymore?'

'No, I've been too busy looking after Aunt Lil.'

'May I suggest that you contact the young man? You'll need to discuss things.'

'Why should I contact him? I don't understand.'

'You really don't do you?' he said, sadly shaking his head. 'The fact is Hannah, that as far as I can ascertain, you're about four months' pregnant.'

Her eyes widened like saucers and what little colour she had drained away as she swayed and would have plummeted from her chair had he not acted quickly and rushed to her side.

She came to, with the doctor cradling her head.

'Take it easy Hannah, you'll be all right, you just fainted. Sit up slowly and take a sip of water,' he said kindly.

She sipped the water as if in a dream and then began to shake uncontrollably.

Life's full of surprises thought the doctor; she seems almost as shocked as I was, poor little soul, she's little more than a child herself.

'Do you want to talk about it? Would you like me to contact the young man for you.'

'What for? It's nothing to do with him.'

'I think it must have something to do with him, you can't get pregnant on your own and he should shoulder his responsibilities.'

'No, no,' she said agitaitedly standing up.

'Take it easy, calm down, I won't do anything you don't want me to.'

'Please don't do anything, and don't tell Aunt Lil.'

169

'But, she must be told. You can't go through this on your own and anyway she'll be able to see for herself before long.'

'I WILL tell her, but please let me tell her when I'm ready.'

'I wouldn't dream of interfering but I strongly suggest you tell her as soon as possible. She'll stand by you I'm sure and if there's anything I can do you must let me know. Meanwhile,' he said, now in a more business-like voice, 'I'd like you to come to see me again in a month's time.'

She walked out, oblivious of the cold drizzle.

Never in her wildest imaginings had she thought that she might be pregnant. She'd always thought that you couldn't get pregnant the first time, at least that's what people always said. Did he do it to her a second time when she'd passed out? She wished fervently that she knew more about these matters, but even if she did, it wouldn't help matters. She was having a baby and the father was her uncle; did that make it incest? Oh dear, how ignorant she was, how could she face Aunt Lil?

She walked and walked until she was soaked to the skin. Perhaps I'll get pneumonia and die she thought, I do hope so. Anything in the world is preferable to having his baby. Perhaps I could have an abortion. But as quickly as she thought this she rejected it. It would be murder, no matter how she looked at it.

'Are you all right love?'

Hannah had been standing on the bridge looking down into the icy-greyness of the water. She turned in surprise and looked into the face of a kind policeman.

The light was beginning to fade; she must have been standing there for hours.

'Not thinking of doing anything silly, are you, miss?'

'What? No of course not.'

'Where do you live, love? Are you in any sort of trouble?'

'No, really, I'm quite all right, I just had a little problem that needed thinking out.'

'And have you sorted it out? If so I'd get along home miss. The Jerries like these sort of murky days and there's not an air-raid shelter in this neck of the woods.'

She shivered. Although she'd been thinking that death was preferable to having a baby, when it came down to it she didn't fancy the idea of being blown to smithereens by Germans.

She hurried towards home now. The numbing shock was beginning to wear off and she was aware of how cold and wet she was and a little frightened of being alone so far away. She must have walked for miles and miles.

She wouldn't be surprised if Aunt Lil, who must be very worried by now, hadn't sent Uncle Bill out to look for her.

'Is that you Hannah?' came Lil's voice from the kitchen, where she was making tea, as Hannah's footsteps came down the hall.

'My God, you're soaked to the skin. Go and get out of those wet clothes and then come and get warmed up with a nice hot cup of tea. I'd forgotten how long you have to wait in surgeries nowadays. Is everything all right?'

'Yes, nothing serious, he's giving me a tonic as you suggested.'

'Thank goodness. Well, go and get changed or you really will get sick.'

She peeled off her saturated clothes, had a brisk rub down with a towel and then returned to the kitchen, thinking, I'll tell her tomorrow when I've got used to the idea myself. I can hardly believe it yet, I'll need tonight to think it all out before I can bring myself to talk about it. Whatever will she say? I could never tell her about Uncle Bill now. She'll think it was John's fault but I don't want her to blame him. Oh dear, what a mess!

But as it happened there was no need to confess to her aunt for early the next morning Lil stood outside the bathroom in order to take her bath when Hannah emerged, and she heard her retching violently.

Her first thought was, I knew there was something wrong, how could the doctor not notice it? and then, as Hannah continued to retch, she was reminded of Aggie's early morning sickness in each of her pregnancies and the truth hit her like a bolt out of the blue and shocked as she was, there was no doubt in her mind as to the reason for Hannah's peakiness. It all made sense now.

Hannah opened the door to find Lil standing outside with a look of utter amazement on her face and she knew immediately that she had been overheard being sick.

'Oh love, why didn't you tell me?' asked Lil, taking her gently into her arms. Now she understood fully Hannah's reluctance over seeing John again and she grudgingly admitted to herself that Bill had been right in his suspicions of him.

On her aunt's gentle, unreproving acceptance of the situation Hannah burst into tears and allowed herself to be led and seated in the kitchen whilst Lil made the proverbial cup of tea over which almost any problem could be solved. Nothing more was said for a few minutes while they sipped their tea. Lil, with her arm around Hannah until the crying subsided.

'Have you thought about what you intend to do?' asked Lil.

'I haven't really had time to think much at all, I didn't know until yesterday. I still can't believe it,' Hannah said, shaking her head perplexibly.

'Well, let's not rush into any hasty decisions. We'll take today to ponder on it and then, you, me and Uncle Bill will have a discussion as to what will be the best thing to do.'

'Oh no, please don't tell Uncle Bill,' said Hannah, taking Lil's hand and crying again.

'It'll be all right love, he's not an ogre you know, he's a man of the world, and I know he won't condemn you, he loves you just as I do.'

Oh, Aunt Lil, her heart cried out, if only you knew! But of course, she probably never would.

They tried to spend the rest of the day normally, talking of the war and rationing and mice and kings, everything except that what was uppermost in their minds.

At tea-time, Bill sensed an atmosphere but on an enquiring look at Lil, who subtly mouthed 'hush' to him, he decided to hold his tongue until they were alone.

Much later, when Hannah had gone to bed Lil told him, and to her amazement he accepted it quietly and even when she said he had been right to mistrust John he said, calmly, 'Well, what's done is done, we must now do what's best for Hannah.'

'Oh I do love you Bill and I think its wonderful of you to be so understanding. I expected you to go up the wall and it would have been within your rights to do so. After all, you agreed to having her live here with us and for her to let you down so badly and you to be so noble about it, you really are one in a million,' she said, putting her arms around him and giving him a big kiss.

They talked long into the night and finally reached a most marvellous conclusion, if Hannah would only agree to it.

On hearing their proposals the next day, Hannah was

flabbergasted. She'd thought of all sorts of things from abortion to suicide and even, to her disgust, making it up with John, in order to give the baby a name but, never in her wildest imaginings had she contemplated her aunt and uncle bringing up the baby as their own.

'Oh, Hannah love, do think about it seriously. You'd be giving us the most wonderful gift in the world and we would love the baby as our very own. Nobody but us would ever know the truth. I haven't told anybody that I've had an hysterectomy, they'll think that I was in hospital for treatment to enable me to become pregnant and they won't be able to point fingers at you. We'll say that you've stayed off work to look after me and then when the baby is born you can go back to work as usual. It'll all work out wonderfully, you'll see.'

As Hannah didn't reply she went on, 'Of course I don't expect you to answer straight away, you'll want to talk it over with John won't you?'

'Whatever for? It's nothing to do with him,' said Hannah.

Lil looked from her to Bill, a frown creasing her brow. 'Hannah love, it has got something to do with him. Don't you think you ought to at least tell him of our suggestion? He might want to marry you.'

'Marry me?' said Hannah. 'We're far too young to get married' and, looking at Lil, 'I know what you're thinking, I wasn't too young to get pregnant. But you don't understand, it's not as simple as that and if I do decide to go along with your plan you must promise me that John will never know.'

'If that's what you want, of course you have our word on it but I honestly think he has a right to know.'

'No, no,' she said emphatically, beginning to cry, 'you must promise me, please.'

'All right love, if that's your decision but think over our proposal. I really think it's the best way out. I know you think I'm only thinking of my own selfish desires but honestly, no way could you bring up a baby on your own and I couldn't bear to think of it going to strangers. We don't expect an answer now. Take as much time as you need and remember, whatever you decide, we're right behind you and nobody need ever know.'

'The doctor knows,' said Hannah.

'Yes, but if you decide to go along with our plans we'll let him in on it. You can rest assured it will go no further. What goes on between doctor and patient is strictly confidential, they are sworn to secrecy.'

'Now, we'll all have a nice cup of tea,' she said going towards the kitchen.

As she left Bill went to Hannah and made as if to put his hands on her shoulders but she shivered and moved out of his reach. He let his hands fall to his sides and said, 'Thank you for not telling Lil, I swear you'll never regret it.'

'I didn't do it for you, I'll always think of you as a disgusting pig and nothing you do in the future can make up for what you did to me. Thanks to you I feel unable to have a normal relationship with a boy. Who wants a girl who's been defiled? I always vowed to walk down the aisle a virgin. Now I don't suppose I'll ever walk down the aisle.'

'Don't be over-dramatic Hannah, there aren't many virgins around nowadays, what with the war and everything. People are just living for the day. They could be dead tomorrow; virgins will soon be as rare as dodo's eggs.'

'In that case I would have been a rarity but now no decent boy will want me so there's no point in talking about it,' and she brushed past him, afraid that if she stayed in the same room as him for much longer she would break down and let the cat out of the bag and now that the worst had happened she would cut off her tongue before telling Lil the truth about her beloved husband.

It took her only a few hours to decide that she had little choice as to which path to take. It was either allow Bill and Lil to bring up the baby or have it adopted. If she had it adopted she would never see it grow up and whilst the thought placated her in the respect that she wouldn't have to look on Bill's likeness, she would be denying Lil her heart's desire so she told her that she would go along with her proposals. At which Lil broke down and cried, assuring her that she would never regret it. The child would have everything that life afforded and more and Hannah knew that she had made the right decision.

After the first few months of her pregnancy the morning sickness disappeared as suddenly as it had started and Hannah began to take on a healthy glow. Although she didn't gain much weight, just a little 'football' in front, she had to admit that never in her life had she felt so healthy. She had an appetite like a horse and had only to mention that she fancied a certain food and 'hey presto', it would be there.

Lil spoilt her rotten and in a strange unexplainable way she began to feel quite happy with the situation now that she was resigned to it and she just hoped that she would feel the same after the baby was born. But she had only to remind herself of who the father was and that would stop her from getting any romantic notions about keeping it.

On 30 April, it was reported that Adolph Hitler had commited suicide amid the ruins of Berlin and a few days later on 4 May, the German forces in North Western Europe surrendered to General Montgomery at Luhenburg Heath and on 7 May the German Supreme Command surrendered at Rheims.

The next day was designated as Victory in Europe, but the war against the Japanese continued.

There then followed much rejoicing and for the first time in years the electric lights went on all over.

Once again theatres, restaurants and cinemas were fully lit up and many very young children were bewildered and afraid of so much light.

There was singing and dancing in the streets and the Royal Family and leading politicians appeared on the balcony of Buckingham Palace.

Hannah's baby kicked out strongly as if he too were doing a victory roll and wanted to join in the celebrations and she felt that this wouldn't be such a bad year after all; if only the fighting would come to an end and the war really finish then people would get back to leading normal lives and all the mothers' sons would come home and there would be no more nightmares of loved ones returning with limbs missing.

The year wore on to a hot, sticky August and by now Hannah was beginning to feel that she'd been pregnant all her life and always would be. She found it hard to imagine what it would be like not to carry this little bundle in front of her everywhere she went but were it not for the little bump nobody would have known that she was pregnant, so it had been comparatively easy to keep the situation under cover.

She and Lil kept pretty much to themselves and when they went out shopping or walking they made sure that they both wore very loose clothes, just in case they bumped into anyone they knew and up until now they had been very fortunate.

On 6 August, the Americans dropped the first atomic bomb on Hiroshima and a second one was dropped on Nagasaki on the 9th. This must surely speed up the Japanese surrender, everyone thought.

A few days later, in Heysham, Pam and her mother were busy re-decorating Ken's room in preparation for his return, for they were reasonably sure that the war would be over in a few more weeks.

They heard the familiar whistling of the telegram boy. Thank God thought Peg, that people will no longer shake in their shoes every time he appears, for fear he's bearing bad news.

She dropped the brush once again into the paint-pot. 'On the last wall now, nearly finished'.

The front door bell rang. Strange she thought, I didn't hear anyone approaching, only the telegram boy and then somebody walked over her grave. Her mouth dried up, 'Answer the door Pam,' she croaked.

'OK,' answered Pam, skipping lightly to the door.

'Telegram for Mr Bates,' he said.

'He's out for a few minutes,' she replied.

'Mrs Bates then.' He tapped a buff-coloured envelope on the palm of his hand, trying very hard but not succeeding in looking unconcerned.

Peg had now arrived on the scene and both she and her daughter looked in horror at the dancing envelope.

'Sign here please,' he said, thrusting the envelope at a now-paralysed Peg.

Pam took the pencil from him and signed hurriedly and the boy hastened away, another dreadful duty over.

She held it out gingerly towards her mother, who just stared at it in horror.

'Come on Mum, it's not always bad news, the worst of the fighting is over now so it can't be bad news.'

'Please, love, you open it,' said Peg, wringing her hands nervously.

'Oh, all right,' said Pam, smiling bravely and tearing open the envelope.

Her smile faded as she recognised the War Office note paper.

'Dear Mr Bates,' she read, 'we regret to inform you that

176

your Son Kenneth Frederick Bates is missing, presumed killed. The plane in which he was travelling was reported shot down -' She got no further.

Peg screamed and Norma came rushing in and on spying the envelope in Pam's hand, snatched it from her and she, too, began to scream like a banshee and this was the scene that Fred walked into on entering.

It was two days before Pam could bring herself to write with the dreadful news to Hannah and she envied the past two days' ignorant bliss that her friend had enjoyed but she knew as sure as eggs were eggs that Hannah would be as devastated as she was for she knew her feelings towards her brother.

Hannah and Lil had just enjoyed a glass of sherry, celebrating Victory over Japan Day for the Japanese had surrendered two days earlier on 14 August and all of London was singing and dancing in the streets once again at this final victory.

Hannah tripped merrily to the door on hearing the letter come through the letter-box.

She recognised her friend's writing. Oh wasn't it marvellous! The war was over and soon, with luck, she could go back to Norfolk to see her family and friends!

She smiled in anticipation of Pam's happiness but the smile turned into disbelieving horror as she read the tragic contents.

She screamed and Lil came rushing down the hall to see her niece crumpled near the door, one hand clasping the letter, the other clutching her stomach.

She quickly scanned the proffered letter and helped Hannah to her feet, who screamed yet again, this time in pain.

Oh God, it can't be, it's too early, thought Lil, as she guided Hannah to a seat, but pain upon pain convinced her that Hannah had, indeed, gone into premature labour.

She got her into bed, trying to keep as calm as possible for although she was aware that an eight-month baby could be a bit dodgy she kept the fear to herself, calming Hannah by assuring her that everything would be perfectly all right and between the contractions, when she felt she could safely leave her for a couple of minutes, she rang for the doctor and then Bill at his office.

The two men arrived simultaneously, Bill rushing in, the doctor sauntering as if he were taking an evening stroll.

'Quick, Doctor, in here,' said Lil, clutching his arm.

177

'Calm down Mrs Huggins, I should be very surprised if anything happens before four or five hours. First babies are very rarely in a hurry to make an appearance. You go and put the kettle on and make us all a nice cup of tea. I'm sure we could all do with one and I'll go and see to Hannah.'

His words calmed Lil, making her feel a little foolish for panicking so.

During the next seven hours Hannah suffered agonies that were indescribable. She marvelled that a body could suffer so much pain and live. She had been told that giving birth was painful but nothing had prepared her for this hell and just when she'd reached the end of her endurance the doctor somehow coaxed one more big push from her and this last great effort made her feel as if her soul was being split in half and then, a slither, a slap and a baby's cry.

'All over Hannah,' said the doctor, 'you have a lovely baby boy.' He wiped her brow, marvelling anew at this wonder of wonders. He had delivered hundreds of babies in his time but every time it seemed like a fresh miracle.

Hannah was now crying from relief. It was over; she had done it, she hadn't died. If she lived to be a hundred she could never experience such elation as this.

'Is it all right?'

'HE is beautiful; a little on the small side but nothing to worry about,' he assured her.

He washed the baby and laid him in her arms.

She looked down on perfection and thought to herself, nobody would believe that this was the outcome of rape. Even if he had been conceived in love he could not have been more beautiful, and she was swamped with unbelievable love for the little mite.

She had fully expected to feel nothing but loathing for the outcome of the rape but that was when it was just an IT growing inside her. Now it was a living, breathing person and she swelled with pride to think that she, skinny, non-descript Hannah, had produced such a perfect little being.

The baby was taken from her and laid aside whilst the doctor relieved her of the after-birth, which took a few minutes and was a bit painful, but nothing in comparison to the contractions that had wracked her body all day.

After she had been washed, Bill and Lil were ushered in.

178

The doctor, looking in from the doorway, felt as if he were witnessing the nativity scene all over again. There was such wonder every time it was performed and he felt although the baby had not been born in the best circumstances, with such love all around him he had every chance in the world of growing up to be a normal, happy, healthy child.

13

Hannah's first day back at work was very traumatic.

She felt a little alienated, as if she didn't quite belong any more.

She found it hard to concentrate on the floral arrangements and after only a few hours wanted to rush home to check that the baby was all right and felt like bursting into tears every time somebody enthused over her Aunt Lil and how lucky she was. They marvelled at what wonders medical science could perform to enable someone who was resigned to being barren suddenly to conceive and what a wonderful mother she would make and how proud Bill was, strutting around accepting congratulatory pats on the back, and didn't the baby look the dead-spit of his father?

By the time lunch-time arrived she knew she just had to get away for a while. She didn't usually bother to take a full hour's lunch, just a drink and a snack, and then carry on working but this morning had been such a trying one that she felt she must get away for a while to compose herself.

She was out of the door before the clock had hardly chimed one and in her haste bumped into somebody who was about to enter.

'Hello, has someone been taking flying lessons?'

'Oh I'm sorry,' she began and looked up into John's face.

'It's so good to see you Hannah, it seems like a life-time since we went to the pictures together. I began to feel it was all a dream. I've had to force myself to stay away from the flat, on your wishes, but you don't know how hard it's been.' He gabbled on, 'These last few months have seemed like years. I began to think that you were a figment of my imagination and when I heard that you were back at work I couldn't wait a minute longer. Can I take you for a spot of lunch?'

All Hannah's resolves flew out of the window as she looked

into his imploring eyes. 'Oh don't look at me like that' she thought, 'I'm not worthy of your devotion. If you only knew the truth about me you wouldn't come within a hundred miles of Flower Corner. But she was so miserable and it was good to see his dear, honest face.

'I mustn't be away long,' she said, 'it is my first day back at work and I've been away so long I feel guilty for taking a lunch hour.'

'There's no need for you to feel guilty I'm sure. After all, you've been doing your Florence Nightingale bit and that was more important than selling flowers. I'm sure Lil appreciates all you've done for her, for without your care and attention she might not be in the happy situation she's in now. But,' he went on, 'you do look a bit fragile. I expect you're worn out. Anyway, I won't take no for an answer,' he said, taking her arm and guiding her towards the nearest restaurant.

He gave the waitress the order and as she walked away, scribbling on her little notepad that was fixed to her pocket on a piece of string, he took Hannah's hands across the table.

'I think I shall keep you forever to make sure that I don't lose sight of you again,' he said.

Hannah blushed and tried to pull her hands away, glancing around nervously in case any of her customers were in the room.

'It's all right, there's nobody here that knows us,' he said, smiling at her embarrassment.

'Really John, I think you've been watching too many love films.'

'I haven't been to the pictures since I last went with you but I hope I can rectify that. How about Saturday, Blue Eyes?' he said, in a Humphrey Bogart voice.

She couldn't help laughing at his interpretation of his favourite film-star and, against all her good intentions, agreed to meet him.

He asked about her sisters and friends in Norfolk and with tears falling uncontrollably she told him of Ken's disappearance and once the tears flowed she just couldn't stop. This 'brick' had been glued to her chest ever since she'd received the bad news and the heavy pain had steadily worsened.

He gently mopped her eyes with his handkerchief.

'I'm sorry John, I shouldn't let go like this in public.

Whatever must you think of me?'

'I think you're a little darling who's had more than her share of sorrow. So please don't be ashamed of your feelings. I know Pam and her family are very dear to you, it must be like losing a brother for you too.'

His sympathy made her cry even more. Oh if you knew she thought, that when Ken died my heart died with him.

A couple of people at the next table glanced her way but on seeing John comforting her, looked away so as not to embarrass her.

John allowed her to cry unchecked for a few minutes, then said firmly but kindly, 'All right Hannah, wipe your eyes now and try to pull yourself together or you'll make yourself ill. Anyway, look on the bright side, they haven't reported finding his body. Chances are, he's in a prisoner of war camp. Don't give up hope, I'm sure his family haven't.'

'Is that possible, wouldn't the telegram have said so?'

'Not necessarily. They'll assume he's dead as nobody's been found and they daren't give the family any false hopes but when they start to evacuate the camps I bet there'll be many a young man turn up out of the blue.'

Hannah didn't think for one moment that this was likely but she blessed John for trying to cheer her up.

They went on to talk of other things and by the time they'd finished their lunch and walked back to the shop Hannah felt better than she'd felt in a long time.

At the close of a very long day Bill arrived and although she'd felt that the day would never dawn when she would be happy to see him, she was and couldn't wait to get home to see the baby.

They had named him John Willam after Hannah's father and Bill and he was already being called John Willie by all and sundry. Hannah didn't like the abbreviation but what could she say? He now belonged to Lil and Bill.

Lil had gradually taken command of the baby and although Hannah still gave him the occasional bottle and bath she was quietly being pushed into the role of Auntie. Although this was what they'd all agreed on, it hurt terribly, especially when it was bedtime and Lil was the one to tuck him in and give him his last hug and kiss of the day. But she hadn't expected it to be easy so she gritted her teeth and played her part.

When she announced that John was taking her to the pictures on Saturday, Lil was very pleased for her.

'I'm so glad, Hannah, you're very young and after all, it wasn't all his fault. I'm sure it's just one of these things' she said 'but you must be more careful in the future.'

Hannah winced and bit her tongue. Poor John, it was so unfair.

'Please, Aunt Lil, remember your promise, he must never be told.'

'I gave you my word, love, and I'd rather die than betray your trust in me' Anyway she thought I could never risk his knowing, he might want to take the baby away and it would break my heart if he did; I love him so dearly.

The next few months found Hannah and John courting steadily and although she kept him at arm's length, she didn't know how much longer she'd be able to do so, for he was a man and his need for her grew steadily with every meeting.

Every time she stopped him from going too far he gave in good-naturedly, quite proud of her in a way, for most girls he came into contact with were far too forward, to his mind. But he was only human and it was becoming increasingly difficult to control himself. She knew it was only a matter of time before he popped the question and she didn't honestly know what her answer would be.

She had by now accepted Ken's death and although she knew she could never love John in the same way, she also knew that she would never find a finer man than he and she didn't fancy being an old maid and she couldn't stay with her aunt and uncle for ever, much as she wanted to. She knew the day would come when she would have to break away and the longer she put it off the harder it would be to leave the baby.

At the weekend Bill offered to drive them down to Norfolk to visit her sisters and this time Hannah insisted they go via Norwich in order to see her mother.

Although there had been no change in her condition over the years Hannah felt a strange urge to visit her and then she'd be able to tell her sisters that she'd seen her and reassure them that she was not forgotten.

To Hannah's dismay, whenever her mother had crept into the conversation the children listened politely as if hearing an account about a stranger. As far as they were concerned Elsie was now their mother and had been a far better mother than Aggie had ever been.

John Willie slept all the way from London to Norwich and when they drove into the hospital grounds car park Bill offered to stay in the car with him while the two women visited but Hannah insisted on taking him for Aggie to see.

'But Hannah,' said Bill, 'she won't see him, she won't even know he's there.'

'I still want to take him,' she said firmly. 'She has a right to see him, he is her first grandchild after all.'

Bill looked at Lil, who shrugged in resignation, so they all went in together. Hannah carried the baby in. She had almost given up all rights to him but was adamant in this respect, so once again she was his mother, if only for a little while.

There were about half a dozen patients sitting in the visiting room and a couple were very excited to receive visitors but Aggie just stared ahead of her, rocking back and forth, apparently oblivious of their presence.

They talked normally to her as if she could understand about the end of the war and Ken's death and other little bits of information but she just rocked back and forth, back and forth. They ran out of conversation eventually. It was very hard to keep up when it was so one-sided and when John Willie started to cry they decided to leave.

'Goodbye Mum,' Hannah said, kissing Aggie's pale old face, and although she'd never received any love from her, blood was thicker than water and love and compassion welled up inside her for this poor creature.

As she leaned over to kiss her, she must have unwittingly squeezed the baby harder than she realized for he gave out a wail loud enough to waken the dead and his scream, which was directed straight into Aggie's ear, made her jerk her head and a look of incredulity sprang to her eyes and her mouth uttered one quiet word. 'Colin.'

'What did you say Mum, MUM what did you say?' said Hannah, looking from her to Lil and Bill and she knew from their amazed looks that they also had heard the whispered word – the one and only word that had left her lips since her baby had died, years ago.

Hannah handed John Willie to Lil and flung her arms around Aggie. 'Oh I knew you'd get better one day, I just knew it.'

But Aggie had gone back to her own private world and try as they may, they couldn't coax another word from her.

They looked at each other unbelievingly and had they not all heard it, they would have thought they'd imagined it.

They stopped by the matron's office before leaving, to report what had happened. They were so excited but she took the news calmly with little reaction.

'You don't believe us, do you?' said Hannah. 'but I promise you we all heard her, we didn't imagine it,' and Lil and Bill nodded vigorously to back her statement.

'Of course I believe you my dear but I don't want you to get too optimistic. It takes more than one swallow to make a summer.'

'But surely it's a good sign, it must mean she's getting better' appealed Lil.

'It is a good sign,' replied the matron, 'it means that one of the doors leading to her past has been opened but there are a lot more doors down that corridor and it could be years before she unlocks the final one. I'm sorry, my dear, I don't mean to throw cold water on your excitement but I don't want you to rush away with the idea that she can be released next week. What we musn't do is to force the issue, for if we plagued and worried her in order to wring another word out of her we could send her further back than ever before and this time there would be no return. I'd like you to leave things as they are for a few weeks. Oh, I know how you feel my dears, you want to come back next week and the next week, in order to be here when the next word escapes but it doesn't work like that. Believe me, I know what's best. If, by any chance there are marked improvements before your next visit, you may be sure I'll inform you but if not please leave it for at least a month before your next visit.'

'Can we bring the baby again? I'm sure it was because of him that she spoke,' said Hannah.

'Bring him, by all means. It could have been coincidence but on the other hand his scream may have jarred her sub-concious. It certainly won't do any harm.'

They left, remembering all her advice, but couldn't help hugging the thought to themselves that whatever she said, the fact was that Aggie had spoken and their hearts were filled with hope and Hannah remembered something she'd been told years ago, when she'd questioned Christianity; The Lord moves in mysterious ways, His wonders to perform.

At the time it meant nothing more to her than a passage quoted from the Bible, but now she was beginning to understand. The death of little Colin had sent Aggie insane but the birth of John Willie would, with luck, bring her back to the land of the living and she gave up a silent prayer that this would be so.

It was a happy little company that drew up outside Elsie's house an hour later. Betsy, Maureen and little Tom came spilling out on hearing the car, with Elsie right behind them, standing on the doorstep like a mother-hen watching over her brood, a floral pinny covering her large frame, sleeves, as ever, pushed up above her elbows as if she'd just slipped away from the wash-tub.

On their entering the house, she took the baby and planted a resounding kiss on his cheek, at which he let out a wail. He wasn't used to such rough treatment and when she handed him back a red blotch marked his face from her exuberence.

She'd had the kettle on the simmer for an hour, so in a matter of minutes they were sitting round the freshly scrubbed kitchen table with big mugs of tea and then she received the good news about Aggie.

'Isn't it wonderful,' said Hannah, hugging her darling little Betsy, 'I told you Mum would get better one day, didn't I.'

'What did she say? Did she ask about me and Maureen? When is she coming home, will she come and live with us here?'

The questions poured from her in quick succession and when Hannah explained that she'd only uttered the one word, 'Colin,' Betsy said, disgustedly 'Huh, I thought you said she was getting better. She's still a dummy if she thinks John Willie is Colin.'

Hannah tried to explain the implication of that one word but Betsy had lost interest and said, 'Come on Tom, I'll give you a push on the swing,' skipping out to the back yard.

'Don't be upset,' said Elsie kindly, 'she's too young to understand. She was only little when Colin died, she can't really remember much about him or Aggie.'

Hannah then told her of the matron's cool reception of their news to which she said, 'Don't you fret, she's going to be all right now, I just know it. Good things are going to start happening. Look at this little chap,' meaning John Willie. 'Who'd have thought he was possible last year this time? He's a good omen if ever there were one and the war is over. Oh, good times are a-comin, you mark my words, this is going to be a very good year for us all.'

Hannah left them chatting about good times, while she went off to find Pam. Peg answered her knock on the door and although she looked the same as ever, plump and rosy-cheeked, her eyes had lost their twinkle and Hannah didn't quite know what to say or, indeed, whether to say anything about Ken. But she was saved from her dilemma by Pam hurling herself at her and the two friends hugged and hugged and shed a few tears and Hannah then realised that Pam had received a double blow for Denny had also been in the plane that was shot down and nothing further had been heard of him since his parents receiving the dreaded telegram from the War Office.

She told Pam of Aggie's startling word and of Elsie's incredible optimism regarding the coming year and it cheered her friend somewhat, for she, like many folk, set great store by Elsie's premonitions.

Norma had returned to London now that the war was over and although they'd received a couple of letters from her, fully expected the correspondence to cease, for there were too many sad memories here for her now.

Hannah casually mentioned that she'd been going out with John recently and although Pam knew what Ken had meant to her she was pleased for her friend. Who knows? she thought, perhaps I'll meet somebody else to care for in time? But she thought it unlikely.

When it was time to leave for the return journey to London Hannah didn't feel as upset as she usually did for there was optimism in the air now, thanks to Elsie's cheerfulness, and she hoped that the next time she came to Norfolk it would be to stay.

14

Christmas Day 1945 was a very quiet one at the flat, with Bill, Lil and in the afternoon John.

The weather had been appalling since November and another trip to Norfolk had been out of the question but nevertheless, Hannah had enjoyed this Christmas.

John Willie, at the age of four months, was beginning to sit up and take notice and although far too young to realise what all the fuss was about, was fascinated by the pretty paper streamers on the tree. Where Bill had obtained them from was anybody's guess, for although the war was over, things were very slow in returning to the shops. In fact it was almost as hard to get Christmas fare as it had been the year before.

John was now welcomed by her aunt and uncle with open arms. The animosity that had been there earlier had now completely disappeared. So enchanted were they with the baby that they could afford to be generous towards him.

Lil had always said that blood was thicker than water but this was not the case as far as John and the baby were concerned, for she was sure he felt nothing more towards the baby than any other of their friends and was equally sure that he had no notion as to the baby's parenthood. When people remarked that he was the dead-spit of his dad they weren't just being polite for as he grew he looked just like a miniature Bill. There was nothing remotely like John about him, for where he was slim and fine-boned, Bill and the baby were the opposite. Perhaps, in time, he would trim down, but for the moment there was no reason for anybody to doubt his origin.

Hannah loved him fiercely and at times regretted that she had allowed Lil to take him over, but when she thought about it logically she knew there had been no other choice. For if she had allowed him to be adopted she would never have seen him again, whereas now she could see him every day.

John thought that she loved the baby to excess, very often preferring to stay indoors with him than to go out, but he thought he understood. Perhaps the baby was taking the place of the little brother that had died and watching her with the baby he thought, 'She will make a wonderful mother herself one day.' He now loved Hannah with all his heart and couldn't imagine life without her and he knew that she was beginning to return his love; perhaps not to the extent that he would like but he understood that men were far more fiery than women in the main, so was quite prepared to accept what she could offer in return.

Hannah, for her part, now resigned to never seeing Ken again, was fairly happy with their relationship and although she still kept him at arm's length, something was beginning to trouble her a little. She enjoyed kissing and cuddling with him but when things started to go a bit too far she would freeze up and go cold on him and she began to worry that she wouldn't be able to respond to him. There was nobody she could talk to about it. It certainly wasn't something she could mention in her letters to Pam without telling her the whole story.

It was at times like this that she wished she could pop down the road to see Aunt Elsie, for she knew, if anybody could, she would be able to explain things and reassure her. John was also a bit puzzled at times for although she let him caress her, just when he thought that she wanted him as much as he did her, she would suddenly go frigid.

He knew that most girls played hard to get, it was all part of the game. But somehow, he hadn't thought of her as any other girl and tried to fathom out where he was going wrong. If he tried talking to her about it she would become dreadfully embarrassed, so he tried to be patient and hope that given time she would trust him wholly.

Christmas over, Lil began to cadge and store a bit of butter here, some dried fruit there, and every spare ounce of sugar was poured into a special tin. Hannah suspected that ingredients were being hoarded in order make her a birthday cake and when 13 March arrived she wasn't disappointed.

John and his mother, whom Hannah had taken to instantly, were invited to the birthday tea and Bill fetched them in his car, for Mrs Hodiak was quite frail and had deteriorated since their first meeting.

Lil did them proud, – wafer-thin sandwiches and tea served in lovely thin cups and a beautiful cake decorated with a big 18.

There was even a bottle of sherry, to which Bill did justice by toasting firstly Hannah's birthday, then the war's end and last but by no means least, with tremendous pride in his eyes, John Willie.

Lil could have cried, so overwhelmed by the fervour with which he directed this final toast.

He's so marvellous with the baby, she thought, I couldn't imagine him being more proud if he were indeed ours, and her heart tightened a little with sadness as she realised that he must be equally heartbroken at their inability to have a child of their own. But she refused to dwell on it for, after all, they had the very next best thing. At least John Willie had family blood running through his veins. If they'd adopted a child it would have been a total stranger's and she resolved never to worry about what might have been but to give thanks for the restitution God had made to them.

Hannah stole a few glances towards John's mother as she nibbled delicately at the little sandwiches and her heart went out to her in sympathy.

Although she could only be in her early fifties she could be mistaken for his grand-mother. She was painfully thin and the skin that covered her bony fingers was almost transparent. John's eyes met hers across the table, as if he knew what she was thinking and they gave each other a thin smile.

She knew that if anything happened to his mother he would be devastated but they both also knew that she wouldn't make old bones and their smiles had said 'We must treasure her while we can.'

By seven o'clock they could see she was exhausted and although she hadn't said a word John knew, by her face, that she was trying to bear up and not be a kill-joy. To save her from thinking that she had broken up the party he said, 'I hope you don't mind if we take you home shortly, Mum, but there'a a musical picture on that I promised Hannah I would take her to see, if that's all right with you.'

Hannah looked up, thinking, 'This is news to me,' but on John's little wink, guessed his reasons and blessed him for it.

'No of course I don't mind. You go along, I shall be perfectly all right,' she said, rising slowly.

Bill offered to drive her home and drop John and Hannah off at the Regent. So, after wrapping up well, for it was very cold and blustery, typical March weather, they set off.

When they reached John's front door, Jane, as Mrs Hodiak had insisted they call her, thanked Bill for tearing himself away from his lovely little family and invited them all to visit her in the not too distant future and with John's reminder to take her heart tablet before going to bed, they proceeded to the Regent.

'Thanks a lot Bill, it's very good of you to give us a ride, I won't keep Hannah out too late, about 10.30ish.'

'Don't you worry about rushing home, it is her birthday after all,' he replied, 'you enjoy yourselves.' He gave John a wink.

'Well,' he said, as they stood in the queue for their tickets, 'having a baby has certainly softened him up. He seems a different chap altogether from the one I first met. You must never go by first impressions, he really is very nice.'

Hannah was saved from comment as the queue surged forward and John paid for their tickets through the little round window. They made a bee-line for the back row, where they could have a little kiss and cuddle without fear of being overlooked.

The picture was one that Hannah had hoped to be able to see, *Kiss the Boys Good-bye*, starring her favourite singer, Vera Lynn. The songs she performed were so nostalgic that half the audience joined in, including herself and John and by the end of the picture many were unashamedly wiping their eyes.

Usually, at the end of the performance, the younger members of the audience rushed to the exits in order to get out before the national anthem started, for once it had they didn't dare move until it was over. But tonight the film reminded them of the recently concluded conflicts and they stood silently and thankfully with pride until the music died, before shuffling out soberly.

'Good-night John,' said a voice, on their leaving, 'Oh good-night,' he replied, to a customer of his, putting his arm around Hannah.

She smiled at his obvious show of possessiveness, pleased at his pride in her.

Please God, she thought, don't let me ever hurt him, he's

191

such a wonderful man, worthy of much better than me.

It was a very wild night with the wind and rain lashing their faces, making conversation impossible on the way home and when they reached the flat they fell in thankfully, taking off their wet shoes and hanging their coats in the hall before proceeding to the kitchen. There they wiped their faces and heads on an old towel that hung on the back of the door. She looked in the little kitchen mirror to tidy her hair and smiled as she thought, If Aunt Elsie could see me know she'd say I had a face like a 'turkey cock's arse'; a favourite expression of hers if somebody had a particularly red face, as she now had.

There were no lights on in the rest of the house so Lil and Bill had obviously gone to bed.

Hannah ushered John into the living room while she made them a cup of cocoa.

They sat before the dying embers of the fire, sipping their drinks, the heat making their cheeks glow after the rain's lashing.

As Hannah drained her cup John took it from her and placed it on the hearth, took her hand and led her to the couch where he began gently making love to her, kissing and caressing. But as usual, when he became impassioned and tried to go further she stiffened and pulled away.

'For God's sake Hannah, don't do this to me, what's wrong? You know I want you more than anything in the world but you always slam the door in my face. I physically ache for you. Please Hannah, I swear I'll be careful, I know you're a virgin but I need you so desperately. If I hurt you I'll stop straight away. I promise, please Hannah.' he begged.

'I'm sorry John, I don't know what's wrong with me. Please be patient. Perhaps it's because my aunt and uncle are nearby that I can't go all the way with you.'

'You don't think that any more than I do. It's the same wherever we are, I don't understand you. If you were any other girl I wouldn't put up with your strange behaviour but I love you so much I'll try to be patient but please try to meet me half-way if you care at all about me.'

'I will try John, I'm not having you on you know that,' she said, taking his dear face in her hands and kissing it gently.

He kissed her back, softly at first and them more passionately as he became aroused again. She returned his kisses and allowed him to caress her, but yet again when he reached the point of no return her thoughts returned to that other time on this couch when Bill invaded her, and she felt herself stiffen. But this time, instead of pulling away, she bit her lip and allowed him to take down her knickers and slip them over her feet. He was so grateful, kissing her face, her stomach, legs and even her feet, fumbling with one hand to unbutton his flies, taking longer than usual, so afraid was he that even now she would pull back. Then he was gently entering her.

It was a bit awkward, she was very dry, but he hadn't expected it to be easy the first time, she being a virgin.

So excited was he that it was all over hardly before it had begun.

'Oh, Hannah darling, I'm so sorry it was so quick, but I've been keyed up for so long I just couldn't control myself. I feel like a bumbling schoolboy, it couldn't have been very good for you. I'm sorry darling, I'm sorry,' he said, burying his head in her breasts.

'It's all right John, really, please don't be upset. I didn't expect the earth to move the first time. That only happens in pictures.'

He lifted tear-filled eyes to her. 'Oh Hannah Hardy, I love you so much, will you marry me?'

She kissed him gently. 'It's all right, you don't have to make an honest woman out of me. It's 1946 not 1846. I won't be drummed out of town like a scarlet woman.'

'I'm not asking you because of what just happened, I was going to ask you tonight, whether you'd let me make love to you or not.'

'Please darling Hannah,' he said, getting down on his knees and holding his hands in a prayer-like posture, 'make me the happiest man in the world by consenting to be my wife.'

She laughed out loud at his dramatics. 'Do get up John, you look ridiculous.'

'Not until you say Yes.'

She'd known this time was coming but still didn't know how to answer.

Thank God he hadn't realised that she wasn't a virgin. With the slight difficulty he'd had entering her, he'd assumed it was because of her virginity and although she'd been unable to respond, she was so relieved to think that she'd been able to allow it to happen. Perhaps, now, that other experience would recede and allow her to enjoy a normal relationship.

Seven months had passed since the report of Ken's tragedy so, what was she waiting for? Next to him, she knew she wouldn't find a better man than John but still she hesitated.

'Let's wait a bit longer John, we haven't got very much money and where would we live? You know I want to go back to Norfolk but your roots are here and then there's your mother. What would happen to her if you left? She can't be left on her own.'

'I've thought it all out. Just listen to what I propose, if you'll pardon the pun,' he said, smiling. Then on a more serious note, 'you must have noticed that mother isn't improving, in fact, she is deteriorating rapidly and' he gave a huge sigh before continuing, 'the medical opinion is that we'll be fortunate if she's still with us next Christmas.'

'Oh no, oh John I'm so sorry, I know she's ill but I had no idea it was so serious.'

'I think I've known for a long time but wouldn't accept it and I think she knows also because she's starting to put her house in order in lots of subtle little ways, like keeping all the bills paid right up to the minute and keeping well ahead with the housework on her good days, and she's even made a will, though God knows why. There's only me, so it's not as if there'll be any disputes and she's started quizzing me as to how serious you and I are. By the way she approves of you whole-heartedly. I think she looks upon you as the daughter she would like to have had and I'm sure if we named the day that would give her something to hang on for.'

'But where would we live? Who'd look after her?'

'That's what I'm coming to. You get on well with her don't you?'

'You know I do, she's such a sweet lady, you can't help but love her.'

'Well,' he took a deep breath, 'would you consider us living with her when we're first married? I assure you she is absolutely no trouble and she'd be very diplomatic, you'd hardly know she's there, and when the inevitable happens, well, the house is bought and paid for so that would be ours. What do you say Hannah?'

'It all sounds very nice but I've dreamt of going back to

Norfolk all through the war. My roots are there. I don't think I could ever be happy living in the city for the rest of my life.'

'I know, but won't you please give it a try and I swear to you if you're not happy we'll move to Norfolk.'

'But what about your job?'

'They have estate agents in Norfolk, don't they?'

'Not in the village, but they do in King's Lynn; but John you're used to city life, I couldn't expect you to love the country like I do.'

'Hannah,' he said, taking both her hands in his, raising them to his lips and kissing them, 'wherever you are I will be happy. It's not where you live that's so important but who you live with, so is the answer yes?'

'Yes John, I'll be honoured to be your wife.'

'Yahoo,' he yelled, picking her up and swinging her around, 'you'll never regret it. I'll spend the rest of my life making you happy.'

'Sh, you'll wake the house up.'

'I don't care if I wake the whole world up, I'm the happiest man alive and I don't care who knows it,' he said, kissing her over and over again. 'I've been so worried, I had a terrible feeling there was someone else. I don't know where I got that idea from for I know I'm the only one in London that you've been out with, it was just an uncanny fear I had.'

'No, there's no-one else' she could answer in all honesty – at least, not since Ken died.

They decided that there was no reason to have a long engagement for they'd agreed to a quiet wedding in a registry office and now John couldn't wait to get home to tell his mother the good news.

When he'd left Hannah felt a little panicky. What had she done? Did she love John? Of course she did. Oh, not in the same way she'd loved Ken but she knew he wouldn't want her to mourn forever. But still she felt she was betraying something sacred. But she'd done it now and she vowed to make him a good wife and he would never suspect that he was second-best.

Her aunt and uncle were thrilled at the news, for they'd feared that she might wallow in her shame for years and become embittered. Lil began, at once, to make a list of things for Bill to 'acquire' in order to make the wedding cake, naturally taking it upon herself to play the role of bride's mother.

Hannah wrote with the good news to Pam, who immediately volunteered to be the chief bridesmaid. She hadn't planned to have bridesmaids, just a very quiet wedding, but now she supposed she would have to have Betsy and Maureen in attendance as well or they would be very upset.

The next week John took her to his home where his mother welcomed her like a long-lost daughter. She was absolutely thrilled to think that they would be married and settled down, hopefully, God willing, while she was still here.

When she was told that a white wedding wasn't planned she was a little sad but Hannah made excuses. They just wanted a very quiet affair, especially as her own mother and father wouldn't be there and besides, it was very difficult to get hold of fancy materials for bridal gowns.

The old lady eyed her up and down without saying anything for a few seconds, then, as if coming to a decision, she sent John up into the loft to bring down a large cardboard box and after allowing him to dust it, sent him out of the room with stern orders not to return until she called him.

When she was sure he was out of earshot, she beckoned Hannah to help her remove the many strings that were securing it.

This done, they then removed the many layers of paper and eventually a dress was revealed. Jane carefully lifted it out, gave it a gentle shake and held it up against Hannah.

'This was my wedding dress,' she said, 'and it would make me very happy if you wore it to marry my son. In the early years of my marriage, after John, I'd hoped to have a daughter to pass it onto but as it wasn't to be, this would be equally appropriate.'

Hannah looked at the dress and thought, 'My goodness, it's so old-fashioned, how on earth can I refuse without breaking her heart? Still the chances of it fitting me are very remote, so I'll try it on and then, when it doesn't fit, she will at least know that I didn't refuse out of hand.'

Jane helped her into the dress, her eyes shining like a young girl's, as they had done all those years ago when she had worn it as a bride.

It slipped over Hannah's slim body as if it had been made for her. Jane fastened the buttons at the nape of the high neck line and then stood back. 'There I knew it would fit you, what do you think?'

Hannah gritted her teeth and turned to survey her reflection in the mirror. She gasped in astonishment; it was like a Cinderella transformation.

The dress, which was more a magnolia colour than white, was fashioned high at the neck with tiny pearl buttons. The sleeves were long and close-fitting, ending half-way down the back of the hand in a V, with a row of pearl buttons under the cuffs. It was close fitting to the waist and then fell away into soft folds to the ground, the back hem going into a V to match the sleeves.

'Oh, my dear girl, it's like turning the clock back seeing you looking so much like myself all those years ago.'

'I can't believe it,' said Hannah, 'if I'd had a hundred fittings it couldn't have been better, it's incredible' and, she thought to herself, 'it's not exactly white, for I couldn't have married in pure white, it would have been hypocrisy.'

They gently embraced each other, a little over-awed by the spectacle.

'What are you two doing in there? Can I come in?' came John's voice from the other side of the door.

'No, you can't,' screamed Hannah and Jane in unison, both thinking the same thing. It was deemed very unlucky for the groom to see his bride in her wedding gown before the ceremony.

'I see,' said John jokingly, 'we're not yet married and already you've got secrets. I'll give you two more minutes and then if you haven't come out I'll go out and pick myself another bride.'

Hannah and Jane smiled at each other, as if to say, 'If we believe that we'll believe anything. Nevertheless, they speedily got her out of the dress and packed it away carefully, out of sight until such time as it could be smuggled out.

The wedding was arranged for the first week in June. There was no reason to wait any longer, for unlike most couples they had no house to furnish. The only difference would be a double bed replacing the single one in John's room which, to Hannah's relief, was quite a distance from his mother's.

Pam's mother was very handy with a needle and had offered to make the girls' dresses and was fortunate enough to obtain some pink taffeta from Kings Lynn. The bouquets and button-holes were to be supplied by Flower Corner, of course, and also the fresh cut flowers that Hannah would be wearing in her hair.

John's best man was to be an old school friend called Tony, whom Hannah met prior to the wedding and liked instantly. The Norfolk Dumplings, Fred and Peg Bates, Pam, big Tom, Elsie, little Tom and her sisters, were to travel down from King's Lynn by train and Bill and a friend would collect them from Liverpool Street station and take the bridesmaids to the flat and the rest to John's house, for it would be too harrowing for Hannah to have them crammed in all around her whilst she was dressing.

The great day, which turned out to be a glorious sunny one, dawned and Pam, and Hannah's sisters tumbled into the flat around eleven o'clock, clutching boxes that contained their dresses. These Lil pounced on and carried to the awaiting ironing board. Taffeta was a lovely swishy material but so crushable and once the girls were dressed they wouldn't be allowed to sit down until after the ceremony.

They all hugged and kissed and Pam and Hannah shed a few nostalgic tears, which Lil tutted away, and sent them flying hither and thither, giving them no more opportunity to become 'mardy.'

The wedding was scheduled for two o'clock and whilst Hannah thought they would be twiddling their thumbs for great lengths of time, this was not the case, for when they'd all had tea and a sandwich – which she found very difficult to swallow, but on Lil's insistence forced down – the time seemed to fly.

Her sisters, once dressed in their finery, were like cats on hot bricks, hopping about from one foot to the other.

Hannah was very glad now that she was having brides-maids, for Peg had really done them proud. The dresses were beautifully made and she had also made big double bows in matching material to go on their hair, and they were allowed to wear a touch of powder and lipstick, making them feel very grown-up.

The only blight on the day was the fact that Bill would be giving her away, for there was no other close male relative who could carry out this duty. But it wasn't as if he'd have to escort her very far, it would only be a few steps from the registry office doors to the table at the far end of the room where the ceremony would be conducted. But Hannah vowed that she wouldn't place her hand in his, as was the custom when being walked down the aisle, but would allow it to hover as if resting on his hand. Nobody would be close enough to notice that there was no actual contact and when he'd uttered his two words, that would be his duty over. So she resigned herself.

Betsy, now aged eleven, was much more mature than Hannah had been at her age and in her bridesmaid dress her little budding bosoms were quite obvious.

Hannah had been just her age when Bill had started to 'fiddle' with her, although at that time she had no idea what it was all about, but he hadn't given Betsy a second glance in that respect, thank goodness. He obviously looked upon her purely as his little niece and she wondered why he'd wanted a scrawny little thing like she'd been at the time.

One last trip to the lavatory and Betsy joined the other girls at the car that was to take them to the wedding, along with Lil and John Willie.

She was now alone with Bill and strangely enough, he seemed as ill at ease as herself. 'I don't suppose we'll be alone any more as we are now,' he began and at her guarded look went on quickly, 'Oh don't be alarmed, I just want you to know that I'll be forever grateful to you for not telling Lil about us and I'd like you to know that I've kept my word since she came out of hospital. When I came so close to losing her I realised she wasn't just a part of my life, she *was* my life and I know I've been lucky enough to get a second chance. They say everybody is entitled to one mistake and I want you to know that I'll never make another one and if, in the future, there's ever anything I can do for you, you only have to say the word and as for John Willie, well he has perfected our lives and I swear to you he'll always have the best of everything as long as I live and we'll never push you out of the picture. As far as we're concerned he's got three parents.'

Hannah could find nothing with which to reply to his little speech, so he went on, 'I hope you and John will be very happy but in the unlikelihood of anything ever going wrong between you two, you always have a home here.'

A knock on the door announcing their car's arrival saved her from replying and she went quickly down the hall and the door was opened to 'Ohs' and 'Ahs' and 'Don't she look loverly?' from the little group of people who'd seen the wedding car arrive and stood waiting for a glimpse of the bride and to calls of 'Good luck girl' she stepped into the car for the short journey to the registry office. There another little group were assembled to watch her go in, to more cries of 'Good luck.'

In no way could this room be mistaken for a church but with family and friends sitting either side of the aisle, there was no mistaking it was a wedding, with everybody wearing button-holes and dressed in their finest clothes that were aired only on such occasions as these.

There were huge floral arrangements arranged by Flower Corner, filling the room with perfume. As she began the short walk, all heads turned in order to get the first glimpse of her. Pam's mother and father sat in the row behind Elsie and Tom, an empty seat beside them reminding her that a part of their family was absent, and she said under her breath, 'Good-bye Ken, I'll never forget you' and on meeting John's eyes brimming with love as she came to stand beside him she made a silent vow. 'I'm all yours now and I'll close yesterday's book and concentrate all my love on you. You won't be sorry. I'll make you the wife you deserve, or die in the attempt.'

15

John turned out to be a model husband, always happy and good-natured, and he did everything in his power to please his 'two girls' as he called his mother and Hannah.

The only dark cloud on the horizon was Jane's health, for in spite of all the care and attention that was lavished on her she was quite obviously failing. They knew it and she knew it but there was no point in talking about the inevitable so they all painted happy faces for each other.

Hannah returned to work, although she would have preferred to stay at home and make things easier for Jane but was told by the doctor to allow her to do what she could for as long as she could, for if they treated her like an invalid she would just give up the ghost. So Hannah had to be content with taking over the chores after she returned from work.

On a glorious September day Hannah arrived home a little later than usual, to be met by a very worried husband and mother-in-law at the front door.

'Where have you been Hannah? Mother's been so worried, you didn't say you'd be late?'

'I was hoping you wouldn't notice if I were a bit late, in case it were a false alarm, but I was kept waiting longer than I expected,' she replied.

'False alarm, what on earth do you mean?', asked John, ushering her into the kitchen where a cup of tea awaited her arrival home as usual.

'Sit down and stop fussing and you too, Granny,' she said, smiling at Jane.

'Granny, oh my dear, you don't mean—,' but she couldn't go on and John's mouth fell open in disbelief.

'I've just come from the doctor's where my suspicions, were confirmed. I'm three months' pregnant,' she announced.

'But you didn't say a word, you little minx,' said John,

201

kissing her gently, 'come and sit down and put your feet up.'

'Now John, don't you start treating me like a bit of porcelain, I'm perfectly all right, everything is absolutely normal.'

'Three months you say,' said Jane in wonderment. 'Oh my dear, I'm so very, very happy. When is the baby due?'

'As near as he could tell, about the second week in March.'

A misty look appeared on Jane's face and they knew she was wondering if she would be spared until then.

'I hope that you're a good knitter,' said Hannah, going over and giving the frail shoulders a gentle squeeze, 'for I'm going to need a little instruction. How do you feel about helping with the baby's layette?'

'Nothing would give me greater pleasure. Oh I can't believe it,' she said, tears filling her eyes. 'I hope you have a little girl, I always wanted a little girl,' and looking guiltily over to John, 'but I wanted a boy as well,' she added hastily.

'It's all right Mum, I always knew I was a substitute,' he said laughingly.

'What a terrible thing to say, you know that's not true,' she said, looking perplexed.

'I'm only kidding, you silly girl,' he said, going over and putting his arms around her and Hannah.

That evening, Jane started rummaging in cupboards and drawers and brought forth needles and even patterns she'd kept out of sentiment, that she'd once used for John's baby clothes, and Hannah was surprised to notice that the little woollen vests and matinée coats hadn't really changed much over the years.

She decided to finish working at Flower Corner when she was in her sixth month, not because she didn't feel well enough to carry on but she was getting embarrassingly big and also she was getting increasingly worried about Jane. For although in spirit she was wonderful her health was by now, very, very poor and Hannah prayed with all her heart that she would live long enough to see her grandchild.

On 4 March, at two o'clock in the morning, Hannah awoke to a terrible backache. John sleepily massaged it and they tried to

return to their slumber but less than an hour later the ache had developed to breath-stopping pain and she realised that she was in labour. It surprised her somewhat for she had thought that with luck it would come on her birthday but there was no mistaking these pains.

'You'd better go for the doctor, John,' she said, trying to keep calm so as not to alarm him.

'Are you sure?' he asked, at the same time springing from the bed and pulling on his trousers.

'Yes, I think so.' She knew so. There was no mistaking labour pains; once you'd had them you could never mistake them for anything else, but she couldn't say this to him.

'Shall I fetch mother to stay with you?'

'No let her sleep. I'll call her if I need her before you get back and don't worry.' She looked at his frightened face. 'I doubt if anything will happen for hours yet, it doesn't usually.'

Nevertheless, he rushed from the room, tucking his shirt inside his trousers on the way out.

After he'd left she wished she'd let him call his mother, for the pains became very severe within a short time.

He'd only been gone about ten minutes when her waters broke and it distressed her as much as the pains to think that she was soaking their lovely new bed. Oh she thought, 'why didn't I put a rubber sheet on, just in case' and then she screamed as a very strong pain engulfed her and before it had died away Jane came into the room and Hannah began to cry.

'Don't be frightened Hannah, I'm here.'

'I'm not frightened,' she said, 'but I've wet the bed.'

'Oh my dear girl, don't worry about the mess. Just you concentrate on the job in hand, nothing else matters.'

By the time John returned with the doctor her labour was in full swing and he and Jane were sent out whilst he examined Hannah. Her pains were now coming in quick succession and he could tell that she was well into her labour.

She hadn't been at all worried about having the baby. After all, she'd been through it all before, but she'd forgotten how agonising it had been.

He quietened her between pains and she vowed that she would never go through this hell again, not for John or anyone. At six o'clock, with daylight streaming in, John and Jane were drinking their umpteenth cup of tea and John was about to suggest that his mother get some rest – she really was looking ghastly in the early morning light – when a baby's cry filled the house, loud and strong.

'Thank God, thank God,' said Jane, as she and her son cried together in relief.

A few minutes later the doctor tapped on the door. 'What are you doing sulking in here, don't you want to see your daughter?'

'Is she all right?'

'She's fine, they're both fine.'

'I don't know how to thank you doctor,' said Jane.

'There's nothing to thank me for, she did all the hard work, she was very good but I could do with a cup of tea.'

She quickly made him a cup of tea and then joined her son and daughter-in-law.

After spending ten minutes with her grand-daughter she was so exhausted that she returned to her bed and before falling into her final sleep she thanked God for allowing her to live to this day.

Hannah was nursing the now sleeping baby with John gazing in wonder and adoration.

'My darling Hannah, I love you so much. Thank you for making me the proudest man alive and for making Mother's dream come true.'

'I love you too John and I'll try to be as good a mother as yours but that will be very hard, she's so wonderful.'

'And so are you, my darlings,' he said, including his daughter.

He put his finger into her tiny hand and the little fingers encircled it firmly.

'What shall we call her Hannah?'

'What do you think?'

'How can I choose a name worthy of such beauty? She's so lovely. Her tiny mouth is like a little pink rose-bud.'

'I know we'll call her Rose?' he said, and taking Hannah's hand in his free one, he said firmly, 'yes, we'll call her Rose—Rose Hannah.'